THE BIRTH YARD

THE BIRTH YARD

A Novel

MALLORY TATER

HARPERAVENUE

HarperCollins Publishers Ltd
Bay Adelaide Centre, East Tower
22 Adelaide Street West, 41st Floor
Toronto, Ontario, Canada
M5H 4E3

www.harpercollins.ca

Library and Archives Canada Cataloguing in Publication
information is available upon request.

ISBN 978-1-4434-5824-5

Printed and bound in the United States of America
LSC/H 9 8 7 6 5 4 3 2 1

For Susan Tater

PART I

THE GATHERING SEASON

CHAPTER 1

I T'S ARRIVAL, THE MONTH OF OUR BIRTHS. OUR SKY-light holds low, cool stars ready to celebrate us. The stars seem to savour their light during summer, release their brightest hues in September. When August ends, we are joyful and ready. Everyone on our Trail has been born in the same month for three generations since The Den was founded. Everyone celebrates their births together. On the Trail, September is Arrival month.

I lie on my back with my stomach to the light—the healthy way to sleep and grow. Some Arrivals mean more than others. This is my eighteenth. I'm now old enough to give birth.

I hear my mother's shaky hands stacking plates in the kitchen. My bedroom is on the other side of the wall.

"Turn on the light," she hisses at my Father. "George, my *s*'s are crooked. Too angled. Should I start over?"

"No, Vale," He says. "They're fine."

It's easy to eavesdrop in our homes. Our cottages are thin-walled and small, crisp in the winter, sticky-warm in summer.

I picture her writing our names on the cakes with frosting. She will be focused under the hanging light bulb at the kitchen table, trying to get it perfect. The frosting on my cake will be blue. I'm eighteen and this means sky life. My sister, Kassia's, will be pink for age fourteen. Pink means to dig deep, keep growing, stay hopeful.

All our neighbours on our Trail will dip their fingers and taste my mother's salted tea frosting. It's my mother's job every year to do the Arrival cakes for everyone. She towers them and stacks them in the pantry, wrapped in foil for each family to collect. She does this because our Trail is busy and tired. Celebrating takes work and she has time.

I lie watching the morning grow though I feel my body hasn't. I wear a stretcher hooked to my ankles, a metal rod cinched to my back. I should feel it press into different muscles the more I grow but I haven't felt change in a while. I'm guilty for it. We awaken, expecting to feel older. Even my mother is supposed to feel it this month and revel and dream and plan. She tries but her wrists hold her back. Arthritis. She speaks to the pain quietly at night when knitting or baking. She knows talking loudly of pain only ages her further. We are not supposed to discuss pain.

It's my parents' Arrivals too. I know my Father and mother will hold a small candle for each other. They take turns lighting it and blowing it out in the mostly dark room. My Father doesn't make a wish—He claims He never has. I picture Him relighting it for my mother, who might look back toward our bedroom, think of Kassia and me, then blow. All she has ever thought of is us.

Most living in The Den will feel alive and happy all month. The Arrival celebrations seem to last forever. They're every night for a month. Each girl in The Den gets a new dress to replace last year's—a simple black cotton dress to our knees with one sleeve the colour of our age. My blue-sleeved dress and Kassia's pink-sleeved dress hang in our bedroom closet, waiting for us. Women are frivolous, so we don't have too much choice of clothes to wear to keep our vanity and lust at bay. Men have unlimited clothing, as much as they prefer. They work. They need distinction, more concrete identities. They need those things.

Kassia's breathing is deep. I can hear her through the curtain that divides our bedroom. I like to think she's breathing in a new fourteen-year-old self. I don't know if I'm feeling the breath of eighteen inside me or if being awake so early is what I'm supposed to do. The older I get, though, the more I feel I'm supposed to be awake, soaking in things, listening.

I wait for my mother to finish rinsing the baking bowls and piping tubes in the sink, wait for my Father to wish her a happy Arrival and wait for them to go to their room to dress. I picture their bodies touching, lips and all.

I remove the stretcher quietly—it's hard to reach the straps—and go to the water closet, pee in the toilet. The yellow of it looks darker than usual. I worry about everything inside me. I go to the kitchen, open the oven and find nothing. Mum's done her baking in impeccable time this year. I open the pantry and the door whines. Mum calls out to ask if anyone's peeking. I say nothing as I admire the cakes, pierced with large toothpicks to make them stand up. They make me hungry. Mine, a blue one with *Sable* written on it, leans toward three sacks of white beans as if even it knows what's better for me—as if the cake knows it holds nothing but tradition and sugar.

This Arrival is pivotal for me. This is the first day I will not be in Lessons.

This summer, I ate cold yogourt with Dinah and Mamie at the commissary, a large metal house stocked with food and run by Men, an Elder named Eli in particular, who ration the food to families, giving women and children treats based on good behaviour or how pretty we smile. Dinah has grown taller and more womanly—Mamie and I benefited from this in the form of extra fruit and nuts, yogourt and pastries. Dinah and Mamie seemed excited all summer. They'd stroked their bellies and told me with yogourt-crusted lips that their bodies could feel it coming. I've been haunted by how fearlessly my friends look to their futures. Their bodies widening with anticipation.

My Father is worried I'll be bored without Lessons and get dark and smart like Marissa Tamons, who lives farther down our Trail. I secretly thank Him for giving me so much credit. Marissa took her eighteenth Arrival as a time to stop herself from ovulating. She decided to starve, make her blood stop, make herself ineligible for a Birth Notice.

Marissa Tamons couldn't make a baby because she'd lost so much weight and stopped menstruating. No Men desired her. She was selfish enough not to eat. She twisted and ruined her baby-making body. That year, on our way to Lessons, Kassia and I saw Marissa's Father, home from the plant, sitting with her on a porch swing. Marissa was wrapped in a blanket. Her cheeks looked grey and sallow. Her Father was serving her with a spoon, pleading. He was a plump Man, but the dent in their cottage siding, their rotting front steps, the missing shingles on their roof, told me He was begging for her to find a Man, maybe one of Lynx's Grandsons if she could, to acquire good favour with The Den. He held a bowl of pudding to His daughter's mouth and she sat there looking toward the Trail, freshly gravelled to ready it for another Arrival month that Marissa no doubt wished she could sleep through.

Marissa doesn't live with us anymore. I don't know where she is, where they sent her once it was clear she was barren and wild.

Like Marissa, I'll miss Lessons more than anything. I'll hate how neighbourhood children, young Boys and Boys into their twenties and girls younger than me, will pass by the window each morning to call on Kassia, and I'll remain on the couch learning about my body and the Family Body. Unlike Marissa, I have no will to stop it, to stop myself, to keep my body from birthing by starving it. I'm not wild. I know turning eighteen is an honour.

Kassia and I go down the hall. Mum sets out cake and tea. Kassia immediately gets pink icing on her new dress. She wipes the stain at the sink.

"Messy Mouse," I say, filling a cup with water.

"I'm too mature for that today." Kassia sticks her tongue out, wipes her chin on a cloth hanging by the window. Her dress looks lovely on her—her calves so defined where the pleats end.

My mother defends her. "Fourteen is good, Kassia. You'll be wonderful at it."

My mother turns to me but doesn't say anything about my age or the sky. I'm not hungry. Kassia asks our mother how old she is this month and my mother smiles and says thirty-six. Her new dress is made of linen instead of cotton. It's short-sleeved, floor-length, practical. Women over age thirty are given white dresses, rather than black like ours. It's to challenge women not to dirty them. If they are unruly and wild, the Men will see by their stains and tears. My mother is proud that she usually keeps hers immaculate all year.

Two Boys and a girl tap the window for Kass. She ties her pink sneakers and goes out into a Trail that's dark, rainy and ready to be filled with her voice and her steps. "Happy Arrival," she calls to us and we say it right back.

I'm a virgin. All girls in The Den are supposed to be until eighteen. We've brushed our hair in silence, always thinking of this age, this time. I don't know why it's always during hair-brushing or tooth-brushing. Something about the times of the day we stroke and touch ourselves, face mirrors, seems to root us in the moment, the severity of when a girl turns into a woman.

My mother doesn't put a DiLexa pill out for me today. Kassia's was dissolved in her strawberry milk the way she likes it. DiLexa is imported from Main Stream, the world we've left. I need to wean off the drug and I must become inclined toward the nature of my body. We take DiLexa so all young women bleed at the same time, keep the order of our young, hysterical bodies. Stay synchronized. But they also prevent accidental pregnancy should a Man be ill and wanting. Girls from Lessons have spoken quietly about their rapes. DiLexa erases them. DiLexa ensures no mark of life is left. Feles, our leader, must choose who we lie with, and that's why rape is illegal for Men. Feles chooses our partners. Feles chooses everything.

We are led by Feles, who took over from His deceased Father, our founder. Feles is His oldest Son. I've never met Feles, because I'm a girl. My time will come soon. I'm nervous to meet Him. I've spoken to His photograph on our living room wall for so long, thanking Him for everything we have.

I got my period at Lessons around the same time as my female classmates. I was on a swing set. Blood stained my dress. I covered it with a sweater tied around my waist. Our lecturer made me remove my sweater, be proud of the blood. I stood in front of everyone in the schoolhouse and turned to show all the Boys and girls the dark red stain. The other girls did the same when it was their turn. We took turns in the outdoor stalls fixing blood-cloths to our crotches and upper legs. I remember my best friend, Mamie, praying to Lynx's ghost for breasts as she changed, how the other girls chimed in.

My Gram told me that in Main Stream, women get their periods sporadically, at a time all their own, organically overlapping and syncing up with the women in their family or with close friends. She says this is a piece of magic to them, a wonderful secret.

I can't imagine being alone and bleeding for a week not knowing who else was going through it too. Not knowing who else felt the sharp pains in their hips, muscles contracting, breaking into pimples and sweating overnight. It would be a hard secret to keep. I've learned to like menstruating together because we can quietly complain; quietly, our qualms are heard and understood the same week during the same month.

DiLexa keeps women together. From age thirteen onwards, we take it with breakfast. It makes all of our clocks move in sync. We all begin bleeding on the same day, starting at lunchtime. My mother has packed Kassia her blood-cloth and the lecturer will excuse all the girls at eleven o'clock to wrap them around their underwear in the water-closet stalls. Boys will walk by and try to watch through the high window in the door. The blood fascinates them, attracts them like thirsty sharks.

My Father has already left for the plant this morning. He works there with other Men, under Feles, bottling the clean spring water The Den was built around. We sell it to towns and cities south of us, in what we call Main Stream.

At the plant, they also ensure that the farmers deliver what we need, plan which girls will breed with which Boys, ensure that

9

medicines, from our DiLexa to pain medication, are ordered and delivered on time from Main Stream, plan the next season at the Birth Yard for those expecting.

Feles's Father, Lynx, founded The Den back in the early '60s. My great-grandmother Iris was a student in His gender studies class at Chalmers University, a place of higher learning in a Main Stream town deeply south of us. There are thousands of universities in Main Stream, I'm told.

Lynx was fascinated with women—He never knew His mother. He had no sisters. He was enamoured with the ways women could conceive and carry children, the way women were attractive and could make Men bend with their words and hips. He said a woman's hips hold power and menace. He believed that women were unable to control their power and limit their roles, and it was the principal danger that would soon lead to the downfall of Men.

The course He taught was about how the female impulse for hysteria threatened order and balance. He believed women and their inability to temper emotion with reason were a primary, key cause of many of society's problems. If women ignored their natural abilities to nurture and produce, all would be weaker for it. A return to traditional ideals was vital for social cohesion. To call it misogyny was a deliberate misunderstanding, as my Father always repeats to me. Lynx's course was about His love for women and honoured their innate strengths in a way that was to the benefit of all. He knew He'd be misunderstood but He tried to deliver His message. He tried to be brave.

In His journals, which we read in Lessons, Lynx referred to His students as "devotees." The last course He taught focused keenly and cleverly on returning society to traditional roles—

Introduction to Gender, Health and Power. Many students dropped the course as it became clearer He strongly believed women are not equal to Men but need to be separate. Iris, my great-grandmother, a beautiful woman, a true devotee unpoisoned by the opinions of her bra-burning peers (Lynx's words), sensed Lynx was smart, misjudged. Other women did too, other devotees—and proudly, they'd become our Den mothers.

Lynx knew that if our society became more egalitarian between sexes, the disconnect between Men and women would only grow and all family, family bodies, our communities, would suffer. Women would become uncontrolled and ruled by their innate hysteria. In our textbooks in Lessons, we learn that women's contraceptives, like our DiLexa, became more widely available in the early '60s and led to social unrest, fewer marriages and fewer families.

Main Stream's Family Body suffered. Lynx believed those pills should be used to unify women as a group, not for us to take individually to unleash our immorality. We are too hysterical to be trusted. We need Men to help us tend to our bodies. The '60s were full of fear, but Lynx knew that the biggest threat was closer to fruition, with Second Wave women trying to undermine all of the industrious achievements, greatness, and ingenuity of Men. Lynx described the rampant hysteria as an apocalypse, the ultimate threat to society's well-being. He had to help us.

These loyal students, these women, followed Lynx once the university dismissed Him for His controversial ways. They left their dorms and moved into His home for more teachings, to learn to control themselves, to learn to accept Men's power. The women eventually forged bonds with each other and with Lynx, a kinship, a following, shatterproof and thriving. They all bore His first children. They all became vessels to quietly and firmly pass on the importance of mothering, of following the natural order. *Men have always done the leading and done it fiercely and well. What an abhorrent thing for this to change,* Lynx wrote.

My Gram Evelyn is one of twenty babies born in Lynx's home. Her family was built on women relinquishing their worldly ambitions, to return to what Lynx felt was best.

Government workers who tear apart families began to visit His home, threatened to take His devotees, His family away, if He didn't provide more space, cleanliness, safety.

Gram Evelyn says her childhood was adventurous but crowded. She remembers her younger Brothers seated at the table eating cheddar with fruit and herself on the floor with her sisters waiting for their turn to eat, uncertain when that would be. But Lynx would take her in His arms and rock her and say she'd receive everything she needed and that her body was clever. Girlhood, He'd tell her, is supposed to be lived simply, supposed to be filled with moments to prove sacrifice, maternal preparation, selflessness. When Gram Evelyn and her sisters told this to a social worker with a clipboard in their Father's bedroom, things were misinterpreted. *I've never felt so shamed, like I'd betrayed my Father, my leader,* Gram told me. *I didn't speak to her after that, on any more of her visits. I was not going to give up my Father, hurt my mother, shame myself. I thought we'd be taken away.*

Lynx decided the Main Stream world didn't understand Him, and His family was going to be pulled apart at the seams for our beliefs. He dreamed of creating His own Eden for us. It was a miracle when Lynx's Father died. Time always worked for Lynx. Lynx was made for miracles to fall into His hands. Lynx inherited all the money from Him, a successful filmmaker, though they were estranged. He lived in Hollywood, a place Lynx described as the most poisoned of lands. A place where women hold decadent wealth and kiss and boast on television for all to see. Lynx spent months preparing to take His women north. He found Men just like Him, attracted to the notion of fierce women willing to sacrifice for Men, willing to work and mother for the common good of the family, not their own interests or ego. The Men purchased vehicles, collected The Den mothers' passports and identity cards to keep in safer hands, abandoned what society told them, to seek land that could nurture what Lynx knew was truly right, truly just.

Legally and soundly, He had space and freedom and harvest and economy for His family to succeed and grow. Main Stream, the government, had to hold their tongues, ingest their sharp words and criticisms and leave The Den to thrive in peace.

I'm part of the fourth generation of The Den. We believe Main Stream is in drastic decline, consuming itself in social upheaval and lack of order. I can feel hysteria in my fingertips when a room is quiet. It's like a dark power I have where we women can unleash disorder and harm. If we listen to Lynx's teachings, honour The Den, we will live healthier lives, never cured, but with our selfish impulses bandaged. We women are needed to make healthy children. We do as we are told and keep our innate hysteria under control through any pills or other means necessary. I'm a burden and hope I can change.

Lynx is buried near the tents put up for women and Men to conceive in each year. His gravestone is a severe black granite slab, His name in the centre, hand-chiselled by all His Sons. We gather around it often. The soil of Him breathes through us when we have sex. I wish I'd gotten to meet Him but I know I'd probably be terrified of His voice, His touch. He was filled with a divine light, my Gram tells me, so much power.

My Father's work position is to travel south to Main Stream, in one of Feles's trucks, to collect pharmaceuticals and sell our life-giving bottled water. We are told many places love our water, that their own supplies are dirty or sulphuric. We compete with large companies and even sell our water in theatres, in airports, in museums, I'm told.

Our spring is a constant livelihood. We honour water in The Den. It's how the Men earn enough to keep us all here. Lynx's Father left millions for Him, but these things ebb and flow— money is like water.

My Birth Notice will be under the welcome mat. Feles and His Brothers delivered them last night while everyone on our Trail was asleep. My mother sits in the kitchen with her clove tea and bites her lip.

"You're so beautiful, Sable," she says. "Sable, you'll make a perfect mother."

I try not to cry as she turns a napkin in her lap. She's not ready either. I go to the welcome mat, inhale the whole Trail before grabbing the letter peeking out. The paper is thin and pink. I've seen them before with other girls. Years ago, a girl who used to child-mind us while our parents attended Feles's meetings pinned hers to her chest and paraded it for the whole Arrival month, putting herself out on display for the Boys, showing off her breasts as the paper bent over them perfectly. She's had two babies since.

Matches. I don't know who mine should be. I don't talk much to Boys or even really like them. Their smells or voices. They tower above me. They're like trees, only I'm afraid to wrap my arms around them and they don't rustle softly and bring me peace.

The Trail is full of whispering trees on either side, star-shaped Arrival bells strung around their waists and branches. Fresh gravel clings to the road and each cottage looks alive with morning smoke as the mothers cook on their woodstoves. I go to our lowest porch step and peer at Dinah's window, a few houses down the Trail. Her curtains are drawn but there's smoke coming from her chimney and I know she's probably dancing with her aunt and mother, rubbing her belly more energetically than ever. I rub my eyes until I see dark bugs, my mind's own creatures, and I open the notice:

Sable Ursu, age eighteen, has had the honour of completing Lessons, of learning about the body and the Family Body from her grandmother and mother during the Gathering Season before Winter's Conception with her assigned Match. Sable will then spend the Harvest Season and Free Season at either the Ceres or Lucina Birth Yard. Happy Arrival, Sable. In work and birth, The Den welcomes you. Praise Feles for your health and for this honour!

Seeing the words "Birth Yard" in print is exhilarating. We discussed them often at Lessons. Their purpose is to help us become mothers, better women, harder workers. My mother leans in the doorway and cups her hands around my shoulders as I return to the house. "We can drink port tonight," she says. "I'll set the glasses out."

I get to ask possible Boys to be my Match and then, after I do my cheek swab and fill out a sheet of questions, Feles will take into account my choices but ultimately select who is best for me. The cheek swabs will be driven to a lab in Main Stream. It's to prevent disease and consanguinity and, I've heard, to test how hysterical we really are. I sometimes feel my temper rise with Kass if she talks at me too fast, or with my mother if she gives me more chores than usual. I sometimes feel weepy and sad when Dinah makes a joke at my expense. I sometimes feel wild when the wind whistles through the Trail at night and I'm dreaming. I sometimes fear I may be truly hysterical if these things make me hysterical.

If I had a Boy in mind, I could write His name down as a suggestion to Feles, but I don't just yet. Dinah is going to write down many names. One will be Garrison. His Father came to The Den after Iris and the other Den mothers were already giving Lynx children. Now He works with my Father, collecting our drugs and goods and supplies from the world we don't see. Garrison's Father used to belong to a Main Stream faith and was against the killing of fetuses in women's wombs. This act happens in Main Stream if the girls are raped or unready to be mothers. In some places, they can still choose to do this, but here Feles decides whether a baby should be born or not.

My Father says Garrison's Father was so sick of fighting for His cause, so sick of fighting for what He called infanticide to stop, that He gave up His God and made Lynx His new one. We don't abort here if the pregnancy is chosen and endorsed by Feles. That is that. No choice, either.

Garrison is very attractive, old for His age, confident. He gave Dinah a hit of His pipe once when she was home alone, watering plants in her flower boxes. Dinah tells the story the exact same way each time. It's funny, I imagine, the minute details one would remember when flirting with a Boy for the first time. After smoking with Him, talking, Dinah said she forgot the ferns, remembered only to water her Father's posies. I remember that night too—from my porch, I watched her exhale into Garrison's mouth and I felt for the first time that jealous drumbeat of what it is to have someone who thinks they might love you.

My mother deals us a hand of playing cards on the tea table in the living room and says Gram Evelyn will be over after her coddled-egg breakfast and hair washing to celebrate with me. Gram Evelyn keeps herself busy by making the small things feel big. I envy her.

I count the stems on the flowers of the queen card. They're blooming off vines coiled around the queen's nude body. Over and over, I count them. My mother pours me another glass of water and tells me I'll stay smart forever even without Lessons, and not to worry: women's bodies are innately intelligent, and isn't that all we could want? She knows I'm afraid of forgetting what I've learned at Lessons.

"Will you tell me about the Birth Yard?" I ask, and her green eyes shrink.

She undoes a button on her dress to show me she's hot and tired. I overhand shuffle the cards, deal and stay silent, let her win at cribbage. Our cuckoo clock shows itself twice in ten minutes. The springs are jammed but it's a welcome squeal of noise to split the silence. Finally, my mother speaks. "Sable, would you like Dinah and Mamie to join us for port?"

I picture my friends' smug faces, their ovaries already slowly heating as if under a beam of light, their wishes coming true, their phantom kisses on the forehead of a phantom baby not yet theirs. How maybe in our Birth Yard, we'll be separated and I'll expand and spread into a new person without them. How I'll miss them. "No, not really."

Women aren't allowed to drink alcohol unless it's Arrival month. Men can drink it whenever they please and can start drinking as young as thirteen. Gram Evelyn says she was a little girl when Lynx decided that women wasting time and gleaming with drink was not productive. Women coating their workday with an evening of liquor could erase all progress. My Father, too, doesn't drink much. He keeps one bottle of port above the stove on a shelf. I've always had a feeling that He might open it, toast me and toast the life not yet inside me, the Match I do not yet know.

Almost every woman on our Trail drinks during Arrival. Everyone's craving kicks in, including my mother's. She shows me the bottle. It's rust-coloured and translucent and it seems to glow.

"Sable," she says, "stop your worrying. Tonight will be fun. Your Gram loves to drink port."

We sit with our cards and my belly grows heavier with thought. After she wins for the fourth time, I go to the water closet to pee and fix my hair and scrub my teeth. I lift my dress and turn to the right and look. I've never been too thin, but my muscles are taut and I'm strong. I'm told this makes me what will be a perfect mother. My shoulders are bony but spread into fleshy arms, ready to cradle and hold and lift. Mum knocks on the door and says it's her turn.

I'm thankful sometimes we only have one water closet. It cuts short the feelings of myself, has made me smarter in some ways. I have time to stare in the one mirror above the sink only in calculated increments. I have coached my body into liking itself.

I'm not really sure I'm ready. I daydream of sheets and the body that will lie on top of me and give me life, a life I'm supposed to need. I've never even kissed a Boy.

Gram Evelyn arrives in the afternoon, hours early for dinner. She brings a basket of soft white rolls that she baked. She makes a bun-in-the-oven joke, outdated and lovely. I hug her and guide her white coat off her slim shoulders. I put my arms through the sleeves and twirl quickly like I always did as a child. She says, "Sable, you're too old for that. Besides, I'm cold. Give it back."

I do as she says. She kisses my cheek with her soft wrinkled lips. "You do make us proud," she says. Then she winks and asks about Matches, says she's dying to see the list.

"Your dying kills me," my mother says, taking her mother-in-law's hand and leading her to the plump sofa in the living room. It's our nicest piece of furniture. It has blue roses stitched all over, one inch apart. We have two ottomans to match it—one for my Father, one for company.

"Happy Arrival," I tell Gram Evelyn.

I sit across from her and my mother hands her a glass of lemon juice and sugar cubes in a small tumbler with ice. The way she likes. "Not my Arrival, Sable," she says.

Her long, dark hair is slicked back with a ribbon. It shines. She is in a long dress, starched clean. Her waist is even smaller than the last time I saw her. Gram Evelyn lives in a large cottage with other Elders, says eating with them takes away her appetite because some need soft food and spew on their plates between bites. Her teeth have lasted perfectly. When everyone finishes their meals and walks back to their suites, she stays and watches Den women collect scraps of bread, meat-fat and creamed corn off the floor. Her logic is that the disgust and disgrace on their faces will teach her to age with caution.

She and my mother prattle on about Gram Evelyn's birth and I listen because I know they want me to. It was a November birth because Lynx had not yet synced and scheduled The Den mothers to menstruate, conceive and mother together. She always says the leaves were floating down from their branches, shaking and golden, and though she was still in Iris's womb, she loves to elaborate and give us an aerial view of the story. I love her confidence in being omniscient.

"My mother, your great-grandmother, Sable, her name was—"

"Iris?" I lean toward her.

"Yes, good memory," she says through a sip of lemon on ice. Gram Evelyn sucks lemon rind in her mouth gracefully as if sour things entertain her. Her thin eyebrows perk up behind her thick cat-eye glasses. "Back then, women conceived at any time, so"— she squints—"I was made in March. I derived from spring heat, I suppose. Feles was conceived around the same time as me. My wisest Brother."

My mother bows her head at this.

"Well, mostly wise," Gram adds. She's smirking.

My mother glares at her. "Always. He saves us from Main Stream. He saves us from ourselves. Sable, He is wise beyond what any of us can fathom."

Gram nods and looks at us seriously. "Yes, always wise. Sorry, Vale."

"It's all right." My mother's voice softens. "Just don't forget what good He has done. He has honoured His Father. He keeps us from wickedness. He holds women up."

I picture Iris and Lynx in bed together, believing and starting

The Den with their bodies and the Family Body. How exhilarating to make something from nothing but two bodies and a bed.

Gram gets up to hug me. I love her frail, thin arms, wish for the same body type. If I were frailer and more deteriorated maybe the Men would tell me I could wait to make a baby. "We'll help, love," she says as if reading my thoughts, "when you get back from your Birth Yard, I promise."

Gram Evelyn goes on to my mother that she's heard I'll be made a laundress at the Yard.

Mum nods, fixes her hair. "Sable, you know I was a laundress. Being at the Yard starts off strange and difficult, but then you'll receive DociGens. Once you get used to them, those little pills lighten the work, that's for certain."

I nod, then play with my hands, make a barn roof with my index fingers.

Lynx and The Den have perfected a way to prevent women's hysteria. The four pillars of medication Lynx and the Men have developed for us are in a handbook on our tea table. I open the book for no reason other than to verify how well I have the texts memorized and understood.

DiLexa—birth control pills. Mamie calls it Rape Erase and that always makes me feel rotten inside. Girls in Main Stream take it because they sleep with anyone, behave like harlots. Feles says there is no shame in ours. Ours is different. It's purifying. It prevents pregnancy He did not dictate and keeps our cycles together. I'm so happy I have never been raped.

Reposery—for Men and women, with permission, to enjoy during the Arrival month. They call it ecstasy in Main Stream because in Main Stream, it's used to sinfully bind opposite sexes and to let women get sloppy, unhinged. We do not call it that because ours is to bring everyone a sense of euphoria, community, empathy and energy. I've never tried the pills but I will when I'm older. My mother always says she loves them; they leave her tired body humming and capable of enjoyment.

DociGens—we are given them at the Birth Yards. The name derives from the word "docility," meaning "woman softening, mollifying." Our lecturer says they calm us into servitude. Lynx learned of them on a trip He took to South America. It was used like morphine until the 1960s to put birthing mothers in labour into a kind of relaxed sensation of rest—twilight sleep. In The Den, we are invited to allow it into our bodies, our minds. I fear DociGens the most because I wonder how being forced to be more obedient feels inside one's head. How does a mind feel when it's suddenly quieted? But I know they are important. I know we women need them.

Afterols—age controllers. No one lives past eighty-three in The Den because that's when Lynx died. You can be close to Him only if you live in His steps. The Afterols weaken an individual's health should they be healthier than Lynx was at their age. They are a form of chemotherapy drug, used to fight cancer in Main Stream. In small doses, liquid capsules, they invade— weed killer of the soul, my Gram calls it. To maintain a good garden—a good life—a little poison is involved, and that is okay. We call Afterols *altum gustan*, or taste of the leader. Elders who are weak and do not live to know the taste of our leader are not buried in the Trail's cemetery. This puts their family in bad favour with Feles. Gram Evelyn takes her Afterol once a day. She says it gives her heart palpitations but amazing skin.

We discussed the drugs pretty thoroughly in Lessons, in a way that makes me excited to take certain ones but also terrified

of their newness. I know I'm not supposed to hold so many con-
tradictions inside me, but I do.

Gram Evelyn once told me DociGens are called Devil's
Breath in Main Stream. They're sometimes used to rape and
control women, to zombify them with dangerously high doses.
When Lynx brought the drug back to The Den, He forced all the
women to begin taking it. It seemed to work. Gram Evelyn was
a teenaged girl. She said she made herself vomit and would not
swallow them. She was too afraid. But when my mother received
hers for the first time at her Birth Yard, she loved them, became
addicted to the numbing effect they had.

But sex. Sex mystifies me. I've never tried to be with a Boy.
Neither have Dinah or Mamie, though Dinah came close. She
held a Boy named Jonathan's sex in her mouth one night, then
spat it out when white semen filled her mouth. She talked forever
about the salt of it every time we'd eat dried potatoes at Lessons.
Way saltier than these, she'd crunch at us.

"My Match will be my first," I say.

My Gram's cheeks redden and she fiddles with a crease in the
fabric of her dress over her breast. Her dress is pilling. It doesn't
look new. "You're a good girl, Sable. You're ready."

My mother leaves to slice up the rolls so we can fill our stomachs before dinner. My mother always eats a pre-dinner before
my Father comes home. At dinner she'll touch a few spinach
leaves soaked in oil, my favourite. She'll fork mushrooms dripping in pepper gravy and wash them down with a cup of lemon
water. But the bread, the heaviness, the potatoes or salted things,
she doesn't touch under my Father's gaze, even though I know
He wouldn't say anything about her widened figure or anything
rude to hurt her.

What is it with women and bread? Our fear of it. I find myself doing the same as my mother. I have scraped most of the frosting off my breakfast cakes and bread as the years went on, spooned it onto Kassia's plate until she grew older and also refused to consume it. I suppose we aren't supposed to feel full, satisfied, too comfortable, or we'll get emotional, confident, unbridled in conversation and tone. But being hungry throughout the day is its own challenge, and I do not blame my mother for giving in, for wanting more fuel, more salt and more joy.

My mother comes back with sliced rolls and garlic butter and knives and napkins. It looks so good. We eat and do not discuss sex anymore. My mother dips her problems away, licks butter off her wrist and thumb.

I want to tell her that I've already counted the flowers on all the sets of curtains on each window, that I've already eaten my fill of rolls and had enough tea, that I'm bored of food and flavour, that all I want is to take notes in history Lessons, listening to the lecturer talk of Main Stream, why we left to better our values. I want to learn about Main Stream music and vehicles and wars and celebrities. We are supposed to learn that Main Stream is bad. My secret longing and curiosity about it is something I would never share.

I want to learn why Men hate other Men so much they kill, why people believe in higher powers when all they get is this sole life, why they think that our genders should fill the same roles, not the ones we are made for, and why others don't follow Lynx's teachings or even know of them. I feel sorry for what they miss—they miss order, the Family Body, hysteric restraint built into their routines. They have to make all these elaborate, risky choices—whom to wed, whom to believe in, what to become, how to earn a living, how to do everything and how to do it alone. Sometimes when I have insomnia, I pretend I have such choices and I always fall asleep out of exhaustion and stress. Is that stress worth it? Why is Main Stream so keen on choice? I'd love to know. I also fear to know.

I want to talk to Gram Evelyn about her oldest stories of Lynx and Iris and Chalmers University and ask and share and write it all down. I want to learn the history of Birth Yards and the history of our bodies, but I will be taught only of my own small, insufficient body.

We live at the northernmost tip of Lynx Lake. I don't know what it was called before we arrived, but I do know it's such a beautiful place. The lake is west of our Trail. Our Trail is a long, winding gravel road leading up to the water plant. Dogwood trees enclose and encase it and in spring, it's alive and lush with blossoms. I'll be sad to miss our Trail in springtime this year when I'm away. The blossoms sometimes look like electric lights when the moon hits them at the right angle. It's spectacular. We have limited electricity because we don't need it to fulfill our everyday tasks. Outside light is what Main Stream relies on. They'd go mad without it. We need ours for the plant and for small household things. Other than that, if you hold enough light inside, that's all you need to live.

Where we are, I know of narrow rivers, snowfall and wind. I know the smells of corn and barley and berries, and I know the timing of all the crops with the inner compass of a farmer. Feles pays nearby Main Stream farms for our food, and some we harvest ourselves. That lets our existence stay silent, private.

"Tomorrow, we'll tell you more," Gram Evelyn says. "Today is for celebrating."

Gram Evelyn strikes me as someone who wants to talk about sex and babies more than my mother. My Gram has suggested in the past that she isn't in support of the Birth Yard or Lynx's teachings because the Yards have gotten too tight and too rigid for us girls, but she knows better than to run her mouth, defy the Men. My Father once slapped her across the face after an evening meal when she refused to speak to one of Lynx's photos in our home, the one above the kitchen window, with thanks. She must have feared her Father. Now she fears mine.

I haven't left the house today. My skin wants me to. The rain has stopped. My mother senses this. "Why don't you go help Mamie make supper? She'll have her work cut out for her."

"Yes," I say. "I'll go knock and see."

CHAPTER 2

I LACE UP MY BOOTS AND WALK THE FOUR DOORS down to Mamie's. She used to leave Lessons early to help her mother, who suffers from chronic pain and migraines. Now she'll have more housework and child care to keep up with. Mamie always makes dinner for her parents and her siblings. She has five Brothers and sisters and, though I've known Mamie for years, I still get everyone's ages and names jumbled up. All I know is that she is the eldest and I do not envy her.

Mamie opens her front door before I get a chance to knock, as if she's been sitting alone doing nothing. But she's smiling and has an apron on. Rags choke her brown ringlets. She looks bright and silly, and I'm happy to see her.

Mamie holds me tight in her arms and wishes me happy Arrival. I do the same for her and press my thumb into her palm like we've done since we were kids.

We once learned about Christ in a history Lesson. Main Stream folk love Christ. He suffered for all these people, and we thought it was beautiful but highly improbable that He was real and could turn water into wine or dream away injury and disease. But we were shown a painting of Him and we found His chiselled dying face, full of wisdom and the love of some God, to be very appealing. If that's really what He looked like, then He was blessed with looks too. Christ used to make me think of sex. The thumb press started because we were picturing the nails in His palms.

"Do you miss Lessons?" Mamie asks as she scoops up one of her Brothers and rests Him on her hip. She uses her new black dress to wipe a peach-coloured stain off His face and He looks at me, sticks His damp, chubby hand out. I don't reach back. I stare at the ground.

I tell her I do miss them. "But maybe we can go back," I say.

Mamie puts her Brother down. "Go back?"

"Maybe after we give birth. They have evening Lessons for Boys. Maybe we could."

"That's impossible, Sable. You know we aren't allowed. Leave your family every evening. All to what? To learn more about things that happened and how things will be? What about just now? I like now."

Mamie's face shrinks as she argues with me. I can tell she misses Lessons already too. Mamie is one of the sweetest people I know and she loved the social aspects of learning.

"It's fine," I say. "We're better off in the home anyway, aren't we. What are you cooking today?"

"My mother has a headache. She's lying down. Oat and turkey pie."

"I'll help."

We go inside. The rafters are full of cobwebs, and the floorboards are stained and littered with more dirty clothes than normal. Her mother must be feeling awful. I hear the kids upstairs bouncing a play-ball off the wall. They squeal when they make a catch. How they must drive Mamie's mother mad in her migraines. I don't say anything, don't ask Mamie why she doesn't ask her siblings to stay still. Soon they'll all be old enough to be in Lessons, they'll be gone all day and maybe that will fix her home.

I go to the cupboard and find a sack of dry oats.

"I'm glad you're here, Sable," Mamie says. "Dinah came by today to tell me she got pierced. Her mother pushed the needle into her ears. She said she didn't even scream. Why must she brag all the time? She got three photographs taken, too. With these cute little pins in her ears. She told me one was in her yard, her on a swing smelling a basket of delphiniums. One in the kitchen posing with an apple. One in her bedroom hugging her knees, her window in the back. Yellow curtains touching her legs." Mamie's voice is fast and heated, and I can tell she's jealous.

The Den restricts photo taking. Memories and nostalgia are fine to keep in your head and in history, but not with too much vividness. It's easier to make changes when the past is limited. Even our Lesson books have barely any photographs. This is why I love Gram Evelyn's private photo collections her mother Iris brought to The Den. I caught Gram looking at them once when I came to her Elder cottage to drop off baking. She's so lucky to have them. I would never reveal her secret.

Dinah's mother is in charge of taking Arrival photos for the eighteen-year-olds. This is why Dinah makes a show of all the photographs she's allowed and Mamie is burning with envy.

"Well, you'll get a photograph taken of you this month, Mamie. They've got to track our progress. Before"—I suck my stomach in—"After." I jut my stomach out as far as I can and Mamie smiles. "We'll be famous. And anyway, you know she'll have to take the earrings out eventually. It's too flashy and vain." I flip my hair to make her laugh again, blow on my nails as if they are painted and shining. It works. Mamie laughs.

"Fine," she says. "But I still can't believe she's pierced. My Father would never allow it. Even for a photograph. I hope her ears turn green." Mamie grabs a pan of flattened turkey from the refrigerator. She sprinkles salt and pepper all over it. "When I'm pregnant," she says, "I want one photograph doing something different. Say I cut a hole in my belly, well, in the fabric. Picture just a regular old dress, but a big stomach hole. My mother could draw rays around my belly button and I'll be sitting in a field and you won't be able to tell which is which, my baby or the sun."

I chop potatoes. Mamie's kitchen windows are filthy. There are so many of them in the kitchen but you can't see out. Her younger siblings file in when they hear us in the kitchen. I peel them each a ribbon of onion and they laugh over their spiced, harsh breath and crawl and touch our feet.

Mamie and I yell, "Earthquake!" and jump, and the kids screech and roll.

"I don't know how you do this every day," I tell her.

"I love them."

"Your mother must've spent half her life in the Yards."

Mamie picks up her knife and makes lines in the turkey meat, stuffs oats in the crevices. It looks like art. But I'm sad for her. My mother doesn't need to enhance our protein with grains, because we are rationed enough fresh meat from the commissary. Mamie's Father is in sanitation and He's known to drink too much. My Father thinks Mamie's Father is short-sighted but I don't know. Others on the Trail say Mamie's mother is allergic to DiLexa and that's why she kept having babies, even when Lynx didn't request her to. I don't ask too much. I ask around it.

"Twenty-five," Mamie says. "She spent about twenty-five months in a Birth Yard. She loved it the first time, none of the rest." I place the potatoes on top of the meat and Mamie puts crumbled-up bread on top of that and tosses it in the oven, no oil or butter. "But now we're just hungry and my mother is sick," Mamie says. "You're so lucky Feles loves your Father. I'd do anything to make Him like us."

We chop root vegetables. We'll coat them in a little brown sugar to make them sweeter. Mamie fakes fruit for her family.

"My mother's body was so strong once," she says. "She was so good at birthing. She told me that when the babies are born, after all the pain, there's this high that you feel."

"Like floating?" one of her sisters, Dacey, asks, eavesdropping with a notebook in her hand.

"Dacey! Lessons are done?"

"They let us out early."

"Come help, then."

Mamie ties an apron around Dacey's waist. They have the same shade of brown hair but Dacey's is tangled up with hairpins. Dacey is already taller than Mamie.

"Happy Arrival, Dacey."

"You too, Sable."

"I like your new dress. Pink sleeve like Kass's."

"Yes, I like it too," she says.

Mamie goes back to talking about the floating. "Mum says your whole body heaves over and out and you can hear the cries of your new baby, but for a minute your head is crowned with wind and you can taste whatever you want to taste in the air. If you dream of a shape you can touch it and it's smooth and you'll feel the pressure and kisses of your Match but they're firmer, stickier. Their kisses are objects."

I toss turnips in cinnamon, brown sugar and flour. I don't believe her.

"I should go see Kassia. See you later on, then?"

Mamie nods. "Tell me how the port is."

MY SISTER IS ON OUR PORCH TAPPING THE WINDOW, playing a pantomime game with Gram Evelyn. Kassia licks her paws like a cat and Gram Evelyn laughs before slipping an Afterol under her tongue. Kass sees me on the lawn and runs to wrap her arms around me.

"How were Lessons?" I ask, reaching for her hand.

She says they were slow but good, and that the lecturer says He'll miss me and that she needs to learn the map of Main Stream as well as I had it in my head at her age. I used to fall asleep in my Father's study, which has a map of the world. Countries with beautiful names that sound delicious and regal as sweets. It always baffles me that a world so backward and evil can have such beautiful names for cities, lakes, mountains and parks. I used to close my eyes and say the names of countries out loud, left to right in the dark. Crickets outside the window seemed to chirp the names back at me as if they were once in those places and wanted to love them too but sought relief in the balance of The Den.

"Did He go over anything about Main Stream today?" I ask her.

"Actually, yes," Kass says. We go inside and she removes her shoes on the mat, leaves a small pile of gravel from under the treads. She must've run home. I want to run. I'm too old, now.

I envy Kass. "So today, He said Main Stream is untidy, sense-less, and then—this was very cool; you'll like this, Sable—He compared it to abstract art versus a portrait. Both are ways of approaching art, a big yellow blob or let's say a field of daisies, but one makes sense and the other forces you to leap to make sense of it. The Den is all portrait, clear, pretty. We don't need to leap."

I nod and jump over three floorboards in a row. "Leaping is wasteful. I think I remember that Lesson."

Kassia jumps to meet me. "Fun. But very wasteful."

We scrub our faces in the water closet and Kass asks how my day was. I don't answer her really; just say that Mamie and I cooked. Kassia's bright glowing cheeks shine under the fluorescent light. She plucks a few stray eyebrow hairs with her sharp fingernails. "I get to start making my face nice next year."

All girls receive beauty treatments at age fifteen to make us more perfect than we are born to be. Mine involved weeks of wax burning out my body hair, everywhere. After twelve or so treatments, it doesn't grow back. I miss my pubic hair sometimes because when it started to sprout I felt healthy as a plant. Kass once showed me her pubic hair and said how much it scratches and she can't wait for her beauty time. My eyebrows were shaped, my lip hairs tweezed and serumed to never grow back. I was fitted for a back-straightener to wear during sleep and now my posture is impeccable and boring. Kassia will start to wear hers next year. I don't need to wear it once I am pregnant and I look forward to this. But the Men see it as beautiful so it must be beautiful. I must be closer to something beautiful.

I look at Kass's reddened pores in the mirror, her skinny body in her slightly too big dress, her crooked teeth not yet purified with daily oil pulling, her posture not yet corrected. "I think you always look nice, Kass."

We hear my Father come in the door and set His briefcase down. He treads right to the head of the table, where His appetizer awaits Him. Leading Men in each family get the nicest evening meals. Usually small and ornate. Tonight my mother cut soft cheese into a flower and spooned pickled apricot spread on top; several almond slivers surround it like rays of sun. Kassia and I sit beside Him, watch Him enjoy every bite, watch a bit of spread stain His moustache. We do not tell Him.

He says He loves us and He's happiest for me today. My mother kisses His head as she circles the table, a wooden bowl in hand. She ladles a meat stew into small bowls then goes back into the kitchen for a sprout salad as beautiful as a bird's nest with bright red tomatoes inside like eggs.

My Gram takes her seat next to Kassia, holding the small book she presents to us every Arrival. This year she wants to pass the book around so we can each read a passage silently to ourselves. She says this year feels different because I'm eighteen. Kass and I are her only grandchildren.

The book, called *Seedtime Song,* has lyrics and poetry in it. It belonged to her mother, Iris, and she trusts it keeps our minds in good places for the rest of the year, that the words inside can root us right, that the poems inside are good luck and pleasant.

As women, we aren't supposed to keep books without consent. My Father graciously indulges this tradition. I'm happy He does. We always have His consent. He just advises Kassia and me not to tell our friends about it so their Fathers don't find out and judge Him. It's embarrassing to see women share and read at a Man's table, His place of leadership. I understand the shame He'd feel—the attention of women drawn away from His presence. He holds more wisdom than any literature we could ever access. We are to believe that. I want to believe that.

Gram Evelyn clears her throat and I can hear excitement in her breath as the spine of the book bends and she passes it into Kassia's lap. Kass flips through the dark green book, pretends to read and sips her water. She's slumped in the wooden dining chair. Her head almost touches her bowl. I watch her breathe in her food and relax. Lessons used to make me tired too. It's a lot to be a sponge for a day, to remember what you're told but also hold it in the spaces of your body and retain it all. I used to hold mathematics in my ribs, domesticity and wifehood teachings in my wrists, and The Den teachings in my kneecaps, ankles and feet. I was rooted with those.

Kass has a bigger appetite than me. She takes a forkful of stew and complains that she's burned her throat. My Father laughs at her. Kass slides Gram Evelyn's book to me next. A small golden earring of Grandma Evelyn's is jammed in the top corner of a page near the back like she does every year for me. I flip through the sauce-streaked pages, which have been thumbed through by our family during many Arrivals. My page is entitled "Chosen" and it is a poem about a lark choosing which tree to roost upon. I drink in the pretty words, once over, then again, allow my food to get cold. *And the lark lay down to claim the tree, for there was no oak as fine as she, and this was to be their destiny.*

I nod at Grandma Evelyn, reach under the table and slip the earring into her wrinkly hand. I pass the book to my Father. He licks His finger and turns to a random page, scans it slowly, humouring my Gram. My Father is finished His meal before I begin.

"Sable."

I drop my fork. "Yes, Sir?"

A slice of delight in His eyes unnerves me. "Patrick, Feles's healer, has a Son. Your age. His Grandfather helped build this house, in fact."

Ambrose.

"Do you know Patrick's Son?"

Ambrose. I do. I shrug. From Lessons, I know Him.

We are divided in Lessons by so many things. One being girls and Boys, because Boys go to another classroom after lunchtime to learn more difficult math, economics and hands-on, practical skills to run a home, run the plant.

We girls learn docility, domesticity, diet and active listening, things we'll need to be good supporters, cheerers and mothers.

And then, we are also divided into different classrooms by our social ranks—or, more accurately, our Fathers' social ranks. This meant Mamie, whose Father is in ill favour with Feles, was in a different classroom from me, and Ambrose. I don't know why they do this—other than the punishments for incorrect answers or disobedience are harsher for the less favoured. The less favoured also have to keep the Lessons building clean, and they line up last to eat lunch, so their food is usually soft and cold. When a student's Father gets in better favour with Feles and they're upgraded to a better rank, a better class, the gossip lasts for weeks. When a student's status is docked and they leave our class, we rarely speak of it. We know it could happen to us. We know things are never formed and sure.

Ambrose sat behind me for a whole year during Den History and Main Stream geography. Dinah fancied Him and told me she would one day want to Match with Him because

His Grandfather was very successful in Main Stream before He joined The Den, bringing tons of wealth and devotion. He was a doctor and Patrick became one too. He cares for Feles in His old age. This means Ambrose might do the same, will be in good favour always.

So I know Ambrose. We didn't really speak much. Nothing personal toward Him—I honestly never felt that compelled to speak in class. I wrote like the wind instead and kept disciplined in my essays and reading. I paid no mind to much else. I regret this now in that not very many Boys know or care about who I am, whether I'd make a good Match.

"Well, fine if you don't remember Him, Sable," my Father says before I have a chance to really answer. "But we think He may be a good fit. He's sturdy. His family is in good favour with Feles."

My mother snorts, then turns her head down to her plate, looks nervously at my Father. "Sorry," she says, toying with her sleeves. "It's just that Sable doesn't care that much about a Boy's sturdiness. She's too young."

"Sure, I do." She's right. I don't.

Gram Evelyn leaves the table and, blaming her Afterol dose, says her bladder is calling her.

Kassia says she knows Ambrose and all of His Brothers, wonders why I don't seem to remember. I do. I'm just nervous. Is Ambrose the one to be inside me first? I know His lovely teeth and hair, His impressive height. I've watched Him bite into apples by the creek near Lessons, seen Him walk Dinah or Mamie home with the other Boys and tell them nice things. I know He loves fishing. He once told Mamie He hates His own Father because of His intensity.

Gram Evelyn returns to the table and looks at me, then my Father. "George, Sable is nervous. Please, not now. We can talk about Matches later."

My Father ignores her, tells me to write Ambrose's name down as my choice. He says there are good genes there. There is no consanguinity but good looks and intelligence. He winks. I feel flushed and honoured that my Father insinuates I'm smart.

He reminds me that I have to have Ambrose's permission to write His name down.

"Well, that might be where this plan splinters, Sir," I say, staring down at my plate full of food, embarrassed. "I'm not very keen to speak with Boys."

Kassia beams and says eighteen can't come too soon for her. "I just love speaking to Boys!" I can't tell if she means it or if she's trying to impress my Father. We finish our food and I clear the plates, one by one because I need to think before I accidentally say something cynical to ruin a good day that started with iced cakes, Arrivals, playing cards and my smiling Gram.

I rinse each plate in the sink, pump soap from the dispenser, the gloppy pink of it oozing like blood down each dish. I love my Father. He loves me. He just doesn't know how hard it is to give up a childhood. He can't remember.

My mother enters the kitchen and takes her apron off. She beckons me and, with a cloth in one hand, leads me back into the dining room. She wipes the table. "It's time," she says, beaming.

She and Kass disappear into the kitchen once more. The swinging door sweeps warm air toward my face. Gram Evelyn tells my Father that dinner was lovely, though my mother was the one who did the cooking. Kassia comes in with that red bottle. She places it beside my Father and He unscrews the cap gently.

My mother joins us with a tray of crystal glasses, each silver handle reflecting sunlight streaming in through the curtains. For the Gathering Season, it's warmer than normal.

My Father pours mine first and it makes me nervous. The dark slurry liquid is my first drink ever. He pours His drink second. Next, Gram Evelyn. Then my mother. Kassia gets an empty glass to raise and clink. My Father clears His throat. "To Sable. May her Match be wholesome, her Gathering trimester peaceful, and her Harvest and Free Seasons in the Birth Yard historic. I have beautiful daughters who will make beautiful children. Sable, we are very proud. A toast to Lynx for bringing us here. May He rest in peace."

I lift my glass. "To Lynx. Praise Feles," we chant. My arm hurts. Everything does. I clink my Father's glass and the chime of it sends an ache through me, a phantom pain, a spark fresh from my brain. I drink my port fast. It burns, but kindly. It courses through my body, which for now is only mine—a body I will soon share. "I will love that child," I say. I take another large sip.

Kassia reaches across the table and clinks my glass with hers. Even though my glass is now empty, I still bring it to my lips.

"What did you say, Sable?" Gram Evelyn looks at me with dewy eyes and I remember something she told me about when Iris was pregnant with her.

Iris was twenty-eight when she entered Lynx's home, among sixteen other women. They began The Den with Him. She *chose* to make Evelyn with Him. Iris grew fat and happy as a house cat, still working a part-time retail job and writing letters and seeing anyone she pleased. She ate large dinners with Lynx and The Den mothers. They grew and they laughed and they played. Through all three seasons Lynx named—the Gathering, the

Harvest and the Free Season. Iris chose what clothes she wanted to wear. She decorated Gram Evelyn's and the other children's nurseries, chose the paint colours and constructed cribs. Gram Evelyn has pictures of Iris rubbing her belly in bed at home with Lynx. No Birth Yard. No Matches. The idea of choice was there for her. Why did they take it away?

Gram Evelyn is still waiting for my answer. I turn red in the face. "I said, I will love my child."

My Father pours himself another glass of port and another until the bottle is done. We sit a while until the Trail torches are lit along the gravel road. The idea of fire warms me through the window. "Happy Arrival," my Father says to us all, for the fourth time. I can't help but notice all our hands are on our bellies, even Kass's. Either we are all full from supper or they can't fathom my age either.

THE TRAIL IS ABLAZE WITH LIFE AND CELEBRATION tonight. There's a tent set up by the main square, where Lynx's grave is. The tents and tables will stay there for all of September to hold parties and merriment each evening. This is our one month to seek pure leisure, to socialize and dance and feel victorious for being part of this place. Beneath a gold awning, musicians play and golden-fried hot food and sugary sweets are served on trays perched on gold tables. There are candles everywhere. They sting my eyes. Beer flows from a line of oak barrels on the grass. Men dare each other to kneel under the taps, mouths open. Dinah's Uncle plays the music. He's brilliant with the fiddle and His Match has a lurid, raspy voice. Her ivory skirt blows in the breeze. A silver paper Arrival crown rests on her thick black curls.

Kassia and I watch from the porch. For years, it's been my and Kassia's task to hand out Arrival cakes to neighbours. They are heavy in the baskets my mother prepared. They smell thick and sweet.

Dacey, Mamie's sister, comes to collect her family's cakes. She gives us two of the crowns she crafts each year for everyone on the Trail. She says she started making them long before the Gathering Season. Mine is a bit snug for my head and has golden rice glued all around near the crown line. Along the four jagged points at the front, there are white sticks that resemble fence posts.

Dacey says she chose this one for me because I'm sturdy. My Father called Ambrose sturdy and I'm honoured to be thought of as similar to Him. I think the crown is perfect more in that I feel trapped sometimes, fenced in, claustrophobic with routine, but I don't say this. I would never say this. I shouldn't even be thinking it.

Kassia's crown is pink. I can tell by her pouty face she dislikes that the velvet rose on the corner is wet and soggy. She shakes it in an exaggerated way toward Dacey and doesn't thank her for her hard work like I did.

"Sorry." Dacey raises her eyebrows in a taunting way. "I dropped yours in a puddle. Accident."

I picture her dousing it in a washing bucket to make Kass feel bad. I want to spit on Dacey's cakes. I don't say anything. Do anything. I'm not sure when they started to hate each other. They used to be friends.

Boys run up and down the Trail shooting off Roman candles. After a few more songs, we leave the remaining cakes on the stoop.

We are tired of just watching. I want more to drink. I want more port or some beer to make me float. The thirst in my throat lingers as I walk through the crowds of my crowned neighbours and friends, smile as they whiz around. The mothers and Fathers are allowed to take Reposeries tonight. The small blue capsules arrived in an envelope tucked under our welcome mat two days ago. They stimulate joy, create carefreeness. My Father's eyes are dilated. He's clearly taken His and they've taken Him.

He stands on the small stage with Dinah's Uncle. He lifts a glass of beer out to the group, bestows on everyone an Arrival wish. He mentions my name but I don't approach Him or the stage. I walk a little way from the square, sit on the ground, pulling blades of grass and killing time. I need to speak with a Boy tonight. I need to find the woman in myself. I need to pluck up the courage to show my age and do things proper and right.

In time, Mamie finds me. She sits on the ground too, places a hand on my knee. Dinah glitzes by with her beautiful earrings but barely looks toward us. She is flirting out all that is in her. Perspiring with compliments, oozing praise for Ambrose and four other Boys. She's always trying to act older but, in doing so, makes herself look whorish. Mamie and I want her to knock it off and stop being so showy, because other people can see through it. Other people judge her. I heard some girls at Lessons say they think Dinah is too arrogant and excessive, that she is so lustful Feles can smell her hysteria. I would never tell her that but sometimes I want to. I want her to leave Ambrose for me. I want someone to see me for once and not only her.

Ambrose looks nice tonight. He's wearing a black jacket and black trousers and His hair is combed cleanly, a jagged left part. His Arrival crown is stuffed in His jacket pocket. He's staring at the ground while Dinah touches His arm and tells Him a boring story about pearl buttons on her mother's coat. She shakes her head to make her gold earrings shine. They look like the chandeliers I've seen in our Lessons books about wealth. They look like glut. They swing with greed.

I want to share a drink with Ambrose. I want to force myself into speaking with Him. I don't know where this drive is coming from. The glass of port? The pressure from my Father to find a Boy to Match with? The idea that my friends could outdo me and I'll be Matchless, barren, alone, pitied? I don't know. I feel electric. I feel the need to move, behave, act. I turn to the cottages in a row behind us, smile at the younger girls listening to the music in their evening smocks, the clothes they sleep in, on their porches. I find my reflection in a random front window. I do look older. Maybe I do. I call Ambrose's name. My hands turn clammy once I realize that I just said His name—we've never spoken before. He walks over to us. Dinah and His friends follow. He says hello. He says He knows of Kass, that His younger Brothers say she's smart. "Must run in the family, Sable. You always got top marks."

I shake my head. "Only in geography, really."

Ambrose sits on the curb beside us. "I like geography, too," He says.

Dinah places a hand to her head like she's going to faint, says she's in need of sugar. I ignore her.

"I like a world I haven't seen." I shrug. "Maybe I should see it."

The other Boys march off with Dinah in search of more food.

Ambrose studies me. "You don't mean that." He's looking down at my fistfuls of weeds, the grass piled in my lap.

"No, I don't." I feel sweat on the backs of my knees. "I enjoy our world."

"Right. Maybe if you saw more of the other one, Sable, you'd hate it," Mamie chimes in.

I forgot she was even sitting beside us. I think she knows I forgot. She flicks me in the shoulder. I'm boiling on the inside with nerves but, at the same time, I'm feigning that I can talk with ease to a Boy. I'm holding a conversation.

Dinah comes back with orange fudge on skewers and hands them to Mamie and me. "Time to plump up now," she says, "especially you, Mamie. You're a twig. You'll starve your fetus if you don't have anything to give it."

Mamie looks embarrassed although what Dinah says isn't even rooted in sense. It's folly that Mamie could kill her baby by being thin. It's stupid folly. But Mamie accepts the fudge and jams some into her mouth, licks her index finger. She always lets Dinah win with her taunting words. Dinah's comment was not truly a criticism of Mamie's figure—it was an attack on her Father's status, her family's rank in The Den. Mostly, an attack on her eligibility as a Match.

"Dinah," I say. "Happy Arrival."

She is glowing, with her long, dark hair, olive skin. Her new black dress fits her perfectly. She is so beautiful.

She purses her purple-glossed lips together. Dinah has worn colour on her lips since she was Kassia and Dacey's age. She's not really supposed to but she always wears it until an Elder notices, tells her she's full of impropriety, and she'll wipe it off on a fallen leaf or on the inside of her sleeve. I've seen her do this many times. She's brave to keep colouring her lips, expressing herself. Dinah is fearless because her mother is so liked by Feles. Some people think her mother sleeps with Him, pleases Him in the evenings. Feles is not to Match. Feles has better things to attend to. Feles can have sex with whomever He chooses. If He is choosing Dinah's mother, Dinah is lucky for it. It's kept discreet, however, so as not to emasculate Dinah's Father or Brothers.

Ambrose makes me nervous. I want to ask Him if I can write His name on my Match list. It has to be an *ask*. If the Boys don't know you wrote their names down, you are cheating Feles's wishes, and if the Men find out, your family will be shamed. There has to be consent or you are showing your hysteria, your lust, a woman's inability to take instruction. You have to put the Boy's cottage number on the form so that his cheek can be swabbed too, to ensure you're compatible to Match. The idea of a Match is to prevent disease, prevent any dangerous consanguinity, prevent too much choice, not enough logic.

The adults all begin to dance under the tent. The candle wicks spit fire, like small burning insects taking flight. The candles will burn out and die around The Den's curfew, eleven o'clock. Our parents' bodies glow. I don't know what to do this year. In previous years, Dinah, Mamie and I would sit on the porch with our siblings and clap and watch and wish we could have Reposeries to release the song in us. Now Mamie and I are sitting awkwardly on the ground where the gravel meets the grass with a Boy we barely know, Dinah rotting with pride, and we are jealous of her.

The song in me right now is muted and broken. Mamie whispers into my ear that Ambrose likes me more than Dinah, that Dinah tries too hard for attention. I ask how she knows this and she shrugs, says it's an instinct and tells me to eat my candy. The fruit flavour clings to my teeth. The sugar drips down my throat and I swallow.

Mamie finishes her fudge, then the rest of mine. She says we didn't make enough supper for her family and she was last to eat. Mamie says she can't wait for the Birth Yard, where meals are large and frequent, where she will be able to eat as much as she needs.

Dinah stops talking to Ambrose for a moment. She reaches down and grabs my hand. I know she loves me. But, in her mind, we are competing tonight. We are at war for Boys. I can't stop noticing—Dinah is so beautiful. Josiah and Claude, two Boys I know from Lessons, walk by and see this, too. They ask her to come play bottle-toss with them in their shared yard. Dinah tosses her hair and leaves us with Ambrose. I kiss her hand before she saunters off. I may be jealous but I want her to love me still.

"Do you miss Lessons, Mamie?" Ambrose's friend Isaac pokes Mamie in the shoulder. "Bet you miss 'em. But with you sluts off DiLexa, they better not let you anywhere near the schoolhouse. You'd bleed all over the floor, wouldn't you."

Mamie shrugs.

"It's not so different on or off the pill," I say, trying really hard not to sound condescending or to roll my eyes. He's a moron. "Just the timing of it all. That changes now."

Isaac touches Mamie between her legs. Mamie flinches.

I'm shocked. How could He do such a thing? Touch her there like He owns her body. "Can't wait, sweet," Isaac says.

Mamie's eyes well up but she secures her mouth into a pleasant smile. "Nice to see you this evening, Isaac," she stutters.

Ambrose tells Isaac to shut up and try another approach if He wants to Father anything. I hate the word "Father" as a verb. I don't know why. Fathers are so important and I honour them. But I always have hated the word. It sounds too much like "falter." It sounds like falling.

Ambrose asks me if I want to drink with Him. I can't meet Mamie's eyes—I'm too embarrassed at how Isaac just spoke to her and touched her—but excited that Ambrose has singled me out. My heart beats with the idea of going with Him, alone.

I nod toward Ambrose and we leave down the Trail, back toward my cottage. We still have a nice view of the Arrival tents, of Lynx's lit-up tombstone surrounded by white lilies.

Feles and His Brothers are in the bottled water plant a mile down. I imagine cigarette smoke and hear faint Main Stream music from a radio, music only they are permitted to listen to. Ambrose and I sit under the only raised porch on the Trail. The steps are half-rotten, covered with a lazy-thin layer of red paint. Ambrose pulls a flask from His shirt pocket. I want to tell Him I love Him, if only for giving me His drink and an escape from looking at Isaac, at Mamie. We pass the flask back and forth three times. I try not to cough as the liquid burns. I try to make it seem like I know what I'm doing. My legs are crossed in the grass and I feel it soiling my dress with wet green marks. My mother will be displeased when she does the washing but at least my dress is black. I romanticize the stain, hope it stays—I'll always remember this day.

Ambrose looks at me, half-smiling. "Are you dizzy, Sable?"

"It's good." I say. I love the slight glow of His teeth under the porch. I lean toward Him, feeling brave, the liquor moving in my stomach. "I have a question for you."

He nods.

"Isaac is to Match with Mamie? I didn't know. She didn't tell me."

"Last Arrival, He approached her and said if He could be her Match, her family would be secure. He's direct blood."

"I know. So am I. I think we're cousins." I feel a storm inside me. Poor Mamie. She must have felt so forced. "But she didn't tell me."

"Isaac's Father is a Grandson. He's favoured."

I roll my eyes, immediately regret it. That means my Father works for Him, in the plant. I was hoping for the other way around.

Ambrose continues. "And He wants Isaac to have what He wants."

Maybe I'd be as entitled as Isaac if Grandma Evelyn had been a Boy. If she'd been born a Boy, she'd also be a Brother of Feles. Instead of prone to hysteria, unreliable. A woman. I'm a descendant but it's matrilineal—not as important, less valued. Rightly so. We shouldn't get too much. We can never give enough.

I toy with my hair. The alcohol is making me blurred and light but not happy. I worry about Isaac. He isn't kind enough for Mamie. He could hurt her and no one would do anything.

Ambrose looks up. The sky beams down, sluices light between the gaps of the stairs. "I'd like to Match with you, Sable," He says. "There's something that seems durable about you."

I feel my heart shift in my chest. I feel my throat swell and ache. I'm not a table. Durable. I'm not brick. I feel movement, an eruption inside. I vomit. I vomit hard behind me in the rosemary bush overgrown under the stairs. When I'm done, I wipe my mouth and crawl back onto the Trail. I say nothing to Ambrose.

I don't turn around. I have never felt so embarrassed and gross. I can't turn around. I rush quickly in the dark away from Him before He can say anything. Of all the things He could compliment me on, my durability is not what I wanted to hear.

That I'll make babies, withstand time, stand by a Man like Him. I wanted Him to tell me I'm clever, tell me I'm attractive, friendly, anything. Durable. I'm just a durable girl. A horrid, stupid, durable girl.

KASS IS HOME FROM THE ARRIVAL PARTY AND WE GO TO bed early, undress in the heat, away from the sound and crowd. Kass doesn't want to sleep on her side of the hanging curtain. She wants to sleep beside me tonight. I let her.

"I saw you speaking to Ambrose," she says, stealing the covers off my side of the bed to cloak herself doubly. Kass is always cold. I'm overheated over everything tonight. She can sleep with me, fine, but I don't want to talk about it.

"I did," I say, facing the wall, away from her. "It was nothing."

"Well, then I envy you for nothing," she says. "You smell like something rotting, though."

"Just go to sleep, Kass," I say. I lie awake on my mattress, my back-straightener causing my neck to cramp. My body is tense and anxious, resistant. But, tonight as the brace pinches a nerve near the top of my neck, I feel I deserve the pain. I was so stupid to leave Him. I should've let Him call me durable and said thank you. Why did it bother me?

I promise myself I will call on Ambrose soon to ask His permission to write His name down as my Match and ask if He'll forgive me for storming off on Him and for exposing my despicable hysteria by vomiting like that. I'll say it was the booze, and that's why women shouldn't drink. It wasn't His fault. It wasn't anything He did.

I listen and wait for my parents to come home high and buzz-ing, listen to them in their bedroom through paper-thin walls. I do want this. I need to want this.

CHAPTER 3

GRAM EVELYN SHAKES ME AWAKE, HANDS ME A cup of water. "Good morning, my Sable. Wake up, I have news." I rub my eyes, heave myself up awkwardly in my stretcher. She has come with bags. "I'm leaving my Elder cottage. Your mother isn't sure it's the right thing, but I know it is. I want to help, until you're with child. So, I'll be sharing this room. Just for the Gathering Season, and a few weeks of Harvest."

I'm so happy as she starts settling in, shuffling her bags around. She is wearing her red felt slippers and a red wool blanket draped over her shoulders. She hangs a white scarf behind my bed frame on a loose nail. She tosses black quilts on the floor.

"Gram, I don't want you sleeping on the floor."

She squints toward the low clouds out my window. "Make no mistake, little one. These are for you. I get the bed."

My breath reeks of alcohol and I remember I'm stupid. Gram Evelyn scolds me for leaving last night's Arrival party early. "Your mother says you were asleep by the time she got home. That's no way to spend your time. You need to meet Matches. Get it over with. The longer you wait, the harder it is. You have to be more social now that you're eighteen."

I nod. I know she's right. She's always right.

My mother calls us into the kitchen and fixes us tea. Kass has already gone to Lessons and my Father is sleeping off a night of dancing. Mothers cannot oversleep or fall behind.

Once I feel a prick of caffeine from the tea, Mum asks me to mop the floors before we talk about Birth Yards and sex and the Family Body.

Our home has one narrow hallway, with the two bedrooms at the end, Kass's and mine divided in half by that same old curtain. She gets the window on her side. I got a bigger bed. Our roof slants up in a triangular, delicate peak. I mop the floor in every room, spending extra time in the batter-stained kitchen, the wood darkening with soapy water. It smells good.

I lift the mop to clean a rafter. There's a spider up in the corner. She's spun a large web, like an ornate glass bowl. She tumbles to the ground beside my foot when I push the mop strings near her. I'd normally scream at her fuzzy legs, stretched-out shape, and the unknowns of her venom. Instead I lower my hand, let her crawl up my arm. It feels like a small dance. She walks with poise, exploring my skin.

Gram comes behind me with a tea towel. She squishes the spider's body, says that's enough idling and it's time to come sit.

Mamie is on the couch in our living room wearing one of her mother's old white dresses, taken in at the waist. She's belted it with a necktie. She eats from a bowl of soft oats, saying she has a horrible headache without DiLexa.

I smile and sit beside her. I didn't hear her come in. She's got her cheek swab kit in her lap. My Father will be taking these to Main Stream next week. It's an honourable task. He's proud to do it every year.

Gram Evelyn tells Mamie to be less of a rodent and slow

down with her breakfast, that women should take small bites, that if she's feeling unwell now, eating too fast is only going to make it worse. The side effects of ceasing DiLexa will bother us for the first couple of days. But we need to withdraw from it.

My Gram turns on our battery-powered fan. "Hot in here," she says.

I nod. Mamie explains that her mother is in bed, unwell, talking to herself. "I came here to learn about sex," she says as she slurps up her breakfast.

My mother and Gram Evelyn say it's fine, that they understand her mother's infirmity.

"Two birds, one stone," my mother says, sitting beside us. "Sex is the stone." She winks. "It will hurt at first, a Man on top of you, inside you. You'll bleed if it's new." She looks at Mamie suspiciously.

Mamie sucks the tip of her pinkie. "I'm a virgin, Vale."

My mother looks relieved. "It'll hurt, His weight and the newness of sex, but we'll find you someone safe and good, Sable."

"Do we have to do it in a tent?" Mamie asks. "Can't we do it at home?"

My mother scolds her: "Mamie." She gestures to Lynx's portrait on our wall. He has a narrow face, bright green eyes that seem to see through us. He wears a starched grey vest and trousers. The Den mothers pose behind Him but they aren't in focus. I always pretend that the one who is third from the left might be Iris. Her hand touches His shoulder. "Mamie, respect that you must conceive in the presence of Lynx. He fills the Men with confidence. He fuels the Family Body. All of us."

"Sorry." Mamie lowers her head, puts her bowl of oats on the tea table. "I know, Vale, I'm sorry."

"How long does it take?" I ask.

Gram Evelyn says it depends on a Man and His stamina and the strength of His sex, that it might be quick but we'll each have sessions during ovulation in December until we are seeded and ready. Each session will be half an hour.

I don't feel as sick as I thought I would. It all sounds thrilling, new. Mostly, it still feels far enough away.

"It's best to get to know Him before. Makes it feel natural." My Gram Evelyn says that with a sharp tone as if she believes none of it is natural. "There will be a cloth in each tent, a basin of nice hot water, you can clean the blood and semen off yourself, and you can kiss and feel alive."

"Your Father was kind," my mother says. "Your Father was kind, and the Men are told to be kind. Tell us if that's different."

Mamie looks to her bare feet. I know she's thinking of Isaac.

I don't know what my body will feel like because I don't know for sure who will be on top of it yet. I hope Ambrose doesn't hate me for walking off last night. I hope He will still give me permission and the Men will approve Him as my Match once the genetic test results are in.

Mamie and I go to the water closet and rinse our faces. I have a headache too. Mamie clutches her stomach. I tell her to try to keep her oats down. She flaps her arms like a bird, facing the mirror. "Are we the birds? Or the stone?"

"Birds. Sex is the stone."

"Right."

And my mother's a field, I don't say out loud. My mother is a dense field of wheat and she scratches against me when she speaks of sex. Gram Evelyn knocks on the door and says we need to swab our cheeks. She has my kit. We open them, take out the small stick with a sponge at the end.

"Brush your cheeks on the inside. Get a healthy flap of skin on there."

Mamie and I face the mirror and don't look at each other as we swab. She rushes hers, places the stick in a small box.

"Sable," Gram says, "you're being too delicate. It's not art."

But as I feel the sponge in my mouth, I think, This is me. This is what I'm going to make. Someone else. It is art. Mamie squeezes my shoulder as if she's just read my thoughts. I place my stick in the box, and Gram Evelyn seals them with labels with our names.

"Imagine if we mixed them up," I say.

My mother hears me from the living room. "Good grief, Sable," she says.

My Gram asks us if we have any burning questions.

"Just a burning body," Mamie says, and my mother suggests the four of us take a walk to The Den commissary, get some things to prepare supper.

Mamie says she has to go wake her Brothers up from their naps. The youngest are twins. My mother tells Mamie to take them with us in their carriage, that fresh air will do her good and she deserves to feel good. We throw on sandals and head out down the Trail.

The party has left behind an aftermath, like a good storm. Wet grass, shattered goblets and dirty plates, half-eaten cake and streamers and cloths and piles of crowns. Mamie's Father and other lower-favoured Men will be in charge of cleaning it all up when they awaken.

My mother says that with her Reposeries, she never feels as good as everyone else. She says that during, she feels light as a cloud, but dark for days following. "Thank Lynx, it's sunny today, though. Somehow, it's always sunny after Day One of Arrivals."

There will be celebrations out on the Trail the whole month, but most folk pace themselves and don't attend them all. Only a few people go out to drink and celebrate every night, Mamie's Father among them.

We put the twins, green-eyed and gaunt-looking like Mamie, drool dried in patches on their blue playsuits, in their carriage and we walk to get fresh food from the commissary. It's half a mile from us on the way to the plant. As we walk, I pray we don't see Ambrose or any Boys. I'm thankful they're in Lessons. The chances of seeing any Men are low right now.

The shop smells like carcass, which means the Men in charge of hunting for The Den have caught fresh game. The scent is metallic and fresh. Eli runs the commissary. He is an elderly Man who refuses to live in the Elder cottage because He likes His solitude. He gives small pieces of dried venison to Mamie and says, in a grunted voice, "For the Boys." Mamie feeds her Brothers each a piece of meat and they suck and swallow without chewing. My mother wraps a fresh wild turkey leg in a linen bag and we thank Eli, head to the back screened-in room for fruit and vegetables.

The vegetable room of the commissary is circular. There's a small basin of water in the centre to rinse or scrape off anything spoiled. *The Den is not to be wasteful* was one of Lynx's most prized values. My mother and Gram spiral around the beautiful crates of apples, pears, carrots, lettuce. My Father has high status, being directly related to Lynx and Feles, so we don't have to choose anything that's gone bad or anything less nutritious like potatoes or corn. Mamie pushes the carriage near the older produce slumped in two wooden crates, choosing the less spoiled turnips and apples, rotating them fully to inspect. I don't walk with her. I don't want anyone to think my family is in poor favour with Feles.

My mother puts a carton of dark berries in her basket and tells me not to tell my Father. They're for us, the dark blood of them on our fingers before dinner, a secret. Gram Evelyn grabs a paper bag from a crate and puts four shiny apples inside.

I stand in place. I'm not ready to claim my life as a mother, cook and food-fetcher. Ready to be consumed by tasks and ready to consume for my family. My mother shows Eli her weekly ration card and He stamps it. Once we head back to the Trail, Gram puts the apples in the slotted pocket of Mamie's carriage and says nothing.

Mamie doesn't notice until we're almost to her cottage. Then she discovers the paper bag and hugs my Gram tight. We leave her and return home to cook. What Gram did is punishable, but I love her for it and would never say anything. Her heart isn't obedient, and I wonder how that can make her bad. She's good. She holds so much goodness.

I'M TIRED OF IT. IT'S BEEN WEEKS OF THE SAME THINGS. I'm tired of listening to Gram Evelyn and my mother tell me the birth-control-withdrawal headaches will fade, tired of them telling me the Birth Yard will be comfortable if I'm assigned to the newer, nicer one of the two, tired of being told I'm going to be great as a Match, as a mother. I am tired of them telling me that when I have sex, the Man may not realize the extent of His strength, the excitement of His body, that it may tear and hurt me, that there are many ways of pleasing a Man to make Him seed me. I blush when they talk about it, but I know it's important that I know.

It's been weeks of me wearing the same apron tied tight to my waist, an apron once mildly dusted with flour from helping with baking, now stained forever with streaks and spills from preparing elaborate dinners. I'm a horrible cook. Only my Father has been honest. One night, when He saw my over-charred trout and burnt vegetables, He didn't eat at all, said He couldn't even try.

My DiLexa withdrawal wakes me up once or twice a night. Or it could be just my anxiety. I'm starting to get very nervous about sex. I used to think I wanted it more. My body is telling me otherwise. It feels like my limbs and my sex are whispering at me, *Stay a girl, stay young, stay.* I spend so much time in the water closet at night—peeing and sweating, splashing water over my stressed legs and arms. I leave a trail of my body's tears down the hallway to my room. My mother dabs the floor dry in the morning with a cloth, saying she remembers being nervous at age eighteen too.

I still have not called on Ambrose to ask for His permission. I'm so ashamed for vomiting in front of Him, walking away from Him. I barely leave the house. I have not attended any more Arrival parties. Dinah taps the windows at night, calling for me to come out and socialize, flirt, drink. I'm stupid and small and the excitement from learning about sex has died. I want Him. I think I want Him. I'm supposed to want Him. Mostly, I want myself back. I want Lessons. I'm starting to understand what The Den wants me to give up. I wish it were all different. Or maybe I wish I weren't a girl.

Kass and I wash our bodies and hair before sleep. She tells me Ambrose has asked about me at Lessons. If He wants me, why can't I feel it? Isaac has visited Mamie three times this week alone. He brings her salted caramel taffy, her favourite flavour, and they sit out on her porch. They have gotten to know each other. She says He's outspoken and doesn't let her talk too much, but He's trying to show her He's powerful, strong, interesting. He summarizes books only Boys are allowed to read. Mamie retells them to me but she's a bad storyteller—she scrambles up character names or forgets how the stories end.

Mamie is over every morning after my chores and leaves after my mother has made us our pre-dinner meal. Mamie says her breasts and face feel less plump without DiLexa and the thoughts of Isaac inside her are fiery and relentless. I don't trust Him still. But I don't tell her this.

Day in, day out, I wake and clean and cook. On Fridays, I'm permitted to nap on the couch with the sun staining my skin after the floors are cleaned and the bread is baked.

I can now label my body, all the secret parts of it. Gram Evelyn gave me an old hand mirror to use in the bathtub to admire and learn about the parts I'm given. They scare me—the flowering and openness of it all—my second mouth. My mother tells me some of her friends have encouraged their daughters to touch themselves in private, feel the pleasure and learn, though Lynx always taught that masturbation was for the weak. My mother doesn't agree it's right. She thinks I should wait for sex. I'm afraid to touch myself anyway. I don't want to feel pleasure. I felt pleasure at Lessons. Really, we mostly discussed The Den, but to understand us, they say we need to know where we came from. I'm grateful for this.

Before the Arrival month, before I was dismissed from Lessons, we were learning about Main Stream—how women there are wild and barely kept at bay, how they don't want to mother or devote themselves to family, the earth and sky suffering from poison oils and toxic air spilling and sloshing into everyone, sprawling cities and forged high-rises at the expense of animals dying, lost women who work urban streets and even sell themselves, their bodies and minds, to fool and use Men. Dying from drugs, dying from illness, dying from too much food intake, dying from greed, dying from conflict, the dying and dying and dying, the taking and taking that is Main Stream. We were taught that folk from Main Stream want sex always, will get it through food and lust and bodies and with themselves and even animals. It was our last Lesson before we were out of school. The last Lesson girls are taught. We need to remember and hold in our hearts the terrors of Main Stream, and thank Lynx, and now Feles, for sparing us from it all.

If Main Stream is so barbaric, I wonder if my Father is unsafe when travelling there. He's signed a contract that He can't speak of what He sees to His family or to women. He is under oath to keep the horrors of Main Stream tucked in His own pocket, His own mind. But I want to know. Why do they bother giving girls Lessons if we are meant to learn for only a short while? We are a waste of that space. We are meant only to breed.

ONE NIGHT, AFTER SUPPER, MY FATHER ASKS ME TO MEET HIM in the living room to fill out my Match sheet. I didn't eat much for supper. My own cooking revolts me too. My Father wants to write Ambrose's name down now. He is in a freshly laundered suit. His cufflinks are swans. He looks magnificent, kind of regal. The flowers printed on our couch seem to touch His arms.

I'm about to disappoint Him. "Sir, you can't write that name. I did not ask. I haven't gone to see Him."

He lays the paper and pen back down on the tea table. "Sable, call on Ambrose tonight. Ask. Do not shame our family. Do not be a cowardly girl."

I nod. I say I'll do it.

I clear my throat and bow to my Father and Lynx's portrait watching us. I put my raincoat on in the front entrance. The blue swishy plastic feels restricting but safe. "What cottage number is His?"

My Father smiles. "Twenty. Thank you, girl."

There are Men drinking by Lynx's grave. No Arrival music yet. The silence is nice. I bow toward Lynx's grave and the surrounding Men lift their glasses of dark syrupy booze before turning away and continuing their conversations. I keep walking. The rain is slight and the valley air is so cool. I exhale and watch my breath cloud. I walk on the gravel road past Cottages Two through Five. Five is Mamie's. Through the window I see her mother kneeling, facing the wall. She's murmuring to Lynx's portrait. She looks less pale than normal. She looks healthy. She doesn't see me and I don't want her to. If I stop and say hello, I will chicken out and never make it to Twenty. It's about a fifteen-minute walk and I don't want to talk myself out of it in any way.

When I pass the commissary, the doors shut and lights off for the night, I know I am close to Twenty. The plant looms at the end of the Trail. We girls will be allowed in soon, to meet Feles, meet our Leaders. After conception. I hope Ambrose chooses me. I hope He allows me to write down His name.

Ambrose's cottage was rebuilt last year. The wood is shiny with fresh varnish and the porch is one of the largest on the Trail. Chimney smoke lifts from the roof and it soothes me. I spit on my palm, slick down my hair with saliva. Even with conditioning treatments every week or so, my frizz always prevails. I tie it back with a rubber band and feel the curls flow down my back. I stomp my boots on Ambrose's walkway so I don't dirty the porch with my steps.

I knock. Silence. Knock again.

His Father opens the door.

I bow my head because He is an important Man to Feles. "Sir, my name is Sable."

To my surprise, He bows back. "George's girl. Your Father is a good Man."

I bow my head again. "He is."

I've seen Ambrose's Father before on His way to the plant or at Arrival gatherings, but I never noticed what He really looks like. He has the same ink-dark hair as His Son, but He is far shorter. He has wrinkly skin and two chins. He rests His arms on His plump belly. "What brings you here so late? You off to Arrivals later?"

"Happy Arrival," I stutter back. I've forgotten my manners. I should've led with this. "No, I'm here to see Ambrose. To ask."

Ambrose's Father looks pleased. "I would've liked to breed with your mother, you know. Your Father Matched with her before I had a chance to ask."

I feel my face redden. I can't grasp His tone or how to respond. "Oh."

Ambrose's Father chuckles. "Some time ago. I'll fetch Ambrose for you."

"Thank you, Sir."

Ambrose's Father shuts the door and I stand on the porch, damp and waiting. It seems odd not to be invited in. My Father would've invited me in. I always find Men's different mannerisms interesting. I feel like we're supposed to see them as one but I never can. I pick at loose skin around my fingernails, tucked into my sleeves so no one can see. We aren't supposed to deface our bodies, even if it's as minor as nail biting or picking. We aren't even supposed to get bruises or scrapes, really. Men are praised for their scars and physical injuries because they reflect hard work. Women's scars show clumsiness and carelessness.

The door opens again. Ambrose emerges without a jacket on. His black collared shirt is buttoned all the way up and His denim trousers look nice on Him, show off His slender, long legs.

"Sable, it's been a few weeks. Thought you'd have filled out your form already. Chosen other Boys."

"I've been putting it off, I guess." I force myself to make eye contact, to act normal and unafraid.

"I told you I'd Match with you already."

"I know. But it has to be an *ask*. *I* have to ask *you*."

He nods and pulls a cigarette and matches from His pocket. He lights up and exhales. The wind blows a puff of smoke into my face. It's kind of nice.

"So, will you? Will you Match with me?"

He smiles mid-drag and answers with a solemn tone. "You can write my name down."

I feel relief. He actually meant it when He said it the first night of Arrival. "Well, okay. Great. That's great."

"Okay." He stares at me a bit too long and I back away.

"Then I will go home and write your name down."

"Yes." He ashes against the porch railing. "Good night, Sable."

I raise my eyebrows and pivot awkwardly toward the Trail. "Good. Thank you." I start walking away, wishing I actually had the skills to flirt like Dinah. I wish I could say something witty or gracious. Instead I keep my head down and watch my feet carry me home until I'm back with my Father in the living room.

My Father still has the Match sheet on His lap and is drinking some whiskey on ice, His favourite Arrival treat. "He said yes," I tell Him.

My Father smiles with His teeth, which is out of the ordinary for Him and His stoic personality. "I've never been so proud of you, girl." He takes a swig of His drink and scribbles down *Ambrose* on the form. "Any others you've asked?"

I shake my head. At least I had His pride for a moment. My Father nods, folds the sheet in half, tucks it into an envelope. I sit beside Him on the couch and He kisses my forehead. I stare at the envelope on the table as my mother comes down the hallway, two Reposeries in her hand. My Father and she kiss and swallow them without water, and He escorts her out onto the Trail where they are meeting friends at Lynx's grave.

I lie down in Kass's bed beside her. She's been falling asleep early with textbooks around her feet. Tonight, there's a map of our Trail beside her. A map of grey streaks marking The Den land around the plant, the farmland beside it, the mountains encompassing us. I grab her arm and wrap it around my body. I fall asleep to her breathing, imagining her at Lessons, imagining she'll know every textbook by heart, and that she'll never have to stop.

CHAPTER 4

IT'S BEEN THREE DAYS SINCE MY ASK. I'M MEETING Ambrose after supper. Gram Evelyn calls it courting, and my Father says that's an unhealthy thought to put in my head. We aren't Matched yet, so to Him, it's more social than political and not an ounce romantic.

I ask Dinah over to help with my hair. She sits in during my family's dinner, eats three helpings of my mother's cabbage, leaves to prepare her heated rollers in our water closet. She says she forgives me for stealing Ambrose away, and that she wrote Garrison's name on her list, and they've been kissing behind the chokecherry tree near the commissary at night when the adults are too blitzed and happy on Reposeries to notice. She says she loves the taste of His tongue.

I haven't seen Dinah for a week and notice she looks even older, if that were possible. She wears her dress more unbuttoned in the front and I can see the line where her breasts begin and the mystery of her body starts. That must be her secret to good flirting. Even I'm intrigued.

"You can't wear that out. You look frumpy," she says when I enter the water closet, shutting the door.

I'm still wearing the apron I cooked dinner in, overtop of an older dress. I take my apron off and twirl. "How's this?" I know she'll still disapprove but I like to annoy her. "I'm going to wear my black Arrival dress anyway, you know. That's the rule for public dress." I raise my brows at her. "You don't seem to care about that."

"No one has said anything about it, Sable." Dinah reapplies purple stain on her lips and sticks one finger through a perfect ringlet near her cheek. She removes her green dress with little stars sewn all over it and she is naked, and she says take it. I don't want to but we trade. The flesh of my waist and thickness of my legs make the fabric a bit tight for my liking but I look what Dinah says is desirable. The beginnings of my breasts are exposed and white and plump.

"You're not supposed to wear colours out like this."

"You're not supposed to do a lot of things," she says, "but you can't stand out if you wear the same thing." She puckers her painted lips toward me. She has a point. "My mother made me this dress and she told me Feles approved the fabric and all. So, you see, the rules can be bent."

I take my black Arrival dress off the towel rack where it was drying and throw it over the borrowed dress. "At least, don't make my Father see me leave in green," I say. I hand Dinah the old dress I cooked in.

Dinah winks. "I think He'd be proud of you, trying to catch Ambrose's eye, but whatever you say."

Dinah tames my frizzy hair for an hour, pumping in pungent yellow oil she brought from home. "We decided to practise," she says. "Garrison and I are going to have sex soon."

"But what if you get pregnant before it's a sure Match?"

"He'll just make sure He takes His sex out. Right before. He says that'll work."

"Why risk it? If you're due early, they'll abort it at the Yard. It has to be approved by Feles, our Fathers. And then you'll be shamed. They might hurt shamed girls."

Dinah smiles. "Do they? Is that really what they do?"

She's so arrogant sometimes. I feel myself blush. "No, I mean, I don't know what they do. They could exile you. Is that what you want?"

Dinah clips my ear with a hot curler. It burns. I slap her stomach and call her a witch.

"I'll hang on, then," she says. "They can't take my child from me. I'll keep it inside. I'll clench until I'm supposed to birth. Sable, I will never leave. Okay?"

I don't think clenching will help her, but I don't know for certain to tell her otherwise. I repeat myself. "What if Garrison isn't your Match for sure?"

"He will be," she says. "We are in love. We're both healthy. Feles will choose Him for me. I know it."

I want to tell her that doesn't really do much for her chances but I don't. Gut feelings can fall into all things hysterical. She's acting too hopeful, which is also to act unbridled, hysterical.

"Dinah, do you know about DociGens? Really know? My mother won't talk about it." I look at my friend's focused face in the mirror as she continues to brush out the ends of my hair.

She doesn't look up to meet my eyes. "Devil's Breath. Don't be stupid. You know about them."

"I know they calm us, but what do they feel like? Do we really change? Permanently? Do we know when we're on them? Do we change back after?"

"They keep us out of the realm of hysteria." She says it so calmly, as if I have no reason to worry. "You shouldn't need to know more than that. What, you think Feles would drug us for nothing?"

"Oh." I exhale deeply. I touch a curler by my cheek before unravelling it. The curl is tight, shiny and perfect. "No, I don't think it'd be for nothing."

Dinah laughs. "We'll still be us, you goose. Just better mothers, better listeners."

We'll still be us. I repeat the phrase in my head but find little comfort. *We'll still be us.*

AMBROSE AND I ARE MEETING ON THE BRIDGE BY Lessons. The bridge is small. It covers a muddy, shallow creek. When I see Him, I want to ask Him what kind of Man and Father He'll be, ask Him if He'll write me when I go to the Yard. The Yard is only a few hours away, but He won't be able to visit me during my pregnancy. This detachment, which Lynx so strongly believed in, keeps us more community minded, less lovestruck and able to focus on our bodies, our pregnancies.

I hope He doesn't bring any booze with Him to the bridge. I don't want to throw up again but still want the courage to make Him laugh, try on a different mask of myself. I will probably spoil my questions and get no answers.

Dinah finishes beautifying me and allows Kass to come in. Kassia is already in her nightdress and has been waiting to scrub her teeth. "Sable, you're beautiful," she tells me, and for a moment when I see my hair bobbing up and down, still warm and shiny from the curlers, when I see pale pink stain on my lips, the striking blush on my cheeks making up for my declined appetite, I believe her.

My parents are staying home tonight from the Arrival celebrations. My mother is ironing a tablecloth in front of the roaring fireplace. My Father sticks a cigar in the flames, brings it to His mouth. They tell me to enjoy myself, to speak to Boys and dance and show myself off, that it's not too late to get more Matches. They think I'm meeting multiple Boys in a starched black dress, not one Boy in Dinah's wild, improper dress.

My mother tells Dinah she heard that she has her eye on Garrison. My mother clasps her hands together and looks happier than she has in a while. She and Dinah are perfect for each other—the way they hug and squeal. They seem a better pair as mother and daughter.

I go to the kitchen to say good night to Gram Evelyn. She is quietly reading her favourite illegal novel, tucked inside a binder of Lynx's Family Body teachings.

She hugs me good night and tells me there are people in her book who believe in a powerful Man in the sky and that using a necklace to count prayers to Him makes them more likely to go to an afterlife called Heaven. "It reads like a real tragicomedy." She laughs. "At least we can forgive ourselves."

I kiss her cheek. "Don't get caught reading that, Gram."

"Well, don't tell your mother or Father." She wags a finger at me. "Or I'll drown you."

"I never would." I laugh. Her humour is often morbid. "But if I did, I'd learn to swim first."

Gram Evelyn smiles and shoos me away. I put my shoes on, leave with Dinah onto the Trail for the last week of Arrival parties.

◇◇◇

DINAH HOLDS MY HAND AS WE WALK INSIDE THE ARRIVAL tent beside Lynx's grave. She steals a Reposery from the pocket of a woman's satchel left on a stray lawn chair, slips it under her tongue.

"Do Reposeries feel good?" I ask, shocked by her boldness.

She nods. "I tried them with a few girls two nights ago. They really do give you that triumphant Arrival feeling. Floating. I couldn't stop laughing."

I'm surprised they let women take them at all. Uncontrolled laughter or tears or anything is deemed hysterical. I wonder if Feles lets women take them now because we aren't to be hysterical or too sensitive the rest of the year.

Garrison's Father walks past us. He smiles at Dinah. He has a pink Birth Yard ribbon wrapped around His left arm. It means He has a daughter who gave birth last season. The Men wear them to show their pride in their familial growth, the newly established Matches. My Father will soon wear a ribbon. I bet He'll wrap it around His arm every day, bet He'll ask my mother to iron it when He returns from the plant, keep it pressed and proud.

"Who is Garrison's sister again? Do we know her?"

Dinah says Garrison's sister is a year older than us. She is quiet and always sat at the back of Lessons. I try to recall her name but I can't quite conjure it.

Dinah reminds me. "Her name is Rachel. She's got black hair and has those weird purple marks around her eyes. Remember? She always looked bruised."

Dinah's dark eyes start to dilate from the drug and she lifts more onto her toes, straightens her posture, takes a sip of lemon water that isn't hers from a table beside us.

"Right. I wonder what Birth Yard she went to."

There are two of them, and it all depends on who your Father is, your reputation, your strength and the risk of your pregnancy. Those who are under-height or underweight will need an opening procedure on their stomachs when they give birth. They go to the high-risk Yard east of The Den, Lucina. If all goes well this season, I will go to the Ceres Birth Yard. Ceres has a large lake and dry summer heat, and is near the farmland we get our crops from. The Yard where my mother went. Both Yards—Ceres and Lucina—are named after Roman goddesses of fertility whom Lynx preached would protect us and help us learn to serve.

"Lucina," Dinah says. "I think it was because she needed an opening procedure. She told Garrison there are no trees because of those forest fires years ago, but that she liked the peace and quiet."

I think about how much more peace and quiet I can stand, and then think of Ambrose and my stomach gives a leap. "I have to go soon, Dinah."

She kisses my cheek. "You're dazzling, Sable. I did well with you."

I WALK DOWN OUR TRAIL. I'M GOING SOUTH TOWARD THE pond and the old bridge. Our Trail is around three miles long. Through the windows, I see families gathered around their fireplaces. I see, in a larger home, a Man, probably one of Feles's more reputable Men, watching television. I've only seen a television once and it wasn't even plugged in. It was in the back of the truck my Father drives. He collected it off the side of a road in Main Stream. He said He was excited to present it to Feles.

It had small wires sticking out of the top and a large FREE sign taped to the screen.

I can see the antennae and screen through translucent curtains. Perhaps it's the same television my Father found. On the screen is a mouse in clothing shooting at a cat with a pistol. I've never seen drawings move in such a way. I wish I could hear the music and banter to go with it. I realize I'm staring through the curtains, realize that if I'm caught, I will be called a leech or a nuisance. In Main Stream, their pictures move to tell a story. How beautiful. What a beautiful and silly thing.

Out on the hilly lawn of this wealthier home, a group of young Men smoke cigars. I'm happy they don't see me staring. They are preoccupied with each other's company. They wear glowing bracelets that cast their faces in different colours. They're older than me by at least a decade. One of them must be a Son of the family who lives here.

I linger a bit longer to see the mouse escape triumphantly from the cat. The cat plays on a fiddle and I see the Father of the home laughing alone at this ending. I turn on my heels to continue on my way. When I do, one of the Men finally takes notice of me.

I wave to be polite and hope they don't know how long I was standing there staring at the television. I'm glad I have not unveiled my green dress yet. I, at least, look traditional and proper.

"Happy Arrival," I say as the young Man puffs smoke in my direction. He stumbles down the Trail toward me. He turns and gestures for His friends. All four of them follow.

"Happy Arrival." He blows more smoke. He must work at the plant, because He's wearing the uniform blue tie the plant workers wear. His shoes look a bit misshapen, overly worn, well used for work. "You're a tall glass of water. Where you off to this time of night?"

One of His friends laughs and grabs His cigar from Him. "Can't leave the water jokes even for a night. Proves you're a workhorse." The first young Man nudges Him in the stomach in self-defence.

"Thank you," I say. "I'm off to meet someone."

"You should be at the big party, shouldn't you?"

"I'll return after."

The Man reaches for my shoulder and squeezes it. His friends circle closer to me. They're all ash and bad breath and laughter. "Who's your Father?"

"Ursu. George."

"So, you're almost as fancy as my Father," the shortest of the young Men says. He points up to what must be His family's cottage. "We have a television."

I smile. "Yes, it's really nice." His friend still has my shoulder.

"And who's your other Father, then?"

"I, I only have one. My mother is—"

"You think I care who your mother is?" The friend squeezes my shoulder harder. I flinch. He lets go.

"It's Feles, slut. You know that. He's the Father of all of us."

I remain calm though I can feel my knees buckling. "Of course He is. I get what you mean. My Father is Feles. Of course."

The Men blunt their cigars on the Trail so close to my feet I can feel the heat of them.

"You better not keep the person you're meeting waiting on you."

"Yes, Happy Arrival." I walk swiftly away, praying I don't hear the crunching of feet behind me. I don't. They've stayed.

My fists are each clenched in a ball. My breath is shaky but I'm trying to stay calm, poised, normal. I'm not a slut. I'm not anything. But they were just having fun. They're drunk. They think they're funny. It's just fun.

"Good thing her Father is Ursu," one says before I turn the corner of the trail toward the bridge, "or I'd have made her take her dress off for us."

"Favoured bodies are the good bodies," another says.

They're drunk. They think they're funny. It's just fun. Calm yourself. It's okay. They didn't touch you anyway.

I approach the bridge, where a foul-smelling pond ends the Trail. I'm far from our pure water, far from the plant. I'm too nervous the young Men could catch up to me, so I don't remove my dress to wear the nice green one for Ambrose. I stay buttoned up, stiff, an everyday me.

Ambrose sits beside the bridge on the muddy creek bank, a bottle under His arm. Dead flowers at His feet. I call out "Hey!" and He says it back. I get closer, touch His foot with mine and sit to lean against the bridge with Him. There's a mound of dirt and small rocks where the water doesn't rise and that's where we sit. The curling arch of the bridge feels cold against my spine. My top vertebra aches. I never want to walk alone again. But I can't tell Him about the Men—I'm embarrassed I answered their Father question wrong. I almost denounced Feles. I can't tell Ambrose that.

He passes me a plastic bottle full of white liquid, thicker than water. I take a cautious sip. I like it. It's herbal and smooth. "Gin," He says.

I nod. "Why is your hair wet?"

"I went wading in the pond. Wish it was deeper but I plunged my body in for a bit. My Father read that being immersed in water tunes out your senses. I wanted to focus."

"On what?"

He takes a swig of gin and nudges the bottle back to me. I accidentally tip it on its side and spill a little. I apologize and bring the plastic to my lips once again for the burning. Maybe gin can clean all bad words and idiocy from my tongue. Maybe it can clean away the fear I had with those Men surrounding me.

He turns to me and takes my hands, clears His throat. "Sable, I know we don't really know each other well but I like your mind. I just think we could make it work."

He said "mind" first, and I like this.

"And I don't know if this is what you want, Sable, but I'll work hard. I want to be a healer. Distribute back-stretchers and help clean teeth, help with aging wrists, poor vision, check for infections in students at Lessons. I like helping people. Blood doesn't make me flinch. Feles will hold me in good favour that way. I want to share that good favour with you. I don't want Dinah or the other girls . . . They're afraid to like anything. You seem to like your friends deeper than girls should, but I think it's brave. I like that you get angry. You let yourself get angry."

I can't believe what I'm hearing. I'm so honoured He has studied me, wants to understand me. "It will please our Fathers," I say.

"Feles rations happiness," He says.

That's a treasonous thing to say. I can't believe He's said it.

He shakes His head. "Why is it the most pleasing things—smoking, drinking, Reposeries—are the worst for us?"

I don't know. "I hope we are a good Match on paper," I say. "We still have to wait that part out."

He stares at His sandaled feet. Dirt cakes between His toes and the hem of His pants.

"I can't believe you went in that water. It's filthy."

"I don't really care."

I smile at Him. "You must get more out of this place than anyone else. No one comes here."

I pass Him back the bottle and He polishes off the whole thing, then lights a hand-rolled cigarette. He offers me a drag and I try it. Exhale and cough and feel a strength and pulse in my veins that I don't want to feel again.

I'm happy Ambrose wants to be a healer. You can't become one until you pass tests at age twenty and then you go live at the plant for a year of training. It's a position of high status and good favour. I wish women could be healers. We can only be midwives at the Birth Yards, and only if we are barren.

We stumble up the bridge's ladder, across cobblestones with cattails shooting through unfixed cracks. We are blurry and hold hands and we walk awhile. We wind our way back to the Arrival tents. Dinah finds me instantly, clutches me tight and we sway to her aunt's far-off voice as she serenades a group of Men beyond the tent. Two Men grip the hem of her aunt's skirt as she performs, their Matches watching from where they are gathered around a bowl of punch like witches at a cauldron.

Ambrose walks toward His house. He lights one more cigarette. I see the smoke in a snakelike haze. The ground hisses with heat. Everyone's eyes are celebratory and tired. Everyone's bodies look tired. The end of the month is near. I like Ambrose.

◇◇◇

WE MEET MORE EVENINGS TO GET TO KNOW EACH OTHER.
My parents are pleased I have a Boy who has shown interest in
me. They tell me that in September it's important to keep yourself happy, that as an adult, the rest of the year is about hard
work and proving yourself. My mother irons a new black dress,
which came from the plant. I find myself learning what impresses
Ambrose. I have learned to paint my lips without Dinah, learned
to braid my hair nicely so He'll take notice and compliment me.

Sometimes I drink with Ambrose and sometimes I just watch
Him drink. He says His liver must be angry with Him but it
clears His head.

One night it rains. We meet anyway. It's eight o'clock and dinner is still heavy in my stomach when we meet. When Ambrose
greets me, He kisses my neck. We've only kissed on the lips a few
times. His kisses are strong. I think I like them on my neck more
than my lips.

The rain has made my dress feel heavy, and my nipples are
pointy and Ambrose asks if He can touch them. I hold His hand
against my chest. The heat of it feels okay but I also feel I am letting Him do something I am not supposed to. My breasts aren't
as beautiful as other girls' so I hope He isn't disappointed. But He
asked and I respected His ask.

Ambrose removes His hands from me and says He has something for me in His bag but it could become ruined from the rain.
He shows me quickly, an atlas of Main Stream from Lessons.
He says maybe I'll want it for the Birth Yard, to occupy myself.
Ambrose says His mother and older sister often complained of
growing sick of people, of wanting something to escape to. If I
keep the atlas secretly, it could provide some solace.

I clutch the atlas. It's maroon and burlap, titled *Great Frontier*

Road Atlas, 2002. I don't want to tear up but I do. "You can't give this to me. You can't show me this. Are you crazy?"

"But I thought you'd like it. I thought you'd be saying thank you. I thought you'd be excited to read it."

"Put it away, please. If they saw me with that at the Yard, they'd think I stole it or that I think I am above my rank. Breeding is more than reading. You know that."

Ambrose nods. "Don't you ever want to know more about it? Main Stream?"

Of course I do—I think we all do. "No, it's an evil place. It's full of witches and promiscuity and disorder. I know enough."

Ambrose leans in. "Sometimes I want to know more. See it. See what it would be like. I remember you saying the same the first night we talked, when we first really talked."

I want the same. I can't admit to that, though. I could be in trouble for wanting more like this. It is punishable to want more than is meant for you.

"Can I ask you something, Sable?"

"Yes." I reach for His hand.

"Have you been raped?" He asks me, so bluntly I let go of His hand.

"No."

"Would you tell me honestly if you were?"

I think on it a moment. "No, I guess I wouldn't."

"But it happens to girls here. And in Main Stream. It happens everywhere."

"So?"

"So then, how different are they? If bodies are had here and there like that? Men aren't supposed to but they do. How different can the two worlds really be?"

I study His face. He's so earnest. He really means what He's saying. My breath feels rattly and I feel heady with a sort of doubt that He could be this forthright. "Why do you care? As a Boy, why would you care about this?"

Ambrose shrugs. His cheeks redden. I've embarrassed Him. "I don't. I was just making a point."

"Sorry," I say quickly.

"You're sure you don't want the book, then?"

I do, I desperately do. "I'll shame my Father if they catch me with it. I'm not supposed to study or learn anymore."

Ambrose steps away and lights a cigarette. "I'm not envious of you. Being a girl."

"I don't know if I'm ready for a baby yet. You're so brave. I want to be brave," I say.

"You have to be." Ambrose exhales, takes another swig of rum and fixes His hands to make a frame around my head. "You're beautiful, Sable."

I thank Him. "I should go home," I say. "I'm a little bit drunk."

"Don't blame me for it," Ambrose says. "Enjoy it. It's freeing, I think."

I walk home in the rain alone, excited, but tired.

When I'm finally far enough away that Ambrose is the size of my thumb, a small speck, I let regret slick over me. I wanted the book. I wanted to have it. I am not a coward, though—it was the right thing to fear such a gift. I did the right thing.

I walk back to my house. My parents are sitting out on our neighbour Polah's porch under torchlight, waiting for the night's fireworks. They wave to me and that is all. Polah helps with administering our medic tests and conception arrangements, so I'm thankful she has no urge to speak with me about anything.

I go to bed, hearing the hiss of fireworks going off at the plant. Feles loves fireworks. I crawl into my blankets on the floor, listen to the sound of Kass on her side of the curtain, shuffling in her sleep. Gram Evelyn, breathing heavily too. They both snore in a deep peace and I want that for myself but can't get there.

CHAPTER 5

IT'S NOW OCTOBER. MAMIE SAYS ISAAC HAS GOTTEN strange toward her. He followed her into her family's water closet one day and touched her without her permission. She said His touch was gentle but she wasn't ready. When they left the water closet, Mamie's mother was at the sink fixing tea and asked what was going on. Isaac said Mamie had a fall at the Arrivals the night before, that He was looking at her hurt leg, and Mamie said it was true and thanked Him. Her mother fixed them sandwiches and went on about how nice it is for Mamie to have someone who looks out for her.

Mamie says she can't let her family down. She just answers Isaac's invitations to get together less often, tries not to be alone with Him. She says these are the only things she can do. She makes me promise not to do anything or tell anyone.

She breaks my heart and it keeps reminding me of what Ambrose said the last time I saw Him—about how there is evil everywhere. Even here, in The Den. I know my family loves me. I keep trying to convince myself there is no ill will or evil in my home or on this Trail. I know I have to be right. I need to be right.

Tomorrow we find out who our Matches are. My Father and

other drivers took our cheek swabs to the Main Stream labs weeks ago. He returned tired, saying they were able to get DociGens for the Birth Yard season now that they don't need to buy September Reposeries. The trucks were filled to the brim with crates on their return. Men from the Trail helped unload and stack them inside the plant. I saw the trucks drive by from my bedroom window and felt the weight and change they hold. The answers. The orders. Our Match results lie inside those boxes. Feles has examined them with His most trusted advisors and they will decide who can Match with whom this year.

I hope I'm enough. If Ambrose's name is not on my sheet, it will be because our genes don't align in Feles's eyes. Because our child will be littered with allergies or deformities or brain lessening. Or because Feles thinks my Father and I are not good enough for Ambrose. It will be for the best. It will also break me in half.

I daydream of Ambrose's atlas. I fantasize I accepted His gift. I imagine my grandmother and me staying up late into the night trading books and secrets and reading. That I memorize every mountain chain, every city, every farm. But even in my daydreams I'm fearful. I picture the atlas itself turning to black ash, ash I'll have to sweep off the floor so no one will discover my secret, no one will find out I question what we have here and whether it's enough for me.

I'M ENOUGH. MY FATHER WAKES ME AND PUTS THE notice right into my hands. Gram Evelyn sits up in my bed and bites her nails. I lift the silver seal and before I focus my eyes I make out the shape of Ambrose's name in bold letters under mine.

"Praise Feles," I squeal, and my Father and grandmother repeat the words back to me. We are fine to breed and my Father will continue to be in good favour. Feles has penned that we are a clean Match. My Father hugs me and says He has to go to the plant to thank Feles, but He promises to return with a new bottle of port.

"I know it's October but I'll pour you a glass, Sable. Besides, soon you won't be drinking anything at all for months." He winks at me.

Soon I will get pregnant.

The sun glows through the window. I'm enough. Leaves stick to the roof from yesterday's rain. I'm enough. Kass runs in yelling and she and I dance at the foot of my bed. Gram Evelyn laughs at us. She knows I feel relief. Relief smells like dew and roses and the fresh tea my mother steeps.

Mamie comes over early. She announces she got Isaac. My mother hugs her. I don't say anything, force a smile when asked what I think of it.

We walk to go see Dinah.

"I know it's not okay, Him touching me, Sable," Mamie says, splitting the silence of our walk. "I know it's not okay, but what should I do about it?"

"Nothing. You do nothing." I wrap my arm around Mamie's waist. "We can't do anything."

Dinah's mother answers the door. She's smoking a cigarette. She says Dinah has cramps and now is not a good time. "Did she Match with Garrison?" I ask.

Dinah's mum says plainly, "You may ask her another time."

When we get back to my house, I can't eat my breakfast or focus now. I want to speak with Dinah. I'm worried she had sex with Garrison but then got Matched with someone else.

My mother tells us to sit in the living room. Today we are going to talk about breastfeeding. The babies latching and sucking, little leeches, and what we can do to help keep our bodies strong and supple.

I ask her if it can wait so I can speak with Ambrose, share the news. She shakes her head and says Ambrose will be at Lessons and it's ill of me to want to distract Him. I take a slip of parchment and draw a small heart, fill the inside of it with black ink.

I give the paper to Kass as she leaves for Lessons. I ask her to slip it to Him before Lessons begin. She tucks it into her bag beside her DiLexa bottle and blood-cloth. She walks through fog down the Trail.

We learn we'll have to feed our new babies every two hours, that our bodies will feel wet inside, dry outside, and that we can't nurse in the presence of Men or other children. Gram Evelyn says we'll be given a nursing smock to wear when our babies are born. The smock has thick curtain-like fabric draping across the shoulders so when we place our babies to our breasts, no one will see our chests. We'll stay warm and our breasts will stay hidden. We learn our breasts will go up in size, swelling with milk. We'll need to take care of our backs and keep our posture strong. Mamie stuffs her fists under her shirt while my mother and Gram brew more tea.

Today Mum sends Mamie and me to the commissary for cheese, bread and grapes for supper. She gives Mamie one of our stamp cards so she can get milk for her Brothers and sisters. Mamie bends her head and accepts. Mamie and I grab empty baskets and tell her we won't be long. But we don't go straight to the commissary as we were told.

◇◇◇

"Girls." Dinah's mother unlocks the door. "What did I say earlier? Dinah is feeling faint."

In the living room, Dinah stands and tells her mother she wants to talk with us for a few minutes. "Just a short visit," she pleads.

"All right," her mother says. "Then back to what we were discussing."

Dinah comes out on the porch to hug us. She's wearing her mother's breastfeeding smock and I ask why. She says she is just excited and she wants to know what it will one day feel like. She looks vacant, tired. Her body is already a marvel, womanly—she believes in it, unlike me who can't imagine white milk leaking out of my areolas to feed another.

Then she starts to sob and I smell pomegranate in her hair, hold her close. Mamie is a terrible hugger but strokes Dinah's back and tries to show her support.

"I didn't get Garrison on my form," she whispers. "Feles must think I'm not good enough. The eyesight in both our families is too poor. Such a small thing. Such a stupid, small thing."

"You have bad eyes?" Mamie asks. I crunch my foot on hers to tell her to be quiet. Mamie isn't always good at consoling people.

"Mamie, can you get Dinah some water?" I ask.

"Fine." Mamie shuffles off into the kitchen.

Dinah's mother scolds Mamie for not removing her boots, tracking mud on the floor. Dinah's house is always freshly cleaned and shining in a sickening way. Not a hair out of place on her mother's head or on the living room carpet. I think it's what makes Dinah so erratic but I'd never tell her this.

Mamie is out of sight now so I ask, "Dinah, did you have sex with Garrison?"

She nods.

"Did He . . . ?" I make a pulling gesture with my hand. I feel my face go pink.

She shakes her head, bites her lip. "He came inside me."

"Okay," I tell her. "It's okay."

Dinah's mother shoos Mamie out of her kitchen, mumbling about how Mamie smells like dirty laundry and booze from her Father. We need to leave.

"I'll come over again later," I tell Dinah. I wave goodbye to her mother and Mamie lifts her middle finger at the house once we're down the laneway and calls Dinah's mother a witch. I get one last look at Dinah through the window in her oversized nursing smock. She looks so anxious. She pushes her mouth against a sofa pillow and presses violently, firmly, but only for a second.

AT THE COMMISSARY, MAMIE AND I GIVE MY FAMILY'S ration cards for purple grapes with black seeds in the center, soft cheese, day-old sourdough. We get apples for ourselves and eat them sitting on the curb of the Trail. The leaves are starting to turn. In December, we can start breeding. There will be Men pitching the tents for us soon near Lynx's grave, where the Arrival gatherings were held.

I think back to Marissa, the girl who starved her body until she was too underweight to breed, how she didn't menstruate or ovulate because she was so frail. I think of how Dinah's baby will be given away or aborted before birth if she's pregnant with Garrison's child, if Feles finds out. He hates things He cannot control.

I think if Dinah's not pregnant, everything will be okay. But I feel horrible by the time I get to the core of my apple. I miss the Arrivals. I wish I had gone to all the celebrations now. I wish Dinah had gone to fewer of them.

"Did Dinah do something wrong?" Mamie finally asks.

I nod. "I think so."

"Oh," she says.

"Why is Dinah's mum so horrible to you?" I ask.

"That's easy." She smirks. "It's a difference of good favour. I think the question is why is your mum so kind to me?"

"I think our mothers were good friends. Before yours got sick. I think that's what it is." I reach for her palm and make stigmata pokes, our inside joke about Main Stream religion.

She laughs. "I wonder if Jesus had sex."

"I'd have sex with Jesus. He has such firm-looking arms."

We link arms and walk home. We discuss who, between Isaac and Ambrose, is stronger. I think it's Ambrose but we settle on Isaac. A dark part of me thinks that whatever strength Isaac has, He uses it on Mamie. It occurs to me that power can be an ugly, ugly thing.

I KNOCK ON AMBROSE'S DOOR AFTER SUPPER. THE DOOR remains closed but I see His eyes through the peephole screen and hear His breath.

"Don't answer," His Father barks at Him, staring at me from the kitchen window. "You're not to see each other until your conception times! Bad luck, says Feles!"

"Okay, Sir. I'm sorry," I call to His Father, glancing again at the door. I return home, lie to my parents about where I was. Ambrose and I are to be fresh and together during conception. December. I won't sleep until then, I swear.

It's one week into November. Dinah and Mamie and I are on my sofa at home learning how to cross-stitch quotes from Lynx to gift to Men at the plant. I have the words "Woman Shall" but I'm struggling for the O in "Obey" to go next. My nails are too chewed down to grip the needle properly without eliciting small but vibrant pains from the peeling skin around my cuticles.

The silence is awkward and thick because Dinah is here and there is so much to say. She must, she needs to test if she's pregnant. She says she's been feeling nauseated and clammy and strange. "Sable, help me," she whispers. "What if I'm . . . ?"

She recently shared her secret sex with Mamie, too. Mamie's response was infuriating—she told Dinah you can't get pregnant if Feles hasn't blessed you and that she's not worried for her at all. She is so birdbrained about some things, superstitious to a fault. How does she think women in Main Stream have children? Babies are made without His blessing—it's good and righteous pregnancies that are in His control.

A bitter part of myself wants to shame Dinah, tell her she should've never lusted after Garrison or practised sex, but that won't fix her or help her. "You need to take a test," I repeat to her for the third time. "Did you hear me?" I accidentally kick Mamie's ankle instead of Dinah's. We are so close together in the same black dresses, I can't separate our bodies from each other.

Mamie flinches and kicks my leg back. "Dinah? Deaf or what? Did you hear me? A test."

Dinah places her cross-stitching hoop down on the tea table, the word "honour" thinly embroidered above what looks like the outline of a jagged fir tree. "You're dumber than Mamie, Sable."

Mamie looks upset. "Don't get surly with me just because you defiled your honour."

Dinah ignores her, a regular reflex for her. "The test you want me to take, Sable, is at the plant. You want me to just walk up, knock on the door, say, 'Hey, can I grab a pregnancy test? I had sex before being Matched. Okay, thanks, Praise Feles, bye.'"

Mamie accidentally pokes her wrist with her needle and winces. "Hey, would you stop it? What if Vale hears us?"

"She's at the commissary. Canning pears with Eli and some of the other mothers. I think she wanted a break from us."

Mamie nods. "I don't want to talk about it. Okay? It has my nerves on edge. Feles would kill Dinah if He found out. And you know she can't be with child. It just can't be so."

Mamie has a small pearl of blood on her wrist, and I hand her a tissue. Dinah just flicks her in the arm. "Right. If we keep talking about this, I'll stab your eyes with my needle, okay? I'm not going to die."

"Calm down," I say. "We are going to get a test. You'll piss on the stupid stick like all the other girls, ourselves included, will do soon. It's okay."

"Then I can know if I ruined everything, and then we won't speak of it again, okay?"

"You didn't ruin everything," Mamie offers. "There's no way you ruined everything."

"I'll ask Ambrose. He'll get one from the plant for me."

"Don't you dare. You can't trust Boys. Any Man." Dinah looks afraid. "Promise me you won't. We'll sort something else out."

I nod, though I can't think of anything else. I just need to not think of it. Of poor, stupid Dinah. My poor, dear friend.

GRAM IS BEATING ME BADLY AT CRIBBAGE. SHE NEEDS only two more points to my measly thirty. My mother is still out canning and my friends have graciously left me alone.

Our cuckoo appears from the clock and coos seven times before getting its wing caught in its own spring. "Your Father should really fix that damn thing," Gram says.

We both burst out laughing but it barely gets my mind off Dinah. "Gram, since you've already won this round, would a walk be okay instead?"

"I'm too chilly, Sable. Let's play another round."

"No, I want to go—alone. May I?" I'm allowed to walk alone but it's good to ask permission because I'm supposed to be spending most of my time with her and my mother.

"Yes." Gram Evelyn cocks her eyebrows. "I won't even ask where you're off to if you don't tell your mother or Father. I'm going to my room. Maybe I'll read. Who knows? It's such a quiet, good day in this home. I do love pear canning season."

I need to find Ambrose at Lessons, ask Him to steal a pregnancy test for Dinah. Without telling Him who the test is for. Without anyone seeing me ask Him.

The Lessons yard is lush with trees lining a narrow concrete laneway. The building itself looks like our Trail cottages—wooden, simple. There is a flag of Feles waving high over the roof.

I can smell the familiar fireplace and shelved books through the open window. I'm envious of Kassia and her classmates sitting on the floor, cross-legged with their books. The lecturer is probably eating lunch in His private room. Kassia bites into an apple and focuses on her textbook. I recognize the book. It's the history of The Den, the textbook we read almost every week. Older Boys are outside kicking a ball around a muddy field. Some bite into sandwiches, nestled under trees. They're allowed outdoors during lunch. Girls are not. The Boys cannot see me because I'm concealed by a dense row of rosemary bushes. I wait for Ambrose. He's not outdoors yet. I crane my neck and focus my eyes and steal more glances at the girls' books and braids and warmth by the fireplace. I don't know where my boldness is coming from.

A few minutes pass and the back-door knob twists. Ambrose and Garrison and a few other Boys exit without jackets on though it's cold. They join the others in their sport. Ambrose runs very fast and scores a goal between two sticks planted in the grass. The other Boys cheer Him on. How do I get His attention? I wait until the door opens again and the lecturer whistles for the Boys to return to their classroom for math Lessons. This is my chance. I haven't seen Ambrose for a while. He looks the same but stands taller, prouder in the presence of His peers. I can tell He is well liked. I remember Him as always being well liked in Lessons. The Boys file in and I crouch against some bushes on the right side of the stairs. I reach for Ambrose's leg and He looks down, startled. I put my finger to my lips and He says to the lecturer, "I'll be right in. Need to use the outhouse." The door closes and it's just the two of us.

"Sable," He says. "What are you doing over here? You're supposed to be home."

"I know. I'm sorry," I whisper. Ambrose crouches beside me.

"Are you all right?" He asks.

"I need your help. When you go to the plant for training, I need you to access a pregnancy test."

His face crinkles up. He looks down at me like I'm a whore. I reach for His ankle because I cannot stand and hold Him. "It's not for me. I swear it's not for me."

"Why should I do it, then?"

"Because I need to help someone. If I could do it myself, you know I would. It's like you said, remember? How you're happy you're not a girl. Now you can show me by doing something I can't. And doing it for me."

Ambrose tugs away from my touch and heads to the out-houses across the field. "I'll try, Sable. I'll try for you. Once," He says before He enters a stall and locks the door. I crawl out from the brush and run down the laneway, praying no one saw me. I pray, too, He will keep His word. For me. For Dinah.

I TOUCH MYSELF THAT NIGHT THINKING OF AMBROSE. I feel nothing from it except the moisture of my sex and fingers afterward. I laugh at myself, half-naked on the floor touching myself while thinking about the Boy I want to trust, with the old woman I trust most, my Gram, sleeping soundly beside me.

My sex feels mushy and I imagine its taste is sweet. I imagine the taste is nothing compared to how I feel inside.

◇◇◇

A WEEK LATER, AMBROSE KNOCKS ON THE DOOR AND MY mother glares at Him through the peephole.

"He's supposed to be in Lessons. He's not supposed to see you, Sable."

I'm on the couch with my mother's knitting needles in my lap. She's trying to teach me to make dishcloths. But the raw skin around my chewed fingernails is flaring and burning.

"Ambrose might have a gift for me," I say. "He just wants to keep us close."

My mother slips off her glasses and stares at me with a look that says she understands but He's not permitted to see me. She'd be so angry if she learned I went to see Him and that I asked Him for a favour—and one that is so dangerous. She rises from her chair and answers the door. I hear His voice. His polite, sober kindness.

I watch through the window. He's in a smart blue suit with a blue tie. He's got a satchel full of His new course supplies. His hair is slicked and looks funny. I feel as though I can smell His cologne from here. He knows He isn't going to see me, doesn't ask to. He hands my mother a small pink envelope. She thanks Him and shuts the door.

I stand as soon as she turns toward me. "That's mine. May I see?"

"May I first?" she asks.

She looks excited but I feel nervous. If she sees the pregnancy test, I'll be shamed into speaking the truth. I'll be unimaginably shamed. This was a stupid idea.

I tell my mother she can open the envelope and feel myself open and unravel at her possible reaction.

She rips the top of the envelope. The whole thing is cushioned with light pink paper. In the centre of the paper lies a small stamp. It's a stamp of a floating home, a home on water with a dock nearby. It's small enough to rest on a fingertip. My mother doesn't understand but tells me she's happy I have a Man who wants to bring me things.

I nod and she hands the envelope over. The weight of the package is light. I'm thankful for this.

I go to my room and sift through the rest of the tissue. A thin stick lies at the bottom. Its end is marked with a minus and a plus.

I watch from the porch and wait for Dinah's mother to leave the house. Dinah lets me in. I hand her the envelope and she opens it. "Sable," she says warily, "you stupid girl."

"I did it for you," I say. "Don't you want to know?"

She nods. "As long as you didn't give my name to Him."

I shake my head. "I didn't."

"Do you need to pay Him for this? With sex? Do you owe Him?"

I bite my lip. "No, I don't think so."

Dinah goes into the water closet, slams the door. She runs the sink while she urinates. She keeps the sink running. She doesn't open the door for some time. She doesn't need to. I already know it's a plus. I already know Dinah has betrayed her new Match, that Dinah has betrayed The Den.

I hold her a while and tell her it will be okay, but I don't know how it can be.

She clutches her stomach and waits for me as I brew us

cinnamon tea, a whole pot, let the aroma cling to our clothes and warm us. "Sable, there's a reason I haven't told you about my Match. My mother is really upset."

"I noticed she was off the other day. I never see her smoke. What is it?"

"His name is Colin. He's older. They're doubling Him. I'm to be part of a double Match."

I don't know what to say. To be doubled is supposed to be an honour but it means you have to compete with the other Matched girl, live with her, be bound to her. I only know of a few double Matches because Feles doesn't dole them out often. I wonder why He's chosen Dinah for this. I feel sorry for her. She likes attention and intimacy. She likes the focus of a Boy's eyes solely on her. She'll be competing, she and her child, for one Man's approval against another girl wanting the same. And it's not even His child.

"You know Colin, don't you? He lives with His mother. His Father died of a bad flu. Or at least, I think it was a flu."

I nod. I know who He is, I think. My Father's mentioned Him. Dinah tells me He is six years older than us. He works at the plant as an accountant for Feles. When Colin's Father died, He chose to take care of His mother. This means He has good character.

"Have you spoken to Him?"

She nods, tells me He invited her for dinner so they could meet in person. They went to the small public house on our Trail across from the commissary. I have never been inside. You have to be at least eighteen and with a Man. She says Colin seemed nice but He isn't very handsome. He is gangly and has crooked teeth He's never had to fix because Boys don't have to undergo beautifying treatments. His facial hair grows in patches and He speaks without much eye contact.

"Do you know who the other girl is? Your mother-twin?"

"No, but I already hate her."

"That's the least of it, Dinah. Can't you see that's such a small thing here?"

"Well, I feel hate inside my body for her already. I always go with what my body feels."

"Dinah, that's your problem right there. You need to stop listening to your stupid body. Your body works against you. Our bodies work against us." I hold her tight and hope she understands what I am telling her. Fight your body's currents to be loud or fierce or lustful. Fight it. We are expected to fight it.

"What a dumb device," she says, turning the pregnancy test in her hand. She tosses it into her roaring fireplace. The smell is plastic and scorching and it stinks. "Such a funny little thing that ruins us."

"Brings us joy," I say to correct her. The stick slowly melts into embers beneath two logs. I breathe it in, dioxin-heavy and disgusting, watch the fire swallow it all.

"Right," Dinah says, her eyes watering with flame and fear. "Brings us such joy."

LATER ON IN THE AFTERNOON, DINAH SEEMS TO BE IN denial—she seems back to her old ways, shallow, carefree. She tells me she's never been less attracted to anyone than Colin. But she has no choice. "Sable, my plan is if I have my baby early—"

"You'll clench," I tease her, though I know I shouldn't be joking about her adultery.

We're inside the commissary. I'm getting seltzer water for my Gram's indigestion, a fresh chicken to roast for supper. I seem to overcook and blacken the edges of everything, but I still receive encouragement, praise. Dinah digs her nails into my arm and places a jug of cranberry juice into our shared cart. "If I can't clench, I will have what the Men will see as a premature birth. And that's honourable and innocent. Especially if I give birth to a Boy."

"In a double Match, are you together at the same time?" I ask.

"Well, we'll be in the same home, right? I think we'll do a lot together."

"No, I mean, together-together. Sex."

"No," she says. "And what a handful for Him. Many tent times until we're both up the spout."

"Seems dreamlike for most Men," I say. "Have you seen Garrison?"

"No, and I won't. It's too hard," she says and then frowns. "He tried to ask my mother about me when His mother was hosting their embroidery evening."

"Bet she ignored Him. Your mother is a real treat," I say.

"Sable, I'm assuming you're being so curt because it's almost our tent times and you're nervous."

She's right. Soon, it will be December. It will be time. "I am nervous. What if I'm bad? What if I can't make Him fill me?"

Dinah places a box of custard-filled buns in the cart. They smell heavenly. "We can eat these on the way. My mother is watching what I eat at home. She wants me to be thin for as long as I can, only get round in my stomach."

Dinah seems too light-hearted about her pregnancy. I know she probably makes herself ill with guilt and fear at home in her room. Here, with me, in public, she can resume her role as the prettier and louder one.

We hand over our ration cards and go around to the back of the store. We sit on a bench. Dinah eats four custard buns and I nibble my way through one. They're too sweet and she's acting too false. "Will I like sex?" I ask.

Dinah licks powdered sugar off her wrist and raises her eyebrows. "How am I to know?"

I nod. She's pretending to be a virgin now. She needs me to look at her and see a virgin.

"Let's go," she says. "I feel sick."

CHAPTER 6

SEX IS AT NOON. I GO TO BATHE AND DRINK TEA and put on my black robe. My initials are stitched into the sleeve but it doesn't fit well and doesn't feel like mine. Every eighteen-year-old girl gets to wear one when she is introduced to sex. My robe arrived in late November but I was too shy to try it on. My initials, *S* and *U*, embroidered on it look too real. I feel too identified, too coordinated. I face the water-closet mirror.

"I can't wear this in public. Everyone will know."

My mother sticks her hands on her hips, squints at me. "You want them to know. It's an honour."

Ambrose is coming to walk with me to the tents. He'll hold my hand and escort me. Gram Evelyn used to tell me about a time when there were bonds between a woman and Man before pregnancy. Now babies are what make a union. We aren't solidified until the day our child is born. But we can parade and walk and hold hands and feel a sense of union. I haven't seen Ambrose in so long, I feel as if we are meeting all over again.

He comes to the door and He looks pale, tired. Is He still drinking a lot since Arrivals? Why doesn't that bother me? It doesn't. I get it. I get Him. He hugs me and says my robe is soft and I smell nice.

My mother pours Him tea and He sits on the sofa. The flowers printed on the arm of the couch seem to stretch to His slender hand. He grips the mug of tea so tight I can see His hand pulsing, shaking. My mother offers Him breakfast cake and He says He's not hungry, that we need to go soon. My mother is doing all the talking. My body feels heavy, like my skin is simply a casing, a wall sealing in all the mania and nerves inside.

"I'm glad it's you," my mother tells Him. "I really like your family. I'm glad Feles chose you to be Sable's Match."

My mother barely knows His family. Ambrose nods and says He likes our family, too. Gram Evelyn has not come out of our room. I know she is nervous and maybe wishes I had a choice. She lives for her mother's old life, the free thought that she felt guided Iris's actions. Iris chose to join Lynx. Iris chose to mate with Lynx.

Ambrose is in denim, no stupid robe and no floral crown in His hair. My mother sets mine on my head and it digs in. "You can take it off during sex," she tells me.

We have ten minutes to get to the tents. I'm worried my body won't smell sweet or attractive. I'm worried I'm almost too hairless and dull, doll-like for Ambrose. Too clean and prudish, even though every girl is the same. We have been taken off DiLexa and I hope that I can get pregnant but that I can also please Him. How do we even start? What do I do with my legs and hips? I think we kiss first. I think that's how it's supposed to begin. Then what will I say and how do I look at Him? How will He see me?

Off DiLexa, none of us are protected any longer from sex

and semen. We are vulnerable and perfect, fertile. We are how the Men want us.

Ambrose clutches my hand and His palm is clammy. It makes me feel better. I kiss His cheek. We walk toward the tents. Women and their daughters and young children eat lunch and drink tea on their porches even though it's cold. So they can see us. So they can know and gossip. We pass at least six girls I went to Lessons with whose tent-times will be later in the month or this week. I'm in one of the first sessions.

There are tall candles lit once we get to the square, and the fence that surrounds the area is laced with large white flowers with red centres. My mother's friend Polah is at the main tent, the tent where the food and drink were during the Arrivals. She stands inside with a clipboard. Her glasses slip down her nose. She clears her throat and greets me. She bows her head at Ambrose, who lets go of my hand and nods at her.

We sit in metal folding chairs and wait with the other Matches scheduled this afternoon. I'm glad when I see Mamie. Isaac is shirtless and isn't even wearing shoes. Primal and regal and strange. They aren't holding hands when they arrive at the tent.

My former female classmates trickle from the tent with former male classmates and ones I don't know who are older. They have just had sex and they're flushed. Some look in love and happy, with a lightness to them, holding their partners' arms tight. Some look like nothing in their lives has changed at all, and I wonder which way I'll feel and which one is better.

Mamie twiddles her thumbs and says I better be first. Her robe is too big on her and I step on her foot gently so she knows I'm here and I care. We are not supposed to speak or distract from anything happening in the six small tents to the left of us.

I wonder which will be mine. I hear a few shrieks from Tent Five and wonder if the girl in there is all right. My mother says sex makes you moan and shriek and I hope it's because her partner's sex feels good and tight inside her, not because He is hurting her.

Ambrose says He is a virgin and I believe Him. Polah calls our names. She takes us into a screened-off area behind her. A healer I don't recognize is sitting on a stool and says, "Welcome," and we nod. The healer tells me He wants to check my ovulation with a small tool. He tells Ambrose to stay and me to remove my robe and expose my sex to them. Ambrose has never seen these parts of me. I lie on the small blue fold-out cot and, looking to the fabric sky of the tent, open my legs.

The healer has liver spots on His hands. He tells me to wrap my legs around metal bars at each side of the cot. I do so and He inserts a small plastic stick inside me before I can breathe. The pain is startling but manageable. He makes a small circle and pokes at my cervix and counts to twenty, asking Ambrose to join in. Ambrose only mumbles with Him until twenty is up and the healer removes the stick. I realize Ambrose has not let go of my hand and is not at the foot of the bed with the healer, staring at my sex. He's waiting.

The healer shakes the stick and it starts to turn a pale, pale green. He says I have a good chance of impregnation today. I put my robe back on. We go back to our chairs and wait for a breeding tent to be freed up for us.

Polah calls Mamie and Isaac in to see the healer next. We can hear them in there. Isaac calls her "baby" and cusses when the healer starts counting, as if He is either disgusted or in love with her sex, as if He's never seen it, never touched it before. I know that is not true, even though unregulated sex is forbidden. If the healer discovers what He has done the punishment will be severe. I swallow hard and feel helpless.

Ambrose says we should've brought some cigarettes to occupy us and I nudge Him in the ribs and rebraid my hair, the crown still sitting in place, digging into my head with pins. Small curls fizz above the rest of my hair. The air is wintry. I must be sweating but the robe protects me.

A girl wearing a darker robe leaves Tent Four alone. Polah tells us we are next. She goes into the breeding tent with a fresh gold cloth and a basin of water. We see the curtain of the tent fall over her, her backside sticking out slightly. I want to make a joke to Ambrose, make Him laugh, but the pit of my stomach is so tight I could vomit, even though I skipped my morning meal, threw it into the trash when my mother wasn't looking.

Polah snaps her fingers, tells the Boy still in Tent Four to follow His Match and leave the breeding tent. His half-hour is up. It's Claude from Lessons, whom I haven't seen in months. He follows Polah, leaves with His pants half-unbuttoned. His sex is peeking out, limp and exhausted. I look away. Claude fixes His trouser buttons and offers a hand to Ambrose. Ambrose nods but doesn't touch Him. Claude says His girl was amazing. He says hi to me and I lift one hand, then He says He's off, back to Lessons now. I wish I could go, too.

Polah comes to us and says it's our time. We shuffle down a small runway of green carpet whose mouth stretches into little lanes leading into each tent. We enter Tent Four. There's a mattress, the gold cloth over it, lit candles, soft music playing that sounds like Dinah's Uncle's fiddle. There are no pillows or blankets. There are two large plants with long stems stretching to kiss the light above in the centre, a dangling pendant light that switches from red to yellow. A bright projection hits the back of the tent.

It's Feles's face on the screen. He tells us to lie down and face the screen, not to touch each other before the talk is finished. I haven't seen Ambrose's face since we got inside. I hear Him zip the flap of the breeding tent. We lie on the mattress, a wide space between us. Feles welcomes us, says that He is proud and congratulates us on getting to the conception stage.

Feles says, "You have half an hour. The Man must ejaculate into His Match in that time. It must be sufficient. There must be a sense of cordial approval between both. Afterwards the woman must use the sponge and water at the bedside to cleanse the Man after His loss of semen. The Man selects the positions that are comfortable during the half-hour. The Man must report to the administration at the main tent if the woman does not bleed. Should the woman bleed excessively, or if either Man or woman experiences problems or excessive pain during the half-hour, ring the bell under the pendant light. Thank you and enjoy. Thank you for your gift of life."

The projection turns off and I'm dry and afraid. Ambrose touches my hair. "What's the point of a safety bell we can't reach?"

I stand on the mattress and touch it. "Sure we can. But we won't need it."

A clock begins to tick. We are at twenty-nine minutes.

A voice from a speaker in the pendant light tells us to remove our clothes.

I'm stiff and scared. Ambrose removes His clothes quickly, down to His socks and shoes, kicks them to the corner. I feel like I'm adrift in water and His body is dry land to me now. I don't know how to touch it or navigate its shores. His body is strong and dark and He has lots of arm hair and leg hair and a thick briar of hair framing the top of His sex. His sex looks like a caterpillar. *I'm not ready for Him.*

He removes His socks and shoes now.

"Sable, please stop looking at me. Take your clothes off."

I undo my robe and my legs shake violently. I turn to face Him. He reaches a hand out to my belly. "We can do this," He says. We lie down.

He slides His hand down my arm and I flinch and ask what we should do. He says, "Let me touch you," so I press my hands flat to the mattress and try to stop the shaking, try to make this work. He tells me to spread my legs and asks if He can touch me, says it's supposed to firm up His sex.

I nod and slide my left leg over His. His sex is hovering below mine but I'm floating, holding myself up with my hands. His hand comes out and strokes under me. It feels both tender and like lightning, but not as good as when I touched it myself at night. I feel my labia softening and widening under His finger and I now know why some mothers call it our flower. Ambrose is kind. He takes a break from touching me when I want to let out moans but I'm too afraid. Our candles are dripping wax. They weren't replaced. They've been lit for others too and I find this comforting. We aren't alone here, the two of us.

Ambrose says His sex is hard and can I suck and touch it. I say okay but I've never. "Just touch it," He says. "It'll be fine."

His sex is so slim and long and it feels odd to the touch, like it could be its own animal separate from Ambrose. Like it could burst out from His body. Ambrose's crotch is covered with hair and I think this is wonderful. He smells like soap—the soap has clung to His sex. How could hair make a person smell cleaner?

I'm straddling over Him now on my knees, the tarp floor not saving me from rocks and sticks digging in. I grip His sex with one hand and place the other flat on His thigh. I tug. "Sable, we can do this. Sable." He keeps saying my name.

It makes me tug slower, more focused. His sex rises and falls and His breathing sounds excellent. I'm pleasing Him. He reaches in between my legs to please me back. I tense up with His finger inside me, plunged deep along the small walls I barely know. He's a tenant in my body. I'm surprised to find that I like it just fine.

The clock is moving. We need to move with it. Should we? Can I? I push myself on top of His sex. It burns and chills me at once. The tearing of myself. I yell out. There's blood on the gold cloth now, some leaking out onto Ambrose's thighs. I'm mortified I've stained His sex red.

"Are you okay?" He asks.

I nod. Keep going. I ride and move over Him and try to imagine pleasure. His hands reach out to my waist and He guides me along. He says we can stop if it hurts.

"You need to ejaculate," I tell Him. "You have to."

"Sable, if you're hurting, it's fine."

My legs are scorched and my belly churns with nausea at the blood and the scent. It's ten times worse than a monthly. He's breaking my barrier. We are connecting. We need this tearing to be with each other.

"Tell me something," Ambrose says, sweating.

His eyes roll back gently. I reach for His hair but miss and slam my hand on the mattress. I tense my sex as if this will stop the bleeding. I feel His testicles with the back of my buttocks. They're round and make me think of fruit. I reach back to touch them. He calls out to me. I nod and keep squeezing His fruit. It doesn't take long after that. He fills me.

I know I'm supposed to look at Ambrose but I can't. I feel shame. Our clock ticks down. We are finished. He removes His sex from mine slowly. It doesn't hurt. I feel a loosening and breathe deep. He says He could sleep but He grabs the small cloth in the basin beside us, begins to wipe the blood off His sex. My blood. I want to apologize but I can't. I let Him wash me. He moves the cloth up my legs, gets the few dark clots of blood on my thigh. He dips the cloth back in the water and squeezes it over me, grabs the small bar of soap in a dish beside the tired, dripping candle. He washes me, though I'm supposed to wash Him. To comfort Him. To make up for what He lost inside me. A small stream of Himself. I wonder if it worked.

He says that trying again wouldn't be awful. He keeps rubbing the cloth up my leg. His touch is so nice. His fruit and His sex are darkened in colour from when we started. His sex snakes against His legs as He rubs the cloth against my nipples. I reek of soap. His sex is still firm and starts to loosen, starts to relax. I exhale.

"I think I believe you."

"When I say we can do this? Be together?"

I nod, reach out for His head, crowned with a layer of sweat, and kiss it. I mean it.

The pendant light turns red. I slip my shoes back on before my robe and Ambrose laughs at me. He takes longer to get dressed and I leave Him to go see Polah. Polah rubs my back and congratulates me. She's standing over a new group of Matches. They can probably see I'm flushed and changed, and this makes my cheeks brighten even more.

Polah says to tell my mother hello, hands me a pregnancy test, and says if she doesn't see me again it must have worked and happy December. I chew my nails and wait outside the tents for Ambrose. Mamie and Isaac have gone to their breeding tent.

"I wish we could do that whenever we wanted," Ambrose says.

I tell Him one day we can, when I'm back on DiLexa to control my bleeding and ovulation, once we know I won't get pregnant in off times. I'm itching with blood, itching to take a real bath, unnerved that I have to go home and face everyone who knows Ambrose was inside me and when. I think of the privacy that Iris once owned, how I'd give anything for it.

"When do you take the pee test?" Ambrose asks. He means the pregnancy test.

We walk home, cutting behind tall rosemary bushes so we don't have to see His friends or children leaving Lessons during their lunch break. So my friends do not see me after sex. I need to collect myself. My hands are shaking and I'm staining my robe with cool sweat.

"In two weeks," I say.

I think of Dinah, who is already pregnant by a Boy she selected herself. I don't know what Dinah will do but she needs us as witnesses, and I'm going to help her fake it. Going to help the best I can, even though I'm afraid. They'll take her baby away and ruin her, possibly even exile her. No one will want her here. She will never make another baby. I dread it all for her. Why did she do it?

"Come see me. When you know," Ambrose says, lighting a cigarette.

I wish my Match took better care of Himself but I also don't know Him well enough to say anything. He reaches for my hand

and I take it. I don't know what we are or where we stand, but for now it's nice and it could be worse.

KASSIA IS ON THE COUCH WAITING FOR ME. SHE CAME HOME from Lessons early to see me. Her hair drips with bathwater. "I drew it for you," she says, "but then I got in first. It's still hot."

I nod and go to the water closet. She follows me as I undress again. My body is a display piece. I get in the tub. Kassia sits on the toilet seat and asks me how sex was. She's upset I didn't tell her it was scheduled for today.

"I couldn't," I say. "I felt too sick to say it out loud."

I rub my belly. What is growing? What seed was sown, what wasn't? My sex is still moist and strange from Ambrose. Kassia looks into the mirror and tells me she's proud of me. I touch a finger to my sex and stare up at the ceiling tiles. I move my feet in small circles in the warm water, revive myself. I feel no pleasure. I'm nothing but a vessel occupying water. "If you do get the Ceres Yard," Kass says, "do I have a good chance to go there too?"

Ceres is the best Birth Yard, according to the women who have given birth before. I say nothing. I don't know. I don't know where they will send me.

THE WIND SWALLOWS MY ANKLES WHEN I SIT ON THE toilet. It's four in the morning. I can't sleep. My mother has been frugal with the heat, says our walls are too thin and it's wasteful, that my Father hasn't been doing as well. My parents need my good favour to repair their home, to get Lynx's money and attention. My urine won't come. I've unwrapped the pregnancy test from its golden foil, pushed the stick between and below my legs.

I have had three glasses of water throughout the night. My bladder is squealing with fullness. But I can't make myself. Can't do it. I breathe into my free hand; the other hand shakes with the stick beneath my crotch. I pluck a small hair from my knuckles. I tense my pelvic muscles, push out. I do this over and over until a small stream forms. At first, the urine flows on my hand, wet and warm. Then it lands on the stick. I count to ten. Shake it. Shake it. Nothing. Let it rest on the counter. Put my lips to the faucet. Drink. Scrub my hands. Twice. I look back. I see such a small thing. A small thing that gets bigger quickly. A plus winks back. A plus turns me blue.

I jump in the shower with my nightclothes on. The hot rain stifles my crying and warms me, warms the both of us.

I want to tell my parents in a way they'll find smooth. Want to tell my Gram it will be good. And tell Kassia this will be good. I pace the house with wet hair and clothes. I sit in the kitchen and stare up through the skylight. People who once believed in a creator believed He sent this baby inside me from up there. That it wasn't conceived from the body but from above. I steal a scoop of my Father's coffee grounds and boil them over the stove in water. I only drink half. I'm a strange vessel.

My Father comes down the hall an hour later to eat and read before work. He'll be the first I tell. He asks why I'm awake and I tell Him I'm no longer just an I. I'm going to be a "we" for some time. I've become a we. He cries. He bends over and kisses my belly. He sinks to His knees, holds my hand, kisses me again, calls me an important girl, which He never has before. He says He will tell Ambrose. This is what Men tell other Men. This is news meant to travel from Men's mouths to Men's mouths. I wish it weren't. I want to. "Okay," I say.

My Father removes His jacket and there's sweat under His armpits. He's so relieved, He's melting. He says He'll miss me, but I'll grow and be so much better in the Birth Yard. "Can I just go one week at a time?" I ask Him. I get no answer.

My Father has a birthmark on His left cheek. It's red and resembles the paw print of a small animal. Its spread fingers touch the corner of His eye and the rounded pad of the animal reaches toward His ear. I stare at it when I can't look straight at Him. When He sips or chews, the paw moves with His tensing temple. The animal walks. The animal settles. I wonder what birthmarks my baby will have. I wonder who my baby will be. I wonder how it will smell. I wonder whom it will love. I wonder whom they'll Match it with.

My Father was the first to touch my pregnant belly. I haven't yet. I smooth my hand across it as my Father brews Himself coffee in the dark. The small orange ring around the stove lid flickers.

In the bedroom, I lift the curtain to Kassia's side of the room and crawl into her bed with her, hold her tight around her middle. She turns to me and says it's too hot in her bed and what do I want.

"I'm pregnant," I tell her. "It worked."

She rubs her eyes. "Sable, really?" She tosses a pillow gently at my arm and says I'm lucky and perfect. "Does He know?"

"Father is going to tell Him."

Kass nods.

"You're the second to know," I tell her. "You're the first woman."

Kass lifts her floral quilt off her body and walks toward the window, opens the curtain. "It's sunny for you. I've heard the baby can see through your belly toward light."

Maybe it can. I'm not sure. I've only known the body inside me for minutes.

Now that I'm with child, I no longer have to wear my back-straightener at night and I feel more like an adult. That and my mother has finally unveiled the pamphlets. She's been hoarding and savouring information on the Ceres and Lucina Birth Yards. She sits me on the couch and tells me which one of the two has the cleanest lavatories, which has the largest beds and most free space. Which one is on the water, which one on a stretch of dreamy yellow fields. We sit in the living room with the two Birth Yard pamphlets spread on the tea table.

I speak up. "Kass wants me at Ceres."

"That's where I went." My mother fluffs a pillow against her legs and stuffs it behind my back. "Ceres is beautiful."

Gram Evelyn walks down the hall and sits across from me. Her white dress has acquired new stains. She says she misses the heat, and congratulations. She says Ceres. She says if I'm on my best behaviour I will be sent to Ceres, because my Father is in good favour with Lynx.

My mother says we can discuss it more later and that I should be with my friends. I knock on Dinah's door. Her mother opens the window when I say hello, says Dinah won't leave her bed and now is not a good time. I won't give up on her. I wait for her mother to go to the backyard where she gardens. The door is unlocked. Through the kitchen window I see her mother bending over her garden, smoking tomatoes on their stems with a small torch. This is my chance to see Dinah.

Dinah is a lump beneath blankets and I lift the fabric on the left side of her bed, crawl under. Dinah feels small. I reach for her hand. "Did you fake it?"

"There wasn't any blood. I cut my wrist on a rock from my robe pocket, smeared it on the sheet when He was on top of me, looking at me. Colin didn't see. He was overcome. He saw the blood and I screamed out as if I was being torn for the first time. Even I believed myself."

I'm proud of her. It'll be okay. I rub my belly and Dinah lifts the blankets. Her cheeks are flushed red from her own heat. She watches me. She puts a hand on my stomach.

"Congratulations, Sable. First try, too. We are made to be mothers."

"I miss Lessons. I want my baby to be smart, to look at the map and go anywhere and never feel like they need to do this."

"They'll want to," Dinah says, "like we do."

The honour is too heavy to lift. Everyone is proud of us. For opening our legs. For breeding. It's an easy way to live. We carry life without living our own. Why would my child want anything different?

"I haven't seen Ambrose. It's killing me."

"He'll be so happy." Dinah melts into my arms and her cotton nightdress is damp with sweat. She cries into me. I let her for some time.

"Your mother doesn't know I'm here."

"She'll be fine with it. She's just firm on letting me rest. She's worried my brain will ruin this. If only she knew rest won't cure anything for me now. I can't have this baby, Sable."

"You have to." I stroke her greasy hair. "You should take a bath, Dinah. You should clean up and feel brighter."

Dinah shakes her fist toward me and spreads open the palm of her hand, a joke we learned at Lessons. The gesture mimics a Boy touching His own sex. "Fine, Sable," she says.

"This is an honour and we have no choice. I'll help you. We can do this."

Dinah lifts her fist again. "My baby will never know its real Father. And now my whole life will be coated in this horrible lie. Honour is heavy but so is this." Dinah props herself up and faces the window. "I haven't been able to think."

I tell Dinah I feel like bees are stinging and swarming my mind too. "Can your mother or my Father get Mamie and me and you in the same Yard? I think we need it."

Dinah shrugs. "Mamie doesn't care about me anymore. She's occupied with her own anxiety. She's too tired to be my friend."

"I don't think so. Mamie is a good listener. She just doesn't make leaps in conversation or read faces well. Our children need to be born together, sleeping beside each other. We can grow and heal together. We can get you through the testing. We can figure it out. We need each other. I can't be the only one to help you, Dinah. I'll get tired and so will you."

Dinah nods but I can tell she wasn't listening. "You know what I'm starting to hate about everything?"

"What?"

"You look outside and some days it's the most beautiful, per-fect place you'll ever see. Not even just when it's sunny. Sometimes it'll be night out or storming, but I'll look out the window and just get a good feeling. There's goodness here. A small light. But where does that goodness go on the other days?"

I picture what Dinah sees: a bright light lacing the trees and the grass and the square and our homes and people's faces. A small glow that could be goodness. I picture it being drained deep into the earth. I picture it never returning. I picture our children's children digging, uncovering the light one day, the beams of goodness on their faces and how they won't know what to do with it. They can't hold it. It moves. It shifts from the earth and back into the sky.

"At least you can still see it." I walk to the window and pull shut a curtain. "And I know what you mean. I can see it too."

It didn't happen for Mamie. It didn't work. She is scheduled to go back to the tents with Isaac next week. She has to take four pills to shift and swivel her hormones so her ovaries will shine and refuel with Isaac's sex, so that they can conceive.

I made Dinah come with me to see Mamie. We left the house without her mother hearing or seeing. Dinah was in her nightgown and her hair curled all around her cheeks. We walked to Mamie's. It's strange to think that there are things floating inside us.

I couldn't help but want to abort my baby for a moment, bring everything back to normal, bring myself back to youth and yogourt and summer and talking about things that would never find us, like fame and love. But I did find love. I keep it at bay because the other girls aren't sure. Because my parents would be concerned. Love isn't what makes a Match. If I love Ambrose too much, how will I be truly devoted? Love wastes the time of The Den. Respect does not. Love moves and distracts and ruins our minds. Respect keeps them pleased. I'm afraid of the love inside me; it leaks out of me in slow drips onto my pillow at night through my face and underarms. I can sweat the love out but it always returns.

Mamie is sitting with her mother in the front entrance of their home. Her mother has made it down the staircase and is sitting on the lowest step. Mamie feeds her oats with a large spoon. Her mouth opens and accepts it, like a small ship on an ocean breaching the mouth of a whale. Mamie's mother's eyes are glossed and tired. She lifts her head at the sight of Dinah and me.

I sit on the stairs beside her, remember her telling us what to do and how to help only a few years ago. She used to make me and Dinah and Mamie sort the clothes when her colour-blindness set in. Lights and darks were easy but the deep blues and reds of her children's socks and mittens were too much, tormenting, headache inducing. Now Mamie's mother wears her same plain white shift and plain, sturdy sandals. Her hair is up in a towel, drying.

I take the bowl from Mamie. Her mother smiles at me as I feed one scoop into her mouth. Dinah is behind me ready for the next scoop. Women and feeding and serving make the sick feel better. We know this. We abide. Mamie thanks us and walks her mother back upstairs.

I begin organizing all the chairs in the kitchen, stained with vegetables and malt drinks and her siblings' and cousins' finger-prints. The children are on the floor. There are six of them. They are on their knees. Dinah goes down beside them. One asks to braid her hair. Dinah says no. Dinah is in no mood to entertain. The children have pencils and paper on the floor. They draw

Dinah's hair in small coils, a crown of ribbon around her head instead. They dub her the queen, and I begin to help scrub a pile of dirty plates. My blouse is stained and we've been here less than ten minutes. Record time for Mamie's place. But I just want to help. I got pregnant and she didn't. I feel like I need to do something.

Mamie says Dacey got the news from Kassia that I'm pregnant and she's happy for me. She rubs my back and helps me dry two pots still crusted with fish skin. The skin's been there forever. We call it the scaly pot.

"Isaac and I need to go back. Sable, I don't want to do it. He hurt me. He jammed His sex in all parts of me. My anus, my mouth."

I stop scrubbing.

Mamie presses a finger to her earlobe, reaches around and tugs on the bow of her apron behind her. "I know. That's not okay."

"Did He ask? Did you say no?"

"He moved me. He moved me and dumped me and flipped me like a sack of chicken feed. Like nothing."

Dinah says stop. "Stop saying this and stop it." She gets up and crushes the kids' drawing with her bare heel. The kids laugh. Dinah claws her hands and shrieks like a vicious bird at them, caws and chases them into the yard. She shuts the door and watches them take refuge under a fig tree, their hands stuffed into their sweater sleeves to keep warm. Their breath visible and unfortunate. Mamie looks angry.

"Just two minutes. They won't freeze," Dinah says.

I'm so frustrated with Dinah, with Mamie. "Can you both please talk to each other? Can you both, please? Mamie is in pain. He's bruising her, touching her like she isn't a person."

"He thinks I'm a person, Sable," Mamie says, lowering her voice. "He must think that. Don't say that again."

Why am I okay? How did I escape Mamie's predicament, Dinah's fate? What did I do? I want to give them Matches like Ambrose. I want to give them my baby. I want to give them this normalcy that makes me so ridden with guilt that I feel sick. "Don't you ever wonder if everything Feles says is true?" I ask nervously.

"No. And to wonder that is a misdeed," Mamie says. She removes her apron, lifts her shirt. She sticks her skinny, lonely belly out as far as it can go. "Look, Sable, we will be Earths together." Mamie can't face anything that scares her—she's too smart for her own good.

I comply and pretend I never said anything. "We need to get sent to the same Birth Yard. I'll die without you two."

Mamie says let her focus on getting pregnant first. She lets her siblings and cousins back inside. They leave muddy, ugly footprints all over the kitchen floor I tried to tidy earlier. I realize that in Mamie's house, there is never any point in trying to make things clean.

A MONTH HAS PASSED AND MAMIE KNOCKS ON OUR front door during our family's supper. My Father stabs a fork straight into His slice of salted lamb shoulder and seems irritated. Gram Evelyn says she'll get it. Mamie rubs her belly from behind the lace curtains on the door—she knows I can see. She bites her lip and I squeal for her. Kassia kicks me under the table as if her legs are asking the question. I nod. I go to the water closet and hear my Gram open the door for Mamie, tell her it's a bad time and my Father is tired from working.

Mamie says, "Tell Sable it worked. Tell Sable it happened!"

I open the water-closet door and hug her.

"I haven't even told my mother or Father," she says. "I came right here."

Her pregnancy test is still in her pocket. She pulls it out and Gram Evelyn says, "Oh, foolish girl, that's private!" The stick is soaked a nice canary yellow and the plus looks larger than mine did. As if Mamie is somehow more pregnant than I am.

My mother calls me back to the table.

"Mamie's pregnant," I say. The thought of Isaac dampens any excitement for her I could have. I wish I could tell someone how He treats her.

My Father says with meat in His mouth that Mamie barely made the deadline. The cut-off for the Birth Yards this year is tomorrow. Anyone pregnant too late must abort and wait. We made the cut.

Mamie walks home in the dark. Through the window I can see her scrunching her hands to keep warm. Her breath looks white and thick like chimney smoke. But in a way she has become house-like and I can tell she feels it. I feel it too. I wonder how Isaac treated her body. I wonder how Mamie is treating herself. I wonder where we are going, and when.

CHAPTER 7

YOUR BABY IS THE SIZE OF A PEA."

"Smaller."

"Right, smaller." Kass braids her hair in the tub and I hand her a ribbon and a fresh towel.

"My turn. Out."

"A grain of sand. Bigger. A snowflake." Kassia climbs out of the tub.

"Ambrose is coming over tonight. He's finished some coursework at the plant," I tell her. He's been doing His coursework the whole month of January and I've missed Him.

"I know. Mum says it's why you've been such a cow today. She told me you wouldn't eat."

"I know. I'm just so nervous. I swear the baby is, too. My gut's been churning all day."

I'm not going to eat only to vomit again. Kass dries her body. She faces the mirror and lets her towel slip to the ground. The mirror is steamed up and she wipes it just where her face is.

"My face will be my undoing," she says. "Why didn't I get one like yours?"

Kassia has developed clusters of pimples on her chin and

cheeks this winter. They're red and angry, but to me they also make her look wholesome and young.

"They say eat less fruit, they'll go away. Eat less grain, they'll disappear. What does that leave? Broth and vegetables. I don't want that," she says.

I sink into the bathwater and it's lukewarm. I feel like a charitable good sister. Normally I get the hot water first, but Kassia has been upset since Lessons.

"Did someone tease you?" I ask.

"Dacey."

"Dacey is like Mamie. They say things they don't mean. Who cares about a few marks on your face? You'll start beautifying soon and miss when you had distinctions between you and everyone else. My face has the same smoothness, pigmentation and proportions as all my friends. And getting that treatment hurts, Kass. It really does."

"Nothing hurts as much as Dacey telling you you're ugly in front of everyone. She said my face looks like a used blood-cloth." Kass starts to shake and I leave the tub to hold her.

"Sable, you can't leave," she says. "What will I do?"

I hold my sister and say nothing. But I don't hold her as long as she needs. My Father yells down the hall that Ambrose is here and I leave her. I choose Him.

AMBROSE REMOVES HIS SHOES INTUITIVELY, AS IF HE knows that my mother prefers it. I hug Him and He breathes in my bath-damp hair. My mother watches from the sofa in the living room. She lights our large oil lamp. Ambrose leans into my ear and says, "We're three." I tell Him I wish we could have a stiff drink! He laughs and kisses me on the mouth, full well knowing my mother's eyes are glued to us. I imagine my Father used to be as sweet as Ambrose. I promise myself to keep Him from souring, as Men with power tend to do. Ambrose is in a baggy shirt and it's coffee-stained.

I touch the stain by His collar. "How was it? The plant."

He says it was interesting to be there overnight and really get to know it as a sacred place. His Father introduced Him to other healer students, Feles, and His Brothers. Handshakes. Buying rounds of port at the public house for Him and His classmates. "It was wonderful, Sable. I felt part of something. I felt special, worthy. I was surprised I'd feel like that, you know? Feles isn't right about everything but He really does provide, and shows this sort of generosity to all of us."

I look pleased for Him but inside I am confused. How could one day shift His judgment? Alter His strong attitudes toward things where we live? How could He one day go against the rules and steal for me, then the next say He's akin and loyal?

My Father comes into the room and shakes His hand. "Ambrose, congratulations."

He hands Him a drink that's charcoal-coloured, with two ice cubes. "It's grey coal whiskey. I brought it fresh from Main Stream a couple of days ago," my Father says proudly.

Ambrose clinks drinks with my Father and holds my wrist with a firm sorry before swigging it down. We sit with my mother for a while. We talk about blending our families, Ambrose's prospects as a healer. Most people are pleased by and proud of healers. I'm lucky to be Matched with one.

My mother is dewy-eyed after a hot glass of tea and she says that Ambrose is perfect and that He'll need me to come out of my shell to serve and help Him. I nod. Ambrose nods. I know she's trying to imply, *Wait until Sable takes DociGens. What a Match she'll be!*

I ask my Father if Ambrose can stay the night on the sofa with me. My Father says not tonight. Ambrose leaves through fresh snow down the Trail. He's left His satchel of course books and my mother doesn't want me to run down the laneway to hand them to Him in such cold weather.

"Your stomach lining isn't thick enough. You'll freeze!"

All I want is to hand the Father of my child His books and kiss Him and hold Him in the middle of winter.

All I get to do is watch my mother strut after Him in her coat and boots and tell Him a stiff but sincere good night.

THE BABY IS GROWING. IT'S THE SIZE OF A LENTIL, THE size of an apple seed. I pretend I know its exact location in my tummy, where the small heart of it echolocates to speak to my own. I worry already that my child will be born lacking a limb or feeling slow or anguished in the head. I worry already that it hates me for making it.

My bladder needs to empty more often. I awake constantly nauseous. My mother whips up all sorts of hot ginger drinks with crushed cloves and garlic to calm me in the morning. They don't seem to work but I tell her they do. Mamie feels the same as me. She vomits so hard and fierce, she keeps a bowl next to her bed because her mother is sick of the stink in the water closet. Mamie thinks she might vomit out her own baby.

Dinah says she wishes she would get sick or have achy bones, tighter temples, the weight and fatigue of knowing another life is growing inside her. She is symptomless and this makes her more nervous that the baby she made is wrong.

"An omen," she mutters, as we sit on the floor on my Father's new braided rug. The rug has four regal-looking lions stitched on it. A gift from Feles for my pregnancy. Only Men in good favour get gifts.

Mamie likes to press her stomach to mine so our babies can talk. Mamie's pale skin on mine is comforting. Gram Evelyn always tells her we look erotic and foolish doing this. Dinah wears her mother's old maternity clothes though she isn't showing and has barely plumped up or swelled at all, even though she is a month ahead of me.

Gram Evelyn asks what we need to keep busy this afternoon. She is too tired from her Afterols today to teach us anything and my mother has fallen behind on her baking and washing.

"It's hard to keep busy with nothing to read or look at," I insist.

Gram Evelyn nods and goes down the hall to our shared room. I hear her lift a floorboard. She walks quietly back past the kitchen, undetected by my mother. She brings us an old photo album with cards taped to the pages.

"They're called tarots," she says and Mamie laughs because it rhymes with carrots. "Special, strong women in your Gram Iris's day used to read them aloud, flip them to someone across the table, tell them of a fortune, a fall, their fate. They're quite romantic, really."

"Let's see it, then." Dinah speaks to the cards: "Show me my fate." She flips four cards over.

A duchess sucking a stem of lavender. A bird with six wings

resting on a nest of blue eggs. A Man with a trumpet at His side. A woman with a tail and long hair covering her chest submerged in water, eyes closed.

"Does it work if you do it for yourself?" I ask. I gesture for my Gram to sit on the floor with us. She sits on the carpeted lion's mane, her back toward the roaring fireplace.

"Dinah," she says, "I think this means you'll see sweetness, from the lavender, many children, a quiet union with your Match, a painless death."

Dinah's smiling down on her results. She seems relieved, so pleased. Such comfort in a thing so random. When did people stop believing in these tarots? Gram Evelyn flips through the pages of the book to peel off more cards. When did we stop believing?

Eliminating Main Stream religion was important to Lynx. When too many people have faith in the sky and in matters bigger than us, how can anyone think right? I can't fathom having that kind of bond with the Earth and with a voice, a Man I've never seen called God, who could promise me things but I couldn't *see* Him because He had no physical body.

In The Den, our God is before us. Our God isn't mist, He's a Man, my Father always says.

My mother enters the room before it's Mamie's turn to get her tarots read. Her face twists in disgust. She lifts the album from the floor, slams it shut and feeds it to the fireplace. The tarots burn. The thick purple cover burns. "We won't speak of this," she says. "Those are prohibited, vile."

Shame scorches my spine. Dinah and Mamie leave, embarrassed, apologizing profusely to my mother. My mother tells them not to tell their mothers and shuts the door. "Prepare supper now, Sable."

While I chop turnips in the kitchen, I overhear my mother speaking with Gram Evelyn. My mother tells her if she shows us that much of Main Stream again, we will no longer speak to her. We won't be able to. She will tell Feles. "No one is to invite the Devil into this home. There is a baby growing here. Our Family Body. Our Family Body is at risk if you do these things. Do you understand?"

I peer through a crack in the door at my mother, exasperated, weeping in my Gram's arms. Her mouth on Gram's ear. "Do you understand? You must. You must."

Gram's lips are pursed tight. She says nothing, rubs my mother's back a long time until she stops weeping.

IT'S TIME FOR US TO MEET FELES. ALL THE GIRLS ON THE Trail pregnant with their first child get to meet Him today. My Gram Evelyn's Brother she never sees. My mother brags she's met Him twice. Once, pregnant with me. Second time, pregnant with Kass. We get to tour the spring. We get to introduce ourselves to the Man whose Father, Lynx, made us who we are. We get to see the water, our livelihood. We all drink it but we've never seen it babbling, then bottled before our eyes. I've rehearsed what I might say to Him when I meet Him—my name, our shared lineage, my deep thanks for The Den and the spring and how we live.

I wake early to fix my hair. I slept with curlers tightly binding every lock. They pinch my scalp as I turn them outward. I toss them into the sink. Blond strays cling to the tubes so I know I did them properly, tight enough. I wear the black dress that my mother took out a few inches in the waist because I'm showing. I rinse all the way up my blue sleeve, soap-stained from cleaning dishes after supper. My belly sticks out slightly and I feel proud of myself. I look presentable, tamed.

Ambrose will escort me to the plant. Feles prefers we walk with our Matches. This means Dinah will see Garrison for the first time since they had sex and she'll see the girl He Matched with. I hope Garrison does not try to speak with Dinah. I hope Garrison has told no one He had sex with Dinah illegally. I wonder if He's done so with other girls but I would never bring this up with my friends.

I chew an apple over the kitchen sink to ensure no seeds or flesh spill onto my dress. Kassia wakes early to wish me well. It's still dark out and a fresh coat of snow has covered the Trail. We are low on firewood and I've been shivering at night.

I meet Ambrose on our porch. He's dressed in His starched blue suit. His hair is gelled again. He doesn't touch my stomach or embrace me. He must be nervous too. We walk hand in hand like we did the day of conception. Only this time, we walk farther, all the way to the plant. My Father is staying home. All Fathers and Men remain home today except our Matches. Feles wants to be devoted to meeting only us, seeing only us.

I've got my thick grey cloak on and the toggles choke at my belly. My mother has not yet taken out the waist and I look a little foolish in its tightness. I try to glance sideways toward Ambrose but He does not change His forward-facing gaze. The Trail is lit up for us, lights draped between the trees and bushes. Other girls and their Matches trudge across the snow beside us. More and more couples accumulate as we continue walking. We look like ghosts in this early morning dark.

I see Mamie to the right of me. Isaac has a tight grip on her arm. He has a waistcoat on and it's too big for Him. He looks like He's pretending to be important.

The walk feels good this early. It's a nice way to wake up my body, stretch my tired, cramped legs. Dinah is up ahead. She's linked with Colin's right arm and His other Match holds His left hand. How odd for Dinah. How odd to share her Match. Or maybe it will be easier to be doubled: shared work, shared housekeeping, shared respect. I recognize the other girl. Her name is Meadow. She sat next to Dinah in Lessons. They used to get along. I wonder if they will now. I wonder if that's all different now.

We arrive at the plant grounds and walk the long path lined with fir trees. I've never been as near to the building as we are now. The plant is painted red and stretches six storeys high.

We gather silently by the stone front steps. Lions with large manes are carved on the doors and windowsills. There are two flagpoles draping large banners of Lynx and Feles. Lynx's face is crinkled in the wind, but I catch a good look at the portrait of Feles, like the one on top of the Lessons house, the one in my parents' bedroom. The eyes are too familiar for someone I have never met.

Two wooden doors creak open. A Man is opening the doors. He must be a Brother. He looks a little like my Gram, with some of the same facial features—the same nose and chin. "Good morning," He says, projecting into the crowd, into the cold.

"Good morning," we speak back in unison.

"Feles is eager to meet the women who are continuing the legacy of The Den. In work and birth, we welcome you."

We bow our heads to thank Him for His words. Soon we're

all marching up the steps and filling the main room of the plant. Some girls remove their jackets. Some girls are showing more than I am in the stomach and hips. I know every face but not every name. The Boys I don't recognize as well because we were separated in so many different settings—certain classes, our cottages, recreation.

"We will tour you around the spring," the Man says. "But do not touch the water. The plant is shut off for the morning so you won't need ear coverings. If your Match is in good favour with Feles, then they've been here before, and they can tell you the noise is quite the cacophony."

Ambrose and Boys with favoured Fathers chuckle, proud to be insiders. I squeeze Ambrose's hand. I hope I make Him proud. I remove the hood of my cloak and hope my curls have stayed intact despite the winter winds.

The front entrance has stone flooring and beautiful tapestries of lions on the walls. It's both glorious and menacing. There is one that catches my eye—a lion outstretched in a grassy field, lionesses with flowers for tails encircling Him. For a moment they look to me as if they are preparing to attack. I shake my head and force my mind back.

I take a deep breath and wink at Mamie as we are herded through a corridor that leads to the spring. She's a few couples behind us. I don't see Dinah in the crowd. It's strange to see so many girls with pregnant bellies.

I hear dripping sounds from the concrete walls as we file into the spring. It's a well in the centre of a massive room—the largest room I've ever entered—and the well alone is as wide as four of our cottages combined. We surround it and the Man instructs us to join hands in a circle. Because there are so many of us, we make two circles, an inner and outer. Ambrose and I are on the inside. I stare down into the stream, the water so dark, all black. It looks like night air, not like water at all.

Above us are conveyor belts with plastic bottles, some labelled and full, some empty and waiting to be filled. There is a large bin full of narrow rubber plugs. "What are those for?" I whisper to Ambrose, the first time we have spoken in here.

He doesn't make eye contact but whispers back, "They block the filled bottles from dirtying until they're sealed."

"Oh," I say. I'm sad He knows all this stuff and I don't.

"And over behind that metal screen is where they do UV light treatment. Kills bacteria."

I nod.

"Let us bow our heads over the spring," the Man says loudly, making our ears ring. "Thank Feles for what we are given!"

Everyone bows His or her head. I lift my eyes to see the conveyor belts that circle the room and cross each other all the way up to the ceiling's large white rafters. This is more than I imagined. It's a labyrinth, a marvel of water.

I now understand why we have minimal electricity and technology in our cottages. Why we live so simply. The plant needs our energy. Hundreds of plastic bottles dangle above us from piping like light fixtures. They catch the rising sun through the plant skylight. Magnificent. It is something magnificent.

"Next," the Man announces, raising His arms for emphasis, "Feles awaits. You'll file in. He'll be sitting in a chair. He's rather tired today. Afterols. He cannot outlive His wonderful Father. And this is what makes Him a good, honest leader. I need you to file into two lines. Men. Women."

The Man separates His outstretched arms to indicate Men

to line up on His right, women on the left. I part from Ambrose and scramble to get a place in the line. Our line curves awkwardly around the large well and extends all the way back out into the front room. It takes a while to get everyone organized. Ambrose ends up way ahead of me and I'm disappointed we are apart. He will not be able to see me meet and converse with Feles. I wanted to impress Him.

So many girls meeting Him are not descendants, merely spawn of Men who came to join His Father, Lynx, in founding The Den. I know He will be impressed or at least interested in meeting me, a descendant, for the first time. I feel a small prick of superiority that clashes with how I normally feel about being a direct descendant. If my Father had a Son and not me, that Son would already know Lynx and the Men, be in good favour.

"Boys will go first." The Man leads them through the doors in a procession. This will take a while. I can't see Feles because the doors are closed. I imagine Ambrose speaking my name. I'm so excited to tell Feles my name.

Some girls begin to chatter among themselves. I crane my neck and finally spot Dinah behind me. I leave my place in the line to go stand with her.

"Sable," she whispers. She puts her jacket hood up to conceal herself from any lip-reading by others. "I saw Him. Garrison."

"Did you speak?"

"No, I saw Him. He didn't see me. Or He pretended not to."

I feel relief. "Good."

"What are you going to say to Feles?" Dinah asked me.

"I rehearsed it while I did my hair. I'm going to thank Him for the water first, then mention my Father, then Ambrose, then tell Him my lineage."

Dinah rolls her eyes. "Right, I forgot your special descendant story. You know, my Father is in good favour just for being a hard worker, a good Man. No need to mention blood. Your hair looks nice today."

Leave it to Dinah to be smug and complimentary in the same moment. I smile. "Thank you."

"Do you think she's beautiful? Colin's other Match?"

I nod. "Meadow is very beautiful, yes."

"More than me?"

I shrug. "You know, you may come to love her."

"We haven't spoken two words today. It's so odd. We used to sit together."

"I remember."

Dinah reaches for my hand.

After an hour, the door opens again and the Man returns to us. He's drinking a bottle of spring water. He's perspiring down His neck. "Feles is pleased to welcome you girls now."

Everyone in the line seems to straighten their posture or place their feet together, adjust their hair one last time, smooth their dress. It's time. It's time.

Sable, George, Evelyn, Iris. Thanks and praise. Remember.

When we reach the doors I can see Feles in His chair. A large chair in the centre of a minimal white room with freshly polished stone tiles.

Feles looks as remarkable as He does in His photos. His legs are slender and slightly parted. He looks tired but comfortable. He wears a plain white shirt with no collar or tie. His chin looks cleaner-shaven than in the portrait, which makes Him look younger, though His hair is a sheened silver shade, falling to His waist. He looks younger than my Gram Evelyn, though they are the same age, with very few wrinkles, liver spots or scars.

My breathing increases and I rub my stomach. My baby gets to just exist and feel nothing of this significant moment but still be a part of it nonetheless. Sable, George, Evelyn, Iris. Thanks and praise. Remember.

The Man throws His arm out in front of Dinah and me, halting us before we can enter. "Note that you may not speak to Him. You may kiss His feet like the girls ahead of you. Then you will return home. Your Matches are staying to eat with Feles. You must return home, see to your Family Body, your mothers and grandmothers."

"Yes, Sir," a few of us say in unison. I'm so disappointed I feel I won't be able to breathe. I always assumed my mother had spoken with Feles when she was with child. I should be thankful just to meet Him in person but I'm devastated I won't be able to converse and share our commonalities, see Him as a person, have Him see me as a person, not just a girl.

"Glad I don't need to speak," whispers Dinah. "I'm scared enough to touch Him."

I nod, pretending I agree. We shuffle into the room and Feles says welcome as we each file up to His feet, bend and kiss them. He is in leather sandals. His feet are large, purpling at the toes. His nails are yellowish. I lean down and peck the top of His left foot. It feels bony, cold. I keep moving. His hand lowers and touches my back. I do not meet His eyes.

I wait for Dinah to kiss His feet, then we walk outside in the line, do not stop moving toward the long row of pines leading us back onto the Trail. I think of my baby. We met Him, I tell my own body. You and I—we actually met Him. Why doesn't this feel better? Why am I not floating? The honour I've waited for was nothing—I realize maybe He's just a Man. And He hates me. I think He may hate us.

◇◇◇

MY BABY IS EXPANDING. I DREAM OF ITS KICKS BUT SHUN the thought of it ever being alive and crying. It's too soon for that.

"Sable," my Father calls me from the living room. He lights a pipe and the smoke smells like anise and cinnamon. "Sable, we need to decide." He's sitting on the couch in His work clothes. I sit beside Him and stare at a map I've looked at so often with Gram Evelyn. Both Birth Yards and the nearby farmland, the lake. The names are italicized and blue—Ceres and Lucina Yards. The map touches every corner of the tea table. "We need to choose which one to request."

"I want to go wherever Mamie's going," I say, "and Dinah. Can they come with me to Ceres?"

My Father licks the tip of His pen. "You want a place with temperate weather, with the best midwives, abundant food. You want Ceres. Mamie's future is too uncertain. It's up to Isaac and His Father to decide where she goes. As for Dinah, they'll separate her and Meadow; typically that's what they do with doubles."

I reach for a blanket and wrap it around my legs. "I want to be with both of them."

"You should go where your mother went. Ceres. It's elite, clean. Good nutrition. Good management. Good support for your body before you can return. They'll help you become good as new. A strong worker. A good partner."

Glass clatters in the foyer. Kassia was leaning on my mother's tall white vase. She's chipped the mouth of it. My Father lifts His hands to shoo her away. "I'll strike her for that," He says.

My Father circles Ceres again. He keeps circling it until the blue pen makes a fierce cloud, a storm around my future. "So I have no choice, then?" I ask.

"You never did, Sable. You'll go to Ceres."

Men think they're being kind by ignoring their daughters. I want to tell Him He doesn't know me, He doesn't know my friends or how they're all the support that I have. Instead I pour a sprinkle from His water glass onto a stick of incense, watch it smoke. I think of the life inside me. My baby won't need cleaner fruit or wiser hands. My baby will just need me. And I need my friends. "Place me with Mamie, Father."

My Father leaves the room and goes down the hall to discipline Kassia for breaking the vase. He turns around near the end of the hallway and says He can speak to someone at the plant who helps Feles sort the women and try His best for me. I guess kindness can find Him even when He's angry.

TWO WEEKS PASS. I'M ASSIGNED TO THE CERES YARD. There we will be able to rest in the heat when summer churns the lake and the air.

We'll share four to a cottage. We'll be fed more calories than we are used to and there is fresh bread and even wine, should labour need to be induced. I have my hopes up that it will be pleasant. Thankfully, Mamie is assigned to be with Dinah and me. She will be in the smaller quarters, the tree-cottages on the outskirts of the Yard. But she will receive the same vitamins and medicines we are promised.

I've started taking prenatal vitamins. My mother says they'll make my fingernails sturdy and bright. I keep the pills in a vase on the floor beside my bedding.

The vitamins are so large—it's the first time I can't swallow a pill dry. I drink a small glass of rosewater mixed with spring water. My mother swears it cuts out nausea. I'm nauseous almost every day but I try to keep it hidden. I scrub the toilet after each vomit. It smells so clean and sterile in the water closet when I'm done, I'm surprised no one is suspicious.

Ambrose comes to see me weekly and rubs my belly and plays music with my Father's guitar. We don't usually play music during the week in the house but my mother says it's good for the baby to hear joy. We are never left alone.

My healer's appointment in the tents beside Lynx's grave is this afternoon. It's my second appointment. The first one was so strange: it was all of us pregnant girls sitting on benches facing the same nameless healer who saw me before Ambrose and I had sex. The healer stood beside a screen. It showed proud Men greeting their Matches when they returned from their Birth Yards, clutching their new Sons and daughters. Baby Boys were given a leaf garland to wear around their necks. The Matches lifted their children to the sun and smiled, so proud. The healer told us there will be no greater pride than handing our child to our Match for the first time. As if the moment we push our babies out isn't their real birth.

I picked handfuls of weeds into my lap. I didn't want to stare at the screen too long. Mamie was breathing heavily beside me. Dinah didn't show up.

But today's appointment is just for me. A urine test, a blood sample, a list of questions to ensure I'm meeting my nutrition quota and attempting to get fresh air every day. I've been doing pretty well but I've gotten lazy with my pelvic stretches. We are supposed to do them for twenty minutes each morning and night. My mother sends me to my room to do them. I just close the door and lie on my mat like a lazy cat and soak in the silence. Women have birthed for centuries. My body isn't dumb. It doesn't need to be coached.

I WALK TO MY APPOINTMENT IN THE TENT. I PASS LYNX'S grave and bow. The girl before me has just hung her medic gown on a hook. The girl doesn't make eye contact when she hands it to me, still warm, and I slip it on. A nurse calls her over before she can leave. She sits at a small table and they hook an IV in her arm. She shrieks and bites her lip. They're feeding her the nutrition she isn't getting at home. I worry for Mamie, who probably needs the same treatment. It looks painful.

The healer's breath stinks of coffee and garlic. He's close to my face with a small light. *Look left, look right, look up and look down.* He doesn't ask me how I feel. The tent is cold and the flooring is a clear plastic tarp over the grass. He asks me to stand. My skin is goose-pimpled with cold. I stand before Him with my arms straight out. He asks me to inhale and flap them. Exhale and return. He comes to my belly and touches it. I'm showing but it just looks as if I ate too much.

"Healthy," He says. He reaches under my gown and His hands touch my sex.

"Cough," He says, "to straighten your cervix."

I cough and the second I do so a small wooden stick touches the lips of my sex. I flinch. He takes out the stick and it drips with fluid. He places the stick in a bag. Then I'm dismissed with a cold nod. I taste His horrible breath still on my walk home, taste it into the night as I fall asleep.

CHAPTER 8

I T'S VERY COLD AND SNOWY. WINTER SURROUNDS US in its full-bodied, fiercest form. I'm pinched into morning. Dark, anxious morning. My back throbs. A second pinch. I cuss. Gram Evelyn snorts in her sleep. I shift toward the edge of her bed. A third pinch.

"Sable, wake up."

"Mamie." I can't quite see her in the dark. "What is it, Mamie?" I whisper. "What's wrong?"

But Mamie can't stop crying. She's unable to speak.

I reach and touch her knee. "We'll wake up Gram and Kassia."

I pull myself up from under my warm covers and try to step carefully across the floorboards so none of them creak. Mamie follows me down the hall. Her face is puffy and red from tears. She's wearing her nightdress. Her pregnant belly protrudes more than mine because she is so naturally slim.

She has several bruises. Trails of them blueing and greying down her neck and legs. Her eyes encircled with purple and blue pain. I breathe in sharply at the sight. "Did Isaac do this?"

For once, she answers. "At His home yesterday afternoon. He . . . He forced Himself on me."

I hold her hand. "He raped you?"

Mamie shakes her head. "I don't think so. He's my Match."

I focus my stare hard and harsh at her. "He entered your body? He hit you?"

Mamie says yes.

"I think that's rape."

Mamie says she's still unsure, that it might be within His rights.

"It isn't. Men aren't to hurt us. We're fragile. We're pregnant, for fuck's sake."

"Don't tell anyone," she says. "Please, Sable."

"And what did your Father say when you came home?"

"He asked if I slipped outside and I said yes. It's almost like He sensed it was more."

"You should go home," I say. "To rest. Come back here in the morning?"

Mamie shrugs. "It is morning."

"The morning that's actually bright out," I say.

I'm boiling with anger but I don't know what to say and I don't know what to do. I don't know how to help her. So I let her stay with me. I hold my friend on the couch until sun seeps in through the curtains.

I'M FOLDING CLEAN LINENS ON THE FLOOR IN THE LIV-ing room, still so angry for Mamie. I hope she is getting some sleep and her sleep is unpolluted by Isaac, by the nightmare of His hands, His hurt.

My mother enters the room, pinning a brooch to her white dress. She grabs gloves and scarf and begins to bundle up for the cold snap outside. "I'm late to go to a ceremony. We are praising harvest and fertility today, the mothers."

"Oh," I say, secretly thinking that sounds very boring. "Please think of me."

My mother nods. "I'm late. Your sister forgot her blood-cloth. She needs it today. I will write you a note to allow you onto the Lesson grounds. Please take it to her."

My mother tosses the clean pink blood-cloth across the room. "Hurry along. You don't want her to bleed through her clothes."

She hands me a slip of paper too, saying that it's okay for me to deliver to Kassia. Funny, she'd be so cross if she knew I'd already been on the Lessons grounds, without permission and to approach a Boy. "Yes, ma'am," I say. I want to ask if what Isaac did is punishable but I told Mamie I'd keep quiet for her. I don't want her getting hurt more if I open my mouth. I don't want Isaac coming for me. So I kiss her cheek goodbye. I put my coat and boots on. I carry the blood-cloth through the Trail to give to my sister.

The snow is thick and ashy looking where the trucks have driven over the Trail. Crows caw above me and I try to spell words with my white, fogged breath. The blood-cloth is tucked under my armpit in case anyone passes me and sees it. Men don't like the look of them.

I arrive at the brick building and push open the doors. Students in their seats in front of the large fireplace and blackboard turn at the creak of the door hinge. This is the first hall, the favoured-student classroom where I used to learn. It stays the warmest in winter and is the most spacious. I bow to the photo of Lynx at the front of the room and march bravely up to the lecturer, a Man my Father's age who came to live in The Den around ten years ago, after His wife left Him for a woman in Main Stream.

"Sable Ursu," He says. "You know you're not to be here, girl."

I slip Him the note from my mother.

He nods. "Give Vale my best."

"Where's Kassia?" I ask when I do not see her in any of the desks.

"She's in the outhouse now. Obviously, she was ill-prepared to deal with her monthly."

"Thank you." I nod. I leave without looking at the maps or art on the walls, the things I used to fix my eyes on and soak in and love. This space is no longer for me.

"Praise Feles," the lecturer says. "May your child be healthy."

I turn in the doorway and bow. "Thank you, Sir." A teacher who used to encourage me and challenge me now sees me as a vessel, a vessel to carry on a legacy, and that's all. Fine. He always made spelling errors on the board anyway and He skipped over words during oral reading. I could be a better teacher. I could.

"Kassia," I call for her, crossing the schoolyard toward the outhouse. "It's Sable."

I don't hear her. I go to the decrepit white box of a building, in need of fresh paint and a good cleaning, to the girls' side of stalls. I forgot how badly it reeks. I peer under all four stall doors looking for shoes and don't see any. I turn to the rusted mirrors and the soap bar in a dish above a basin of grey water. I used to see a smaller girl, a brighter girl, in this mirror. I look tired and gross, puffy yet somehow sallow. I retie my hair into a knot at the top of my head. Snowflakes dampen my hair as I melt them with my palms. "Kassia," I call again. "Kass?"

There is a whimper, a small cry. It might be my sister's voice, the voice of a girl. It's not words exactly. It's a teary sound, a sulking. It comes from the Boys' side. Do I dare go to the Boys' side? I've never been to the Boys' side.

I do. It could be Kassia in there, worried about other girls finding her. She could be hiding, trying to scrub blood off her dress. "Kassia?" I open the door to the Boys' stalls on the other side of the wall. Three of four stalls are open and empty. The last stall is where the crying is coming from. I hear, too, someone heavy-breathing. I swallow hard and open the swinging door.

"Dacey?" I whisper toward the young figure on the toilet seat, her dress rucked up, trying to kick off a Boy crouching before her. He's pinned her arms against the wall. His pants are undone and He's pushing her back and pressing Himself in between her legs.

Dacey starts crying louder and the Boy doesn't stop. I think of Isaac. I think of Mamie. I want to make Him stop, scream until His ears burn away. I kick Him. I kick hard, with all my might. The Boy falls forward, banging into the wall, releasing Dacey's arms. Dacey leaps over Him, scrambling to get away. I let her pass me. The Boy turns toward me, holding His head, cussing at me. I do not know Him. He looks no older than Kassia. Dacey runs out of the outhouse.

"You fucking cunt," the Boy spits at me, still touching His head. His pants are around His ankles, His white underwear stained and foolish looking. "What are you doing?"

"I—I'm sorry," I utter, though I'm not.

I run from the outhouse to find Dacey and Kass on the front steps of the schoolhouse. Kassia is rubbing Dacey's back, asking, "Where is He? Where did He go?" Two girls who hate each other brought together by hurt.

"What happened? Kassia, what happened?"

Kassia is crying. "We were in the stalls when the Boy came into the girls' and tried to grab us so we ran to the Boys' and tried to lock the door but it wouldn't go. I ran away, behind the trees over there, but Dacey got caught."

Dacey's face is stone cold. "He was trying to rip my dress off. He . . . He had His pants down."

"Sable, did you hurt Him?" Kass asks me.

Dacey nods. "Sable attacked Him."

The Boy exits the outhouse, His jeans now zipped, His shirt tucked in. The Boy charges toward us, charges past us, into the schoolhouse, yelling out, "I've been assaulted. That pregnant cunt outside. Look. Look at my shirt. There's mud from her fucking boot on my shirt."

I can hear the lecturer. He asks, "Who? Who did this?"

"The pregnant one, I said." The Boy's voice rises in anger. "She shouldn't even be here. It's against the rules for her to even be here."

I hand Kassia her blood-cloth and listen to the footsteps as the lecturer rushes to the front steps. When He opens the main door, His back turned to His pupils, the classroom erupts with noise and horror from the girls, rage from the Boys. I focus on my sister. I only see her. "Kassia, say nothing. You did nothing wrong."

MY FATHER COMES FOR ME. HE TOWERS ABOVE ME IN the lecturer's office. He is dressed for work, His hair combed to the side. He reaches for my hand. I can't feel it. My body is numb and anxious. I've been sitting in shamed silence. He tells the lecturer how sorry He is.

"My stupid girl," my Father says. "Unforgivably stupid."

My Father walks me home, tells me to go to bed and gather my thoughts. I listen. But my thoughts are gathered. Who was that Boy? Why would He try to touch and hurt what is not His? He is so young to be tempted by the bodies of girls. Our bodies. Why is there no consequence for Him? I know I'm in a great deal of trouble. You cannot exercise strength against a Boy or Man. You cannot bruise the body or ego of any Boy or any Man.

HOURS HAVE PASSED ALONE IN MY ROOM. A KNOCK sounds at my door and it seems I can't avoid my parents anymore. My mother sits at the edge of Gram's bed. She stares so hard and so intently at me. She looks fierier than my own embarrassed self.

"What the damned were you thinking? You've never been like this. Your Father says hormones. Your Father says hysteria. Your Father is so ashamed. How could you shame us like this? The whole Trail knows. You've put Ambrose's honour at risk too. It's despicable, Sable."

"Is Dacey okay?"

My mother swallows hard. "She's as unwell as her mother. I'm glad Kassia ran. A young girl showing her body to a Boy of that age. Is Mamie like that too? I always felt empathy for those girls, like she'd turn out different, spending time with you and Dinah. But now this."

"I need to speak with Mamie. Please. I need to know if her sister is okay."

My mother shakes her head. Her angular face scares me in the dark. The jutting of her chin. I can tell her teeth are clenched. I can tell all of her is tensed. Her clavicles are visible beneath her apron. "Dinah is in the living room. I'll call her in. You may see her."

My mother calls me selfish as she walks down the hall, turning the lights off behind her. I put the baby at risk, our family's good favour. There is a price to pay for that. I look toward the window at a hanging painting of Kassia's. It's her holding a small baby. I recognize it's her by the braids and yellow hair. Her arms are just one wreathed circle, a bundle lying in it with black eyes, round circle for a face. I want to open the window, push the painting out.

Dinah crawls onto the bed with me. She puts her hand on my leg, strokes it. "Ambrose knows. His family probably thinks you're a real nut."

"Does your mother know you're here?"

"She does. She told me to forgive you. She says it's stuff like this that proves we need DociGens, Birth Yards."

"He was trying to rape Dacey. And He almost tried with Kass."

"Do you know who the Boy is?" She says this like she knows.

I cover my head with the covers. "Don't tell me He's someone who matters."

"A cousin of yours, I'd think. Lion's Son."

"Are you sure?"

Lion is the Brother who runs Ceres Birth Yard.

Dinah starts to cry in my arms.

"What? Why are you crying?"

"Because I don't want them to hurt you," she whispers. "Or hurt me." Dinah shoots me a look of remorse. "I would've kicked Him too, maybe. If He really was hurting her. The Boy told everyone Dacey invited Him to see her sex. They think she's a whore."

"Well, she isn't. She was using the toilet. And He came at them with His sex and His strength and tried to—"

Dinah bows her head into my shoulder. "I believe you, Sable. I'll always believe you, okay?"

I nod. I take in the heat and the cleanliness around me. I take in the world of Men.

IT'S EVENING, A SUNDAY EVENING, WHEN I'M CALLED TO repent at the plant. My Father drives us through fresh snow in His truck because His legs are stiff and He wishes not to walk. He makes me sit in the back of the truck with boxes of pharmaceuticals. I clutch my knees to my chest in the dark.

For days, I've tried to explain to my Father and mother that the Boy was in the wrong, full of thrust and hurt and lust. No one believes me. Dacey, too, is shamed but nothing she did was punishable. Unlike me, she did not lay a hand on a Boy. "Foot, technically," I told Kassia before bed. "Not funny," she said back to me.

The truck's engine rumbles and everything smells foul, like rubber, like burning. I brace my palms flat in the truck bed to try to keep myself steady as we drive. I wish my Father had let me sit in the back seat at least. I feel like freight, I feel like an animal. I'm not sorry for what I did to the Boy but I know to apologize. I know to lie. I've practised it, sweet and sure, in the mirror. I've practised it, docile and soft, under my breath before falling asleep—*I was wicked. I'm sorry. So wicked. Please forgive me. I'm sorry.*

Soon, the truck comes to a stop. My Father lifts the handle on the back and I crawl out. "It'll be okay, girl," He says to me. "Comply and repent." He touches my shoulders. The front doors of the plant open and the same Man who led us on the tour calls to us. My Father lifts His touch from me quickly, not wanting to be seen comforting me.

"George." The Man bows toward my Father. My Father does not bow toward Him. I'm observing rank and power here. The Man does not acknowledge me, nor should He, I suppose. A girl once here as an honoured guest on a tour, now here to apologize for kicking someone in The Den, her own family, bruising a young Boy.

"Feles's upstairs room," the Man says. "He'd like to be comfortable. He's come down with a fever."

My Father nods and hangs His coat on a rack, wipes His boots on the carpet in the main room, the exquisite foyer, tiled and vast, that used to hold wonder. Now I'm afraid of this place. I can hear the mechanics of the plant, the water hissing and rushing and being bottled down the corridor. We walk up a flight of stone steps to the fourth floor. My knees ache under the weight of my belly. I'm not in very good shape right now. I have been too stagnant, too still at home. My Father clears His throat and knocks on a wooden door with a brass handle. He waves His hand behind Him, gesturing to me He'd like to enter alone.

The doors open and it's Ambrose who greets my Father. Ambrose dressed in formal attire. Ambrose stern and serious. Ambrose who needs to understand what happened, my story, and forgive me but also see me, hear me, believe me.

"I'm sorry, my Boy, for Sable's transgression. She's been in a lot of pain and nerves with her pregnancy. We should never have let her onto the Lessons grounds."

Ambrose doesn't look at me. He reaches out a hand to my Father. "You didn't know, Sir. And the Boy is fine. Bruised ego, bruised head."

My Father half-smiles but I can tell this whole thing makes Him so disappointed, so embarrassed to be my Father.

"Feles would like to speak to you before Sable apologizes."

My Father enters the room. Ambrose stands outside in the hall, facing me. I try to embrace Him. He holds me back. "Sable, was He forcing Himself? Onto that girl?"

"Yes," I say.

Ambrose nods. "Sable, clear your own name. Be remorseful. Show them you're sorry. And you can't bend and tell them about me getting the pregnancy test for you, offering you the atlas. For both our sakes."

I well up. "I know I have to apologize. I don't want to."

"Go in there and just say you're sorry. I wish I could come in with you. But I've been asked to go home." He places a hand on my stomach, then leaves me.

Feles's room is filled with beautiful things. There is a large wooden chessboard on a table. There are large, delicate clocks shaped like animal faces surrounding the room. The second hands all tick together. There are multiple glowing screens, computers in large rows, Men sitting before them, typing, making telephone calls. There are so many telephones with long spiralled cords. Televisions on each wall showing Men playing soccer, lectures from Lynx, and even one of cartoons. I look at the Lynx on television, our deceased leader. He looks directly into the camera, strong and proud, black and white. The Men at the rows of computers wear headsets and laugh when Lynx laughs. They can hear Him.

My Father kneels at the foot of a large bed. Feles's long hair flows down near His shoulders. He's propped up with many pillows. He reaches for a sponge resting in a bowl of water on a side table and dabs His forehead. He's had influenza for a few days now. He then places the sponge to His lips and sucks. "You, girl," He says, "daughter of George Ursu, Match of Ambrose Kent, come into the light."

I stride over to my Father and kneel next to Him at the edge of Feles's bed. I bow my head. I thought the Boy I hurt and His Father, Lion, would be here. I'm pleased they aren't. But facing Feles is like facing your worst fears and best dreams all at once.

All the Men at the computers remove their headsets and rise. They encircle my Father and me. "George, stand with them." My Father obliges. I fold my hands. I don't look at them. I stare at Feles, His shining hair, His intense glare upon me, then the chandelier above us, causing me to sweat and feel heat as if it were the sun.

"Earlier last week, Sable went onto the Lessons grounds, permitted, to give her sister a blood-cloth. A noble errand. But then it seems she found a slut with a Boy and a jealousy, perhaps a lusting, came about inside her, and she misdirected those thoughts, injuring the Boy. Caleb. Caleb, my Nephew. Son of Lion, my Brother.

"Sable, do you affirm this is what happened?"

I clench my teeth together and feel my temples beat with the truth, my heart beat quietly with the truth. Then I speak their truth. I speak a Man's truth.

"Yes. I kicked Caleb. I hurt Him. I'm wicked. Please forgive me. Please hold us still in good favour." I hear the breathing of all the Men behind me. I want to reach out and hold my Father's hand but I know He would not accept my touch even if I tried.

Feles raises both His hands in the air, palms facing down toward me at the foot of the bed. "Foolish girl, you have contaminated us with a vicious act. But Men are compassion. Men are the light. You have tried to dirty our perfect world, so we do so back to you. Penance."

Feles nods at the Men. I do not turn around.

The spitting starts small. A few drops on the back of neck, wetness on my shoulders. The Men spit and spit upon me. I know my own Father, too, is spitting. They wet my hair and my hands, folded on the bed. They hack and gurgle and do not relent. I will not flinch. I will not cry. Some Men begin to laugh. I bite my lip. I remain in place until finally they stop. I bow my damp head toward Feles.

The Men resume working at their stations. They drink glasses of water to replenish their dry mouths. They toss around words like "slut" and "whore," like a foul wind.

Feles dismisses us and says He needs rest now. My Father walks me back to the truck. He says nothing to me. I sit in the back, in cold silence. I weep for my damp body, soaked with spit and hate, until I can't even seem to remember my name anymore.

PART II

THE
HARVEST
SEASON

CHAPTER 9

OUR BAGS ARE PACKED. WE WAIT IN A LINE BY Lynx's snow-covered grave. The Harvest Season aligns with our second trimester. It's supposed to bring warmth, but winter has prevailed. Dinah, Mamie, me, the other Ceres-bound girls and women, waiting. We wear matching brown coats distributed from the plant. Some girls wear long wool shirts and pants. I wish I had dressed warmer. I smile at Flora and Jade, two girls I used to sit beside in Lessons. They smile weakly at me, their bags clasped in gloveless hands. I am the girl who was spat on and punished. I am the girl who holds so much shame. But I am going. I am going to Ceres.

It's freezing. The wind whips through us and chokes our throats. We don't speak. Our families wait in a designated departure line across from us along the Trail. I haven't been able to look at Kass. She has her hair tucked into a knitted wool cap. Her breath reaches me. I will not cry yet.

A shuttle bus is coming to take us to the Ceres Yard. I've never been outside the Trail. It makes me anxious. It makes me excited. Ambrose stands behind me and clutches my waist. He has avoided me since my punishment from Feles. But He came to collect my luggage and escort me this morning. And His touch right now is comforting and sincere. He must not hate me.

Isaac stands behind Mamie. Colin behind Dinah. Meadow will be leaving for Lucina tomorrow. It's good for Dinah that they have not been placed in the same Yard. Still, no one is speaking. Some neighbours sit on their porches with their morning tea. We are the first girls to go. The journey to Ceres is around four hours. It's a secondary property Feles purchased from an old Main Stream summer camp. We call the former occupants Jesus freaks because when the Men went to claim the land, renovate the camp for the Yard, they had to remove and burn over seventy crucifixes. That's two crucifixes for every acre of land. I think of our jokes about sexy Jesus but I flush at the thought. It's not time for humour.

We'll be fed a hot meal when we get to Ceres but will have only water and milk to drink on the drive. Feles decrees that our hunger will build anticipation, enhance our desire to be at Ceres.

Ambrose rubs my stomach and whispers that He'll miss me. I look to Colin holding both Dinah's hands. Dinah's child is not His. The secret sours the insides of my mouth.

My Father salutes me as Polah walks by to give Him a pink Birth Yard ribbon, a sign that His daughter is at a Yard, expanding the family, honouring The Den.

I reach for Mamie's hand but Isaac grabs it before she can reach back for me. As if to say she is His. I hate Him. Isaac puts Mamie's hand in the pocket of His coat. Her mother is not here with us. I feel spoiled inside like old fruit.

Dinah's mother takes a photograph of each of us and shakes out the fresh photos slowly. I imagine our photos on display in the

Trail, these photos of our leaving. I imagine I'll look back on the photograph years from now and barely remember this day. That thought is soothing.

The shuttle bus lights beam and blink down the road. Polah blows a whistle. Ambrose kisses me on my forehead. The Boys step back from us as if their bodies are saying goodbye.

The door of the bus opens with a lever pulled by our driver, a woman with large hands in an enormous gingham coat. She is missing teeth but she smiles as if this has never mattered to her. She calls us each beautiful when we board. Polah holds our dresses and long coats at the hems so the wheels don't muddy them climbing in. The driver waves hello to my Father. He waves back.

I am second to board. I sit with Mamie in the front, where there is plenty of legroom. Dinah sits alone across the aisle from us. The bus smells like soil and makes me sneeze. Mamie has tears in her eyes and she lays her head on my shoulder. I know she's sorry to leave her mother behind for so long. But maybe relieved to have space from her too. Her head stays there while everyone boards, while the bus steams out into the dark morning of our Trail. I look out the window and see the lights of Eli's commissary turn on to start the day. Eli chokes a cigarette with His heel and rotates His sign from Closed to Open.

Dinah's face is pale. She rests her arms over her stomach and leans her cheek against the cold window. She leaves a small mark of herself. Mamie begins to fall asleep and I am envious. My body is racing.

◇◇◇

FOR AN HOUR, WE DRIVE DOWN A LONG DIRT ROAD THAT leads out of our Trail. The sun is slowly stretching over the blank horizon and the valley hills, all brown ground but for small patches of ice and snow. I reach over Mamie and clutch Dinah's arm. "Are Birth Yards a test?"

"Of course they are, Sable." Dinah turns away.

The driver meets my eyes in her mirror. "You look like you're strong. Why question that?"

Her eyes are soft. She turns them back toward the road. The road bumps and creates a deep craving in my bladder. I get up to use the toilet at the back of the bus, waking Mamie. She bends her head toward her knees and closes her eyes again. I rub her back and stare down the aisle. Jade and Flora sit near each other in the middle, but not together. I smile at them and they each nod in return. Flora's long black hair curves over her belly. The dark circles around her eyes tell me she's anemic. I feel sorry for her. Flora barely looks pregnant. She was always one of the smallest in Lessons and she still has a severely girlish look to her. Her eyes are very close together and her lips are pursed and I sense she's not new to loneliness.

I sit on the seat of the toilet and move the curtain for privacy. I cough while I pee so no one can hear the tinkling hit the bowl. Then I return. I decide to sit beside Flora because Mamie is making me feel too dark. Maybe I am a bad friend.

"How was your first time?" Flora asks me.

She takes off a bulky sweater and rests her back against it. I see her stomach now. Mine is way bigger.

"First was fine. And my baby seems well."

"Mine kicks already, I swear."

"Really?"

Flora asks about my Match and says she's always thought Ambrose is good.

"He is," I say. "I think He's good."

She tells me hers is a Man named Angus.

"I don't know Him."

"He's a descendant, you know. And He's the only one I Matched with. I have anemia."

I don't tell her that I am also a descendant. I don't tell her I can see anemia in her face. "I like your sweater," I say instead.

"It was my mum's. Nicer than these stupid brown coats," she says.

I nod. "I know, they're not warm enough."

Flora laughs. Jade leans over. "Could you two be quiet? I am so bloody nauseous. My head's pounding."

"Sorry. Morning sickness?"

"I don't know. This feels different. Shuttle bus sickness."

Flora chews her lips and we sit in silence for a while. Mamie is still head-in-her-hands asleep at the front of the shuttle bus. "Will you miss your family?" Flora whispers.

I lie. "No, I'm ready for this. My Gram and mother taught me everything."

I know more about Flora than she knows I do. I know her Father works collecting waste with Mamie's Father, that they aren't really in good favour. I know her family never let her attend the Arrival parties. I don't believe for a minute that her Match is a descendant. Unanswered curiosities ache in my belly. I wonder when my baby will kick, tell me it's here.

I move back to my seat. Dinah is asleep too. I'm too anxious to try. I climb over Mamie and watch out the window as we pull over. There are seven girls in a line. It's too foggy for me to see the faces of their family members but I see their silhouettes across some kind of new, narrow Trail. "Where are we?" I ask the driver. "Why are we stopping?"

"Feles has brought in new families. Main Stream–born. They're to join you. Their Fathers have joined The Den to work at the plant. Their eldest children have been Matched amongst each other."

How did I not know this? Surely my Father must have known this. "Are they with child?"

"Yes."

Fresh genes. Fresh faces. This is exhilarating. What I can see out the window looks similar to my Trail. When the bus doors open, I inhale a healthy cold breath and the air tastes the same. Nobody warned us how similar but strange it would feel to be in a new place, to meet people from this place. Seven new girls file in. They wear the same coats as us. Some wear vests or puffy winterish coats overtop. Two girls touch hands and find a spot behind me. The rest don't seem to know each other well, populate the bus with nerves and silence.

I turn to get a look at the two friends. One is big-boned with two chins. Curly blond hairs sneak out of her hat. She chews her fingernails. The other is tall and lanky. She spreads a bag of dried bread in her lap and places a piece in the other's mouth. A few pieces in, the other girl says that she feels less nauseous. I pluck up the courage to greet them. "I'm Sable." My arm is squished between Mamie's seat and mine as I turn. They look normal. They don't look like they've come from a blackened world of evil, a world of all crime and all hatred, all hysteria.

The slim girl coughs. I turn around. I can't get sick from her. But I sneezed earlier and would hate for someone to think of me as a pariah, as ill. I turn back.

"Mildred."

"Elspeth."

I nod. No one says anything after this. The girls finish their bread. I have their names. That's good enough for now. I kick Dinah across the aisle to wake her up. She cusses at me quietly so the driver doesn't hear her. "What the fuck do you want?"

"I guess company."

"You're so needy, Sable," she says. "I wish they'd let us watch those televisions. They never do." She is gesturing to the small boxes hanging above each seat.

The Main Stream girls giggle at this. I feel hot shame, embarrassed for our world. Well, it's their world now, too. They'll probably take a while to warm to it. I wonder what evils from Main Stream they've seen, and perhaps what goodness too.

Dinah ignores them. "Some shuttle buses have working televisions, I bet. Some shuttle buses give out hot towels for car sickness. Some have individual toilets. One for each girl!"

"I doubt that. Dinah, can we just talk about something else?"

Dinah takes a moment to think. "If you give birth to a Boy, what will Ambrose name it?"

"I didn't ask Him. What about you?"

"Colin likes Roy."

"That's nice-sounding."

Dinah scrunches her face when she pronounces the name again. "*Roy.* I hate it. It's smug."

"I know mothers who select pet names for their children that they like better than the names their Match chose. You can use them in the home."

The driver has been eavesdropping. "My mother always hated my name."

"What is it?" Dinah asks.

"Maddalena. My Father liked un-American names. He knew Lynx from Chalmers University. Followed Him north."

"Maddalena. Is that European?"

Dinah looks impressed. "Sable has a map of Main Stream in her head. Though she really shouldn't."

Out the window, the earth grows drier. The snow has lessened. I wish Ceres were west or south so we could soak in Main Stream. See what my Father sees. Rape and theft and gluttony and carelessness—the devilish reality of Earth. I dare to know it. But instead, this drive is all remote, pastoral, absent of life and people, good or bad. My ears fill with pressure and begin to ring and ring as we roll up a large hill. The bus is half full. There is a line in front of the toilet in no time. Girls in the line are smirking at each other. I think we all share a sense of humour about it. Like the beginning of a joke that could start with *Twenty pregnant girls, one shuttle bus!*

Mamie reaches over my head to crack open the window. Maddalena shakes her head. "They don't open."

"Hysteria?"

She nods. "They don't want you jumping out."

Halfway to the Yard, Maddalena pulls over. She opens a crate by her seat and presents us each with a cup of water, a bottle of creamy milk. The milk is lukewarm and thick. I don't mind. I savour mine for the rest of the drive, taking a couple of sips per hour.

"The mucous texture of milk always grosses me out," Elspeth says to Mildred.

Dinah turns to her. "I'll drink yours," she says boldly.

Elspeth passes Dinah her milk without even knowing her name or where she comes from. This makes me feel wonderful.

◇◇◇

IN TIME, WE PASS THROUGH AN ARCHWAY WITH IRON gates that open, then close behind us. The dirt road seems as vertical as climbing to the sky, a ladder leading up to a large white house with small cottages circling it. There are at least twenty of them. They spread out toward the hillside, small specks of white. It makes me nervous to think of so many girls with babies inside them sharing this land. Each cottage has one window in the front and a small chimney wedged out of a tin roof. If Ambrose could see this.

The lake here is so beautiful, the sun shining, casting small jewels onto each ripple. "Can we swim?" I ask.

"Wade. They allow you to wade to a certain depth," Maddalena says. "No one wants you to drown."

We've been driving for what seems like my whole life and my inner clock is thrown. It's strange not to really know where you are but convince yourself you're safe. Maddalena drives the bus all the way to a chicken coop and a garden. The garden is large and plentiful, rainbowed with vegetables and flowers. I am hungry. I find myself intoxicated by the bright orange bell peppers on their stalks.

"You girls must be starving. Welcome home." A Man steps onto the bus. He is slender, one of the tallest Men I've ever seen. He looks like He's tried to clean-shave but there are whiskers about His neck. He's dressed formally in a dark blue suit but His shoes are ratty, worn out. I know who He is. I feel sick.

"I thought there weren't Men at the Yards," Mamie blurts out.

"Who would keep order, then?" He welcomes us once more. "It will be an honour to serve each and every one of you. I am Feles's youngest Brother."

"What shall we call you?" asks Elspeth.

The Man looks disappointed. "I thought some of you might

recognize me. From photographs? Or the familial resemblance, surely."

Mamie raises her hand, seemingly embarrassed to have blurted at Him the first time. "Sir, she's a new girl. And I recognize you now. You're Lion."

It was Lion's Son whom I kicked. It was Lion's Son who tried to assault Dacey. Standing before us is Lion—gaunt but strong-looking, slight age to His face near His cheeks and eyes.

"My Brother likes for descendants to oversee the Yards," Lion says. "Of all my Brothers, I was chosen." From the sombre tone of His voice, I can't tell if that's an honour for Him or not.

We exit the shuttle bus and stand in a line. We wave goodbye to Maddalena but she doesn't wave back. She looks in a hurry to leave.

My hands are cold. I try to shrink myself down, escape Lion's notice. "You will meet your midwives now. They will help you learn the duty and responsibility of upholding the Family Body, your fetus's health. I will see you all at dinner," Lion says as He heads back toward the house. He turns back once, locks eyes with me. He knows who I am. I feel sick.

The midwives walk down the dirt path to meet us. I've never seen a midwife in person before. They don't leave the Yards. Their job is to serve. Many of them have Fathers who are deceased or in terrible, unforgivable favour with Feles.

They're wearing long black skirts, heavy sweatshirts, winter coats. Their clothes look worn out, with loose seams and patches of dirt stains. Some wear wildflowers in their hair. Some have more than one pair of socks up to their knees. They all seem fragile and cold, not how I imagined them.

The midwife who approaches me looks my age. She leans

in to shake my hand. Her hands are cold, too. She wears a thick wool scarf coiled around her neck, a black knitted sweater.

"Sable?" she says. "My name is Grey."

I never thought I'd be taller than my midwife. It seems funny that it would matter. I just pictured someone older, stern and cruel even, with years of experience, years of being too hardened to belong anywhere else.

Dinah's midwife has red hair and deep crow's feet by her eyes. She is plump and kind and they've already hugged. She tells Dinah her name is Fern. I'm envious. I want someone older, maternal.

GREY ESCORTS ME INTO A CANVAS TENT BESIDE THE lake. There are twelve tents in a row overlooking the shore.

It's dark inside the tent. Grey strikes a match and lights a lantern on an oak table. It's pleasantly rustic in here. There's a straw mat and a pillow beside a medical stretcher. It reminds me of my first time with Ambrose. The thin fabric of the tent walls, the absence of sunlight, the absence of people.

Grey says she's been looking forward to my arrival for weeks, that she was assigned to me in the Gathering Season, that she's seen all my health records, that she's happy I am healthy.

She hands me a green apple from her apron pocket. We stand in the centre of the tent facing each other, my belly between us. I take a bite and watch a small spark of juice erupt onto my ugly coat. "How old are you?" I ask.

"I don't need to answer that, Sable. But I will. I'm twenty."

I focus on my apple.

"I'm barren," she says. "We did Lessons together, you know. I sat near Ambrose."

"I remember," I lie. I don't remember her at all. I hear the steaming sound of the shuttle bus descending farther down the hill. All of a sudden I feel faint. This is it. This is my body. This is a Birth Yard. This is now. I will leave here drugged on DociGens, a child in my arms, older and different. I will leave here a mother.

I can feel my body shaking. I want Dinah and Mamie beside me. Grey reaches a hand to my shoulder, the other to my stomach. "Congratulations."

Grey takes my blood pressure, my temperature, records my height and weight with a scale by the stretcher. I never knew how much I weighed before, so the numbers don't mean anything to me. One hour of every day is assigned to me in this tent. Solitude. Comfort. Medicine. Rest. I am given a morning time slot. I have learned to forsake mornings, not being in Lessons, and want them back, so I am pleased with this. Now I'm forced not to be lazy, to get up and start my day.

"Are we finished?" I ask, massaging my arm where the band tightened like a snake around me.

"Finished," Grey says, sanitizing the thermometer with a cloth and antiseptic spray.

EVEN THOUGH IT'S FREEZING, I WADE TO MY ANKLES IN the lake. I have never seen water this vast and inviting. Across from the lake is a fogged line of green forest. I don't care how cold the water is. It calms me down. I feel so alone here and I turn to face Grey, who stands on the dock, frowning. I look at the rest of the tents and picture the other girls with their midwives. I look up toward Lion's large house. Grey calls it the Domicile. Lion is standing on the balcony smoking a cigarette. He stares down at me and I blush and look away. I walk out in the spongy sand and weeds until I am knee-deep in the icy water. My feet burn with cold. I want to stay out here longer so Grey will worry about me, so she'll know I am not going to listen to everything she says. There is a red cord strung between two buoys to mark our boundary. Soon, Mamie and Dinah join me. We don't speak. We are so tired. But we're pinching ourselves with bliss from the water, nerves from everything else.

After we come out, Grey hovers too closely behind me, so I can't talk to my friends. The other midwives don't seem to stalk their patients like she stalks me. Dinah's midwife, Fern, and Mamie's midwife, a middle-aged woman named Ollie, are sitting in the sun, huddled in coats with the others. I tell Grey that I am fine. She gives us towels and we dry off our legs.

Grey's breath smells salty and too close to me. Her thin shoulders tremble nervously when I toss my towel at her. She thanks me. Dinah laughs. Mamie shushes her. I feel juvenile and know I am behaving this way out of anxiety. The truth is, Grey cares. She's known me less than an hour, and she cares with everything inside her simple, timid frame. She follows us as we walk up to the Domicile for supper.

"So, it's His Son you hurt, Sable?" Mamie says.

I nod. "I wish it wasn't."

"Well, I'm glad you did it. For Dacey. I'm glad."

Grey whispers, "That's an insolent thing to say."

"Well, we weren't talking to you," Dinah hisses. Dinah gets like that when she's feeling nervous or territorial. I reach behind and pinch her shoulder blade and shoot Mamie a look to get her to keep her voice down. We're better than this. We need to act better than this.

CHAPTER 10

ALL OF US GATHER IN A CROWD IN FRONT OF THE Domicile. Lion leads us in. The front hallway has two sets of staircases, like two rows of white teeth. The ceiling is sky-like, a dark shade of night. Hundreds of small light bulbs hang down and illuminate everything. "You can see stars at night so well at Ceres, but I prefer these," He says, climbing the first few steps and turning to face us. "Much more dramatic."

The lights are stunning. Our cabins will have limited lighting, limited electricity. At least we have some to keep warm until spring helps thaw the ground and heat the air.

"I want to sleep here, not in a bloody cottage," Dinah whispers.

Jade overhears her and nods. Jade must have dipped her long hair in the water. It drips and shines with a piece of lake weed caught near the crown of her head.

I have never been in a house so large and I am somehow underwhelmed. I miss my home's supper table. I miss our floral couch. I miss Kass. I even miss Gram Evelyn's snoring already.

Lion leads all of us into a room built entirely of wood. Owls and foxes and chickens carved into the wainscotting. Owls with hollowed-out eyes, wings spread, descending toward foxes. Foxes, jaws open toward the chickens. Chickens, leaping in the air. This pattern around and around and around the room. It feels intensely cold and masculine. In the centre is a long wooden table set with wooden bowls and spoons and plates and knives and cups. Set for us.

"Welcome to what I call my utopia," Lion says, smiling widely. He doesn't sit at the table but stands before us. I note His posture is slouchy but His voice is confident, ceremonious. "A place where you will learn to be mothers. A place you will grow. I praise my Father, my Brother, for keeping us safe, keeping us alive in The Den. We welcome all newcomers who will learn of our legacy, of our greatness. Main Stream lacks greatness, peace, order. We find it here together. We find peace every day here. Now, the rest of your meals will be in your cottages. But I wanted to share this Harvest Season with an offering. To thank you for being daughters of The Den."

Two small pills await us inside the bowls. They are red and tubular; they don't look like my prenatal vitamins at home. Maybe these are DociGens. My feet go numb, I am so afraid. Most girls I know, my friends included, see DociGens as an honour, a milestone, a natural process. I want to think of them like that but they scare me.

Grey and the other midwives hold out our chairs for us and we sit. I hold the pills in my palm. Mamie pops hers in her mouth, chased by a small swig of water from her wooden cup. She doesn't even question. "They're iron pills," she says. "What do you think they'd give us? We just got here!"

Then Fern applauds Dinah for taking her medicine and whispers welcome, rubs her shoulders.

I place one pill in my mouth. It tastes like metal.

"Is there blood in these? Human blood?" Elspeth looks pale

in her seat at the head of the table. Red streaks pour down her chin. She bit into the pill when she was supposed to swallow it. Her midwife holds out a napkin for her. Her midwife's hands are dark and bruised and veiny.

Lion circles the table and lights another cigarette. He shouldn't be smoking around us, but no one speaks up. "They're blood capsules, from last year's placentas. You'll follow decades of breeding here. You'll take blood capsules every day. They unite the women of The Den."

"Is that hygienic?" Elspeth speaks, raspy and quick.

"Everything we do here has purpose," says Lion, placing His hand firmly on the table, leaning over toward Elspeth. His body language is telling her to be quiet, to stop asking questions.

Grey and the other midwives pass out baskets of bread with jam, slices of dry beef with mushroom sauce. I can't eat for the life of me. I pretend to try, rip apart my bread, stuff small bits in my lap. Lion is watching me.

I touch my second blood capsule. The clear capsule sloshes with the small bit of blood when I turn it in my palm—the afterbirth of someone before me. I pretend it's my Gram's or my mother's. This brings me a strange comfort. I pop it into my mouth, dry-swallow so Lion will think I am brave. Grey takes a napkin and wipes crumbs off my lap and offers me tea. I decline. I am tired of watching her serve me and it has only been one day. When dinner is cleared, some of the girls clutch their stomachs in fullness. Some of the girls who eat much less at home, whose Fathers aren't in as good favour with Feles as mine. I am happy for them, but guilty that I wasn't hungry. Mamie is beaming, full. Lion takes a seat at the foot of the table. A fireplace roars beside Him, the flames rogue and wild.

"At Ceres," He says, "you'll be happy. But happiness needs to go hand in hand with work. You all need to learn a sense of duty, community, the feeling of hard work. Learn to set an example for your children, learn to support and aid your Match. The work here isn't much, if you can push and be selfless. You do not serve yourself. You serve The Den."

My Gram warned me they'd present this platform. Birth Yards are meant to coach girls, demand that we work harder, learn to contribute. As if we innately don't know how, as if we're genetically designed to be slothful and incapable. Elspeth chews her thumb at the table. Her cheeks are flushed red. Dinah slouches, disinterested. She's putting on a show of nonchalance. Inside, I'm sure she resembles the angry flames facing us, warming the room to an uncomfortable tension.

Lion takes a sip of orange liquor from a wine glass. He talks about our other pills here, DociGens. The dosage is big enough to work, small enough not to harm our babies. "My Father learned of it, implemented it. To protect our foremothers from hysteria. It's used to open your minds to the beauty of service. DociGens make you open to criticism, open to new ideas. Open."

I hate how Lion says the word "open." His voice seems to swallow the entire room. The tight circle of His lips is menacing. There is spit on Lion's chin. His tie is crooked. I convince myself He is imperfect, something I know I am not allowed to feel.

"The work you do is simple. You'll all be in sections with different tasks. It will not begin until next month. You must adjust to your new home, strengthen your bodies first. You may leave your work to attend your medic sessions. The work will improve your mind and happiness. You'll be making new clothes, laundering, harvesting, cooking, woodworking, for each other. For The Den. For Feles. For Lynx, our great deceased Leader."

Many of the girls smile and look excited to carry on such a marvellous legacy. The Main Stream girls look terrified. They don't seem to understand what The Den is, what it means to people, to the Family Body. But I get it—if I were them on this day, soaking in all this ritual and newness, I, too, would be terrified.

After dark chocolate cake for dessert, Grey walks me to my cottage and asks if I need anything. There are two sets of bunk-beds, a water closet, a small table and kitchen area, a sink and a woodstove. It isn't what I thought it would be. I expected it to be warmer, decorated with birds or themed like the sea. To feel like a home. Dinah and Elspeth are assigned to my cottage. I fall into bed without speaking. Grey leaves with Fern.

"We lock it for the first few weeks. For your safety," Grey says, in a voice strangely too chipper. They lock the door behind them. We become treasures or prisoners. I don't know anything.

THE PENDANT LIGHT IN THE CENTRE OF THE COTTAGE flickers in the early dawn. Dinah is already awake, sitting in the dark at the small table, on a stump seat, scratching her fingers down the grooved trunk of the oak. I roll and turn to the opposite side of the room. Elspeth and the other girl, another Main Stream girl I don't know, stretch and open their eyes.

Elspeth reaches for her morning robe. She strokes her belly and says, "Good morning, little one."

I forgot I was pregnant from all the newness of this place. I look down and silently apologize to my baby.

"That mattress is terrible," says the girl I don't know, whose voice is pungently loud, like a strong odour.

She has thick curls, frizzing off into static. A lot like mine.

She has clear, pimple-free skin and beautiful plump breasts. I wonder if they do beautification treatments in Main Stream too. Her pregnancy is all in her stomach, does not show with fat near her chin or the swelling and veining of her legs. She sleeps in the nude. I look at her sex, but look away before she sees me.

Dinah's voice is as loud as the new girl's. "Sable, you fell asleep before you could chat, you bore. This is Harrio. And you met Elspeth on the shuttle bus."

"Hi, Sable," Harrio says, splashing some water from a glass bottle onto her face. She licks a droplet off her lip. "We're sharing that doe midwife. The one who looks terrified to speak. Shit, it's too hot in here."

The stove burns almost red. It really is too hot. Dinah's midwife, Fern, unlocks our door and fills our water bottles from a glass pitcher. She has deep face wrinkles and bright red hair, trimmed down like a Man's buzzed haircut—we aren't allowed to cut our hair that short on the Trail.

"Any of you girls from Main Stream?" she asks.

Harrio and Elspeth raise their hands.

"You've tried our water?"

They both nod. "It's very good," Elspeth says.

"Now," says Fern, "Lion has asked me to speak to the Main Stream girls. You aren't to compare and share and go on about your childhoods, your lives before your Fathers found us. Assimilate. Be proud to be part of The Den. You dishonour your Father's decision to bring you here if you mention Main Stream. You understand?"

Both girls nod and I am disappointed. I was going to ask heaps of questions. But it makes sense—they need to leave Main Stream behind. Like my great-grandmother Iris did.

Grey enters our cottage with a basket of bread and fruit and more blood capsules. She sets them on the table. She asks us how we slept, asks us if we can feel our babies. Her voice is so cheery. Syrupy and irritating.

"Are we allowed to write home?" Dinah asks, her mouth full of green apple.

"No, dear," Fern says, "not until you're settled."

"Where's our other vitamin? The one Lion mentioned?" Harrio asks.

She has not touched her bread. She sucks pink jam off a knife.

"DociGens. You'll receive them in the evening, typically," says Grey. "It'll take a while for you to adjust to them, for them to get into your system. Even in such a small dose. But don't fret, you'll have them soon enough."

"Are midwives on DociGens?" I ask, peeling the skin off my apple with a small knife. I hate the hardness of apple skin. It coils around as I rotate the fruit, making a kind of curly animal's tail.

"We are not, no," says Grey. "We aren't in the presence of Men enough to really need them. It'd be a waste to give them to us."

Fern purses her lips, eyeing my apple. "Speaking of waste, girl, you'll eat the peel. We don't throw out the beautiful food Feles provides."

"Right. I'm sorry." I pick up the peel from the floor and put it on my plate. Once she leaves, I'll throw it out. Fern is not my mother. She's not my keeper. She isn't even my midwife.

Grey places her hand on my stomach. I flinch. She removes it and apologizes. I hate being so full and sacred to her.

"It's all right," I say. I look into Grey's eyes, the same colour as her name. Her hands in her apron pocket, her bottom lip in her mouth. She's so young. She's so much like us.

Fern hands us some clothes to wear. We each receive a brown cotton dress, simple and long-sleeved, and we each receive black slacks. I never get to wear pants. I strip on the spot and put them on.

"And this sweater goes with it," Grey says, laughing at my keenness. She tosses me a thick black sweater and I pull it over my head.

Elspeth throws her clothes on her bed. "These are gross."

"Oh, sorry." Harrio smirks. "Did you think Feles went to high-end department stores or something?"

This makes Elspeth laugh but I don't understand. "Maybe more like an online vintage boutique. Tasteful Mormon dresses."

"With kittens all over them," adds Harrio.

Fern snaps her fingers at them. "That. Is. Quite. Enough."

"Sorry," says Harrio. "But so you know, online shopping has gone to shit anyhow. Too expensive. Cheaply made clothes."

"And no language," says Fern. "I may be a midwife, but you will use respectful language when I am here. You're not a Man!"

"Fine," says Harrio. She pulls her brown dress on. "Fantastic."

Elspeth sighs. She goes to the mirror in the water closet and holds her brown dress up over her robe. "Yes, don't we all just look fantastic."

MORNING FEELS QUIET HERE, QUIETER THAN THE BUSTLING Trail of Men going to the spring, children going to Lessons, deliveries to and from Main Stream in and out by truck. There is a light sheen of frost on the ground. We're given tall rubber boots. They're stiff around my calves. They don't know the shape of me yet. My neck is aching from resting weirdly on the shuttle bus. I tie my hair up in the brown scarf Grey gave me. Elspeth does hers as well. Dinah and I hold hands as we leave the cottage.

We walk toward the lake. There is nothing to do but wait, maybe wade. We sit in the sand, staining our uniforms, our sweaters and slacks. We sit without thinking of work or life. We sit without any other girls around us. We sit like lepers. The dock ahead is so inviting. We are not permitted to walk along it. I notice a lack of birds here. A surplus of insects. Little sand fleas chewing at our wrists. Worms curling around shoreline rocks.

Spiders big enough to see from a distance, black and hairy, spindle in and out of the wooden boards of the dock. It's infested, Harrio said this morning as a spider spun a web in the corner near her pillow. She'd squashed it dead with her bare fingers. I like her.

"What's a department store?" Dinah asks. I'm so thankful she did.

Elspeth snorts. "A store where you can get anything. Usually there's over five floors. Pots, pans, dresses, pillows."

"Socks, undies, naughty undies," Harrio says, winking.

"Oh," Dinah says. "I just didn't know what it was."

Elspeth says, "Oh, you Den girls, I feel sorry for you."

I shrug. She sounds so arrogant. "Well, what's easier? Being born blind or going blind after an accident?"

Elspeth kicks a rock between her feet and stares up at the sun until she has to squint her eyes shut. "Born with no sight, I suppose."

Dinah nods. "Even if you do have department shops or whatever the hell, I don't care anyway. My mother makes me beautiful clothes. She owns a camera too."

Harrio gives Dinah a look of annoyance. "I used to own my own phone. I used to have sex with whoever I liked. I used to paint my fingernails blue. I used to drive a car. Can we please be done with this now?"

Dinah looks embarrassed. We both nod.

The morning passes quietly. The sun peeks through gauzy clouds. It's red like a wound. It bleeds down onto the water, rusting the world. Our row of cottages is the closest to the water. In this way, we are lucky.

Other girls' homes stretch into the forest. Some are built into the trees. Mamie's is. I look forward to seeing it. I haven't seen Mamie since the welcome dinner last night.

HARRIO, ELSPETH, DINAH AND I EAT SUPPER IN OUR cottage before we're all to gather for the first administering of DociGens. I almost gag on my blood pill, wash it down quickly with milk and think of my stomach lining being dyed a terrible pink by it.

Grey and Fern escort us to the field outside the Domicile. I hope to see Mamie immediately but I can't find her in the evening crowd—girls and midwives and pitch-black darkness. The silhouettes of our bellies terrify me in the moonlight. There is so much life filling this space. It's too much to fathom.

Midwives begin handing us DociGens from little pill bottles. They are green circular pills knifed carefully in half. Lion announces, "To The Den." He lifts His glass of beer. And we swallow our pills. The chalky texture is fine enough. They're tasteless. I can't believe I just took a form of Devil's Breath. My Father would be so proud yet I am endlessly anxious.

Harrio pinches the back of my neck. "She's so pathetic. We may have to care for each other in this mess." She gestures toward Grey, who is standing near us chewing her fingernails. The field is full of us all in the same uniforms, same plain colours. It's a field of plain brown, of blue scarves, of bulging navels.

"Now what?" Dinah snorts and grabs my wrist. "Are these as good as Reposeries?"

Harrio squints at us. "I used to take ecstasy with my friends and go dancing. When my parents were at these crazy long spiritual retreats, marriage counselling stuff."

Dinah gives Harrio a knowing smile. "I think we've been on something similar, haven't we, Sable."

I shrug. I haven't. But I'll feign the rebellious party-girl role for Dinah.

"It's the waiting that sucks," says Harrio. "For it to work."

Grey timidly pipes up. "These are fairly fast."

"Fucking hope so. It's cold out," Dinah says, grabbing my hand.

I can see the lake. I can feel my body humming, coursing with blood and anticipation as I get more and more nervous for the DociGen to take effect. Will I obey everything? Will I still be me? I feel my heart rate sharpen, my breathing grow shallow. I focus on the shoreline water, silver, lapping, humming too. My friends stand in a circle. They're singing. I join them. But I don't sing.

The world starts to smudge. I find myself leaning on Grey, who holds me up. The group of girls seems to switch limbs and faces. They begin to laugh and fade. I hear myself laughing, unable to find any words. The grass starts to separate and glow, burst through the frost and coil up around my boots. Dinah's hair begins to stretch and coil around her own body. What is real? Some girls begin to collapse to the ground around me and midwives guide them down kindly. But some aren't guided. They hit their mouths on the ground and blood mixes with the frost. Everyone still exploding in strange laughter. I sink to my knees. Grey holds my head up to the sky. She says it will be okay. When the world starts to steady itself, the stars spell my name.

WE WAKE ON THE GROUND THE NEXT MORNING. THE girls who bled in their mouths and on their knees from falling have been given towels to wipe away the blood. I see blood and girls. The ground is somehow warm to my body. Dinah lies beside me. I feel a body near me, a warm scalp and hair. I sit up and see that it's Mamie. She found us in the crowd; she sought us out in the dark. Murmurs start to spread and everyone seems plain and dull and distraught, drained of clarity. We lie in confusion for what seems like forever. Lion is not there. A midwife speaks to us all: "The first night is the hardest. But the pills will line the pathway to womanhood, motherhood, Matchhood. In time, you will adjust. You will feel clear."

We spend the day there, exhausted. Our bodies too heavy to move. Not one girl stands. Some are able to speak again. The midwives fill our canteens and tell us we're good, so good. They give us plenty of bread, cheese and fruit. This does not bring me peace. I wonder if my baby feels different with this weight and medicine inside me. I hated every minute of it, the unknowing-ness, the being overtaken by something. Will it always be this way? I want to see Kass. To see Ambrose. I want Ambrose here. I am not supposed to want that. I am not supposed to need Him. Will the medicine change what we have and how I feel?

The drinking water is too warm, makes my mouth feel dry. I

search the crowd for Grey. She is standing at the edge by a poplar tree. She locks eyes with me and runs over with a pitcher, refills my cup. "What did it feel like?" she whispers. I notice the other midwives spelling each other off to go change into fresh clothing, warmer sweaters. Grey is in the same grass-stained denim pants, the same blue corduroy shirt. She won't leave us, Harrio and me. Harrio is over near Elspeth, both perched on a few large boulders in a decorative garden. They look rumpled but peaceful.

I tell Grey I saw my name in the stars. Dinah falls in and out of sleep all day. She never sits up. She drools on the grass. She has a cut on her lip, a small bruise on her cheek. Mamie says something inside her felt like a glowing compass. She says my headscarf glowed across the field. That's how she found me. She says she kissed my skirt and legs before falling asleep. She says she just wanted to serve and help me. She says that must mean the DociGens are starting to work.

I FINALLY UNPACK MY THINGS TO PUT IN MY DESIGNATED drawer in our cottage. A towel, soft nightclothes, face cloths, bars of white soap, a hair scarf. The top compartment of my suitcase has warm wool socks I knitted myself, too loose on my feet to wear outside but cozy on wood or tiled floor. I gather the bright-yarned bundles and place them in my drawer, the one beneath Harrio's. Grey comes to collect my suitcase to store in the Domicile until I give birth. She waits at the door. I check to make sure I've taken everything out. I feel a hardness, a stiff rectangular outline in the side compartment meant for extra shoes I do not own. I unzip the compartment and see a book.

Ambrose's atlas. The one I refused from Him before. My heart begins to pound.

"Sable," Grey asks, "are you finished?"

I slide the atlas under my mattress, keeping my back to her. "Almost."

I hand my suitcase to Grey at the door. Her face tells me nothing. I don't know if she saw. She carries my suitcase and Harrio's toward the Domicile to store. Now I have a secret to store as well.

I WAIT UNTIL MY ROOMMATES LEAVE AFTER SUPPER FOR the second evening ceremony. The other girls at the Yard have been chattering about it all day. In the ceremony we will chant some prayers to Lynx's ghost, to honour the earth, and then we are to write down one thing hysterical in our hearts and feed it to the flames of a raging bonfire. Then we will take our next dose of DociGen. I wonder if I will bloody my face this time when I fall to the ground.

"Sable," Grey says, "are you coming? I'll take you. Where is your coat?"

She looks determined to be my keeper. I roll my eyes and go to the water closet. "I'll meet you there. I'm quite bound up today. Need some quiet."

Grey nods. "Constipation happens with pregnancy. Do you need a teaspoon of dish soap? Just a little to swallow? Supposed to lubricate the body quite quickly."

This makes me laugh. "That's the most bizarre thing I've ever heard. Just some time will do." *Fucking go away*, I want to say, but I don't.

Finally she leaves. The door clicks shut. I go to my bed and lift the mattress at the end and stare at the atlas. If I'm caught with it, I'll be in so much trouble. I am already in trouble for injuring Caleb. I am already a disappointment to my Father.

I love the maroon cover, the burlap texture of it. I love the delicate drawings of maps and the wriggled lines of mountains and lakes swarming each page. I flip and flip through mostly Main Stream, things I do not know and can hardly picture. I notice a dog-eared page and flip to that. "Ceres" is scrawled at the top in pen. I see the mouth of the lake. "Lynx Lake" is hand-written over the body of water. This is where we are. This is who I am. I search for a note from Ambrose, a sign He slipped this into my bag. I know it was Him. To show me kindness, to help me entertain and grow my tired spirit, my spat-on spirit. Or maybe to frame me. Maybe He hates what I've done, sees me as filthy and feral. But there's no trace of a note or His name or anything. So His reputation is safe. That makes sense, I suppose. I pretend not to be disappointed. I hide the book once again and walk out to the field.

I write His name down with the pencil and paper being passed around by midwives and stand with the other girls, singing to Lynx and howling. I toss Ambrose's name to the flames. He makes me feel the most like myself and not myself at all. Something about Him makes me feel possible. Maybe I am possible.

IT'S MY FIRST BIRTH APPOINTMENT WITH GREY AND A healer who drove here from our Trail. I lie on a stretcher under the cloak of the linen tent.

First, they test me for hysterical behaviour. A quarter of women suffer from it and can never shake it, Feles says. It's part of the reason we're given back-straighteners when we're young. Good posture is aesthetically pleasing, but it also regulates the flow of our blood, the demonic hormones that could lie in our spines. I don't miss my back-straightener. It pinched and cursed me, gave me insomnia on nights when I had my period and was cramping.

"He needs to touch you, Sable. Rub your sex. If you can release, you're most likely fine." Grey says these words as if she is asking me permission, but I know she can't ask and isn't.

I nod. I focus my eyes to the slit in the tent that reveals blustering trees, a lick of normalcy.

The healer leans in. He's wearing a mask. I recognize Him but He doesn't know who I am. He's never made an effort to know any of us. As if this makes it easier.

"If you release today, we won't do this again," He says. "We are testing if you are worthy of mothering. If you have an open-minded soul. You'll feel pleasure. It won't hurt you."

I wish Ambrose had given me pleasure and light so I'd know what my body feels like releasing. The healer touches me. His latex gloves are cold and feel awful near the mouth of my crotch. Focus my vision. Watch the trees. He moves in small circles on my sex, the petal of it. It feels ticklish and makes me want to urinate. As He keeps going, I breathe deeper. I lose time. I lose my focus on the trees. Close my eyes. I bite my lip. I don't want to make noise. The circles increase. Grey says something about being almost there. The healer whispers for me to relax and I tense. Then I release, well up, feel a rush through my whole body, contract. The waves course through. I become a tree. Quiet but moving. I release.

"Congratulations," the healer says to Grey and not me. "She's clear."

I reach for Grey's hand but she places it back on my heaving stomach. Grey rubs warm liquid on my bare skin. I flinch at her hands. She apologizes.

"Don't. Don't," I say.

The healer removes His mask. He has a pained face. His neck sinks into His shoulders. He carries harshness in His body, in His always foul-smelling breath. He uses a remote to turn on a screen. My baby appears. This is my first time seeing it. A black swamp with little white outlines in the shape of Ambrose, the shape of me. A small furled-up thing I want so badly to own, to love. The head a distinct planet, the legs and arms little constellations of stars swirling about. The tent is filled with the beat of its heart.

"A girl," He says. "You're having a girl."

Grey squeezes my wrist and wipes the blue goo off me with a towel. She gives me a small cloth for my face and it's only then I realize how much I am crying.

THEY CAN'T IDENTIFY THE SEX OF MAMIE'S BABY YET, but she did release and is free from hysteria. She, too, has a soul and is capable of mothering. Her fetus flips and moves around too much for them to see. They think it could be a Boy. Her midwife called in Lion to see Mamie. He says He knows Isaac's family well. He says it must be a Boy if the fetus is this cunning and full of energy. She's getting tested again tomorrow.

Dinah is having a Boy. I cried when she told me. Not because I am happy for her. Because I know too much.

I'm given a new apron to wear. Pink to represent a girl. There is a loose hem near the pocket. I don't complain. The pink is the shade of the sleeve on my sister's Arrival dress. It makes me feel connected to her, something I haven't felt since we got to Ceres.

Bathing days are twice a week. We get twenty minutes in the shower shed, made of lovely cedar beams, with three stalls. The midwives assigned to care for the showers—water girls, we call them—their task is to fill balloon-like rubber sacks with warm water and tie them closed with a cord. We stand in the stalls and pull the cord when we need to rinse and the water streams down warm and slow. It's the water girls' job to go up stepladders behind each stall with kettles of hot water, dump them into those rubber sacks. We can use up to half the bag with each shower. The walls of the shed smell nice, although the whole space is narrow, claustrophobic and in no way private. I miss the constant warmth and immersion of my bathtub back home. Speaking with Kass and braiding our hair in the overly yellow light. We always looked jaundiced in that bathroom and it was so funny to us to look sick but feel healthy inside.

This afternoon, I'm in the shed with Harrio, side by side because we walked over together after we ate lunch. "Lots of girl sex reveals, I see," she says, pointing to the rack of cubbies for towels and clothes beside us. There are some pink aprons strewn about. She pulls the rope around her shower's rubber sack and water trickles out. She scoops it up in her hands and rinses her hair. "A little warmer, please," she says to the midwives working the showers for us, on ladders above us. A young one nods without making eye contact and fills Harrio's sack with a steaming kettle. "I'm having a girl, Sable," she says, pulling the rope again. She looks up to the meek midwife. "Much better. Thank you."

My water has gone cold but I am pretty much clean and too shy to ask anything of the shrew of a woman above me. She looks cranky like Fern, like my mother can get if she is hungry or over-tired. Soon, some of us girls will be assigned to do the shower work. I point to the cubbies too, point to our pink aprons side by side. "Me too. I'm having a girl, too."

"Have you been ever been pregnant before, Sable?" A new voice startles me through the wooden wall. It's Elspeth. She's eavesdropping as she combs her hair outside the stalls.

"No, this is my first. I'm only eighteen."

"My Father is very religious, like Harrio's. But maybe even more so. Pro-life evangelical. Did you know I'm still a virgin?" She squints her eye through a knothole in the wall and stares aggressively at my sex. I take a step back.

She lowers her voice so only Harrio and I can hear her. "He got me inseminated with a total stranger's jizz so we could join The Den. In a hospital! We lied about my age. He made us pre-tend to be a couple. It was horrible. And now my child has no Father. Well, I guess Feles is a Father to us all. My child has that. Because my Father didn't want me having sex. Physically having sex. I'm only seventeen."

Harrio opens the stall door to face Elspeth. "Are you jok-ing? That's insane." She reaches for our towels, hands one to me, wraps hers around her body. "I'm sorry."

Elspeth shrugs. "It was Feles's freaking internet videos—anyone could join Him, live up north here, especially if they had means to repopulate. I was the means my Father needed, I guess."

I can't believe what she's saying. "So, you have no Match? And Feles is okay with this?"

Elspeth nods. "He will be once He learns I am having a Boy."

She holds up the blue apron from her linen clothes bag. "Praise Feles, right? Praise His live streams!"

"Sable doesn't know what you're talking about, Elspeth. I bet she's never even been on the internet," Harrio says.

I shrug and readjust my towel up under my arms and grab my clothes. "I know what it is, though."

Harrio tosses our black shower sandals onto the wet cement floor and we slip into them. "Have a pleasant shower, Daddy's girl." She smirks at Elspeth. We head toward our cottage.

"See you, dyke," Elspeth sings back. Harrio doesn't seem to hear or she pretends she doesn't. We walk in silence until I can't take it.

"She called you a name, you know," I say. The grass is soaking wet in the field. Bits of dirt and grass cling to my sandals. We pass other girls on their way to eat lunch or bathe. I whisper the word. "Dyke."

Harrio shoots me a glance. "Sable, do you know what that word means?"

I shake my head. "No, we don't use that one."

Harrio smiles. "Well, don't start using it. Unless you are one and you choose to reclaim it. Make it hold power versus pain."

I nod, though I'm still unsure. "There are other words I'd reclaim for myself if I could."

"I don't think this place is about that, though, is it."

"No." We reach our cottage door and leave our wet shoes on the mat outside. "It really isn't anything about that."

THAT NIGHT, IN THE FIELD WHERE THEY ADMINISTER the DociGens, we women become a strange singing, glowing blanket of pink and blue aprons littered with a few brown ones like Mamie's, sexes still unknown. I slip my DociGen into my apron hem, like hiding it in a tunnel.

I know I am defying Feles, shaming my parents. I am breathless with my own daring, but I cannot make myself swallow the pill again. I pretend to collapse and then I hold Dinah and Mamie as they tell me how great it is to serve Men, how great it is to be a girl. I look over to Harrio and Elspeth, two strange girls who hold the secrets of the outside world inside them.

THE BIRTH YARD ROUTINE IS SETTLING ON MY SHOULDERS like an ache. I feel it most at night. I wake and attend my tent time, the best part of my day, before I run out of ways to entertain my loosening mind. Each morning in the tent, Grey brews me clove tea. She squeezes half a lemon into my cup and stirs it twice with the spoon she keeps in her apron pocket. The spoon's handle has the face of a woman on it. I don't ask who it is but the eyes are full and open and real looking. We sip and talk. She reads questions to me from a notebook so I can connect with my body. I ask what she's writing down after my responses and she says *good* or *poor*. Good or poor.

"How does your person feel when eating?"

"Full. Fine."

"How does your person feel on the DociGens?"

I fib for this one but it's easy. I believe myself to be an excellent liar and I am not afraid. I haven't taken any pills in two weeks. I fake it, mimicking the other girls. We've started to take them for cleaning and cooking for ourselves in our cottages. Everyone seems adjusted to the dosage. Girls whistle and cheer with laughter before they kick in. Some link arms, form small circles and dance. No one falls to the ground anymore. It's as if our bodies are learning to steady themselves. All the other girls say they feel more in control. They all believe it's working for the best.

I look Grey in the eyes. I even convince myself I take the DociGens, by the sureness of my voice. "They're pleasant. I enjoy their peace."

"How does your person feel near the lake? Is your person heavier when the moon rises?"

"Fine. It is."

"Pregnant women are affected by the moon," says Grey. "It's a kind of guide. It's called the lunar effect. If you are full-term in the Free Season, August, around the time the moon is full, its gravitational pull can influence when you go into labour. It affects water. Not our spring water but other sources of water. And your amniotic fluid inside you, it's a form of water, too. Just as sacred as The Den spring water." She puts her notebook away and presses on my stomach to help me with my indigestion. It's really embarrassing as she relieves me. It's noisy and the smell is sulphuric. I feel sweat on my cheeks.

"It's okay, Sable. I'm not a Man," she says. "It's natural."

I nod, still flushed in the face. "Will the moon be full when we go into labour, into giving?" I wipe my clammy hands on the hem of my dress.

"Sometimes, yes. Not always. But should any girls be troubled or late, the moon normally helps."

"How do you know? Have you seen it happen?"

Grey lifts her fingers from my abdomen and shakes her head. "Just been told before."

◇◇◇

THERE'S AN AWFUL STORM WHIPPING THE LAKE INTO foam. Rain leaks through our cottage roof. Elspeth moves from her bed to the floor under the table to stay dry. Dinah says she doesn't mind the wet raindrops on her face. She opens her mouth for them.

"We used to drink it all the time," Harrio says, standing on a chair between our beds. She jams a rag into a crack in the tin roof. "Rainwater. My mother used to collect it because she said it was cleaner than what we were given in our town."

"That's a load of moonshine. There was always water where I'm from," Elspeth snorts.

"Shut up, Elspeth," says Dinah. "Was it, Harrio? Was it actually cleaner?"

"I don't know. It tasted the same as the taps." Wind shakes the roof lightly, but it's enough for Harrio's carefully placed rag to slip to the floor. "I knew that wouldn't work," she says. She steps off the chair and places the sodden rag back in her dresser drawer.

Dinah crawls into bed with me. "I get scared when the wind's this loud. It sounds like a Man or something. Howling."

Elspeth rolls her body toward us and wraps her hand around a table leg. She sneers her lips and teeth. "Maybe it's Lion. Hungry, horny Lion."

Harrio goes to the sink in the water closet. She jams her toothbrush in her mouth, scrubs her teeth. "Can we not speak of Lion like that?" she says, muffled from sparks of toothpaste flaring down her chin. "I'm scared enough of Him as it is. He reminds me of Men from Main Stream."

"In what way?" I ask her.

Dinah has been quiet. I pinch her freezing feet and she

flinches. "Fuck, Sable. Be my friend or don't. I'm too tired for your games."

I nod. I hold her.

Harrio smiles at us and the foam around her mouth looks shiny in the damp water-closet light. She spits in the sink. "You two are lucky to have friends here."

"I think they should be more subtle about it, honestly," says Elspeth. "It's obnoxious and you're not upholding the community or this cottage. Isn't that against your precious rules? I bet you two are queer for each other or something."

I feel Dinah twitch and cover her head with my arm. She's too tired for Elspeth. I want to be.

"Couple of dykes," Elspeth says. There's that word again and she says it with so much hatred, I think I know what it means now.

Harrio strides over and steps on the ends of Elspeth's hair and drags her foot; a few thin strands peel lose from her scalp, making her scream. "You stupid wench. If you've got something to say, then say it. I'm queer. And I think you know that. I think someone told you. And so fine, do you hear me? I love girls. I like sex with girls. But we aren't allowed now in this fucking place. So why make it worse?" Harrio pulls against Elspeth's hair again and kicks her shoulder.

"Stop it, you're hurting her, Harrio," I say. I reach my hand out to her and she swishes past, leaving a weeping Elspeth on the floor.

Harrio climbs into her bed. "I've lost everything. I don't have time for holier-than-thou homophobic bullshit. Bible-thumping bitch." Then she says nothing after that. I hear her breathing heavily as if she's trying not to tear up.

The rain grows louder than pathetic Elspeth as she sobs into the night, calling us all queer and terrible and unforgivably bad at being here, at being devoted to The Den, at being women.

I WAKE FOR MY TENT TIME WITH DINAH BESIDE ME, HER body sweaty from leaning against mine all through the night. The tightness of the sheets creates a heat and brightness. I feel dizzy. I strip off my nightdress and change quietly into my dress and pink apron in the dark. My stomach is veiny and uncomfortable. I pour myself a glass of water. I have the earliest tent appointment and always feel nervous and guilty should I wake the other girls. Elspeth is still sprawled beneath the kitchen table. She's drooled on her nightdress. Her face is puffy with tears and I wish I could feel sorry for her. I hope she's sweated out her hatred for us, for Harrio. I slip on my sandals. I reach for my wool cap, knowing the rain will have changed the air.

"Sable." It's Harrio.

I walk over to her and kneel beside her bed. "I didn't mean to hurt her," she whispers.

"I barely know you," I say quietly, "but I can tell you're brave. I wish you could love women the way you want to." I reach for her belly. "But this is what has to matter right now. This is what we have."

Harrio clears her throat. "I think it's part of the reason my Father made us come to The Den. My Father caught me with a girl in His car. They used to let me borrow the car Sunday evenings to drive myself to my gymnastics class. I used to be so flexible. Before I got fucking pregnant. I would leave my practice early and pick this girl up at her house. This time we were in the parking lot of a closed restaurant in my parents' blue Mazda. Mazda is the brand of the car. I mean, the lot was near my parents' church but I thought we'd be clear. It was dark. They were supposed to be at confession. That's where you tell all the bad things you've done to a Man who has a direct line with God. Anyway, she and I were kissing. And my Father—He hates women enough as it is, but to know, to see, that I wanted to be with one—He snapped. He dragged me out onto the pavement. And He beat me, Sable. He beat me right there in front of her. She ran away down the street. In her bare feet. I loved her and she left me. She was so scared.

"My Father pulled me out of school, my siblings too, and said we were joining a new church. Finding a new God. The God who is Man. And then I was Matched with a Boy whom I'd never talked to. I had to have sex with this stranger. The last thing my Father did when we sold the house—He'd kept her shoes, her black Mary Jane shoes she'd left in the car—He threw them into our trash can, tossed a match into the can. I drove away seeing the symbol of who I loved, or even just wanted to know if I loved, just burning there."

I try to imagine knowing freedom and love and having it stolen from you by someone who is supposed to love you. That's the most awful thing I can think of. I start to cry. Part of me wonders if her Father did all this because He thought it was right. Like He was trying to save her from something. But that can't be right. It doesn't feel like a gesture of love. "Sometimes I don't want to be a mother," I say.

Harrio sobs back into my arms a little while. Then suddenly she's strong and firm, collected again. She pulls gently away from me. "Turn the light on when you leave," she says, sitting up. "We should get up and help the midwives clean up storm debris. It sounded so violent out there."

I offer Harrio my pillow. It's firmer than hers. I pull it from underneath Dinah's hand. "Just sleep for now if you can. You sound tired."

Harrio accepts the pillow and wedges it under her softer one. "Not tired," she says.

Grey unlocks the door for me and we leave in the morning dark. I leave one storm-brewed world for another one.

CHAPTER 11

A FEW WEEKS GO BY AND I AM PLEASED WE NO longer need to sleep with the door locked and we are allowed to write our loved ones on the Trail. I write to Ambrose that we are having a girl. I put a small sprig from the tree outside our cottage in the envelope. The parcel smells like pine.

I hand the letter to Grey in the evening before supper. We're walking on the beach. I am barefoot and feel the pleasant scratch of sand. The sand is still hard and wintry cold but I like the firmness of it. Some girls are beside us with their midwives, stretching in the sun. They harmonize in rolling their shoulders back, their hands greeting the other hands behind them, pushing back toward the water. I overhear Elspeth and a group of other girls begging the midwife who is leading their stretches. They beg her for their DociGens early, excited about the carefree feeling, the loosening of their minds. The midwife shakes her head, presses a finger to her lips and tells them to stand and reach for the lake.

Grey has changed her apron and her hair looks healthy and clean.

"You finally took a break, I see," I tease her.

"Yes." She picks up on my tone and smiles. "To bathe, Sable. I took a warm bath."

While we girls shower in the shed by the lake twice a week, I don't know how often the midwives get to bathe or how they bathe. They have their own quarters, isolated from us on the property. "You'll mail that, then?" I gesture to the letter I gave her.

"I'll take it to the Domicile. Lion ensures that everything gets back to the Trail."

I nod. "Do you have showers or tubs?"

"Just a small tub in the middy home. But it's always in use. I got lucky." Grey twirls a stray wet hair by her cheek. "And I got through a couple of chapters in my book. *For Whom the Bell Tolls.* Have you heard of it?"

I shake my head. I haven't. "You read?"

Grey's eyes look fiery and offended for a moment. She stares down at my apron. "We'll have to get you another one once the seamstresses start their work. That's starting to look worn out."

"Sorry, Grey, of course you can read. I know you're very smart." I feel my cheeks flame. "It's just, once we are ready to conceive, we aren't allowed books. *Breeding is more than reading.*" I recite the line told to me so often in Lessons.

Grey rolls her eyes at that familiar quote. "I guess we aren't supposed to have books either. But they get confiscated over time from girls staying here. We've a bit of a secret library in our middy quarters."

"Why are you telling me this? What if I reported it?" I would never do that, but Grey doesn't know me that well.

Grey shrugs. "You pity me. You pity me and that's how I know you won't tell."

I stop to think how many Matches The Den might've paired with Grey to help her conceive. How many Men have entered her body to fulfill the only thing she's really meant to do. How many books she's been able to consume since then.

"I'm not meant to be a mother. But I can read. I can read myself to death. I just can't be back on the Trail, back in our world. Ceres is my home." Her fingers have tightened on my letter to Ambrose. "Is He good?"

I nod. "What's *For Whom the Bell Tolls* about?"

"A Spanish war. Main Stream values. Lust. Love. But women get kind of mythologized in war stories. Like we need saving, like we're frozen in place until peace can find us."

"Sounds familiar," I say boldly. I hear raised voices from our cottage. It sounds like Dinah. "I have to go. See you at supper, Grey."

I run across the sand and grass to our cottage. Dinah stands outside the water-closet door, stomping and enraged. She says Harrio is hogging the water closet. She bangs on the door over and over again. "Out! Your hair will never look any different! No matter how much time you spend in there trying!"

"Dinah, be nice. Harrio is nice to us," I tell her.

"Her hair's fucking barbed wire, Sable. It's never going to look good! So stop hogging the toilet."

Harrio exits. She has her scarf over her head. "I wasn't doing my fucking barbed-wire hair," she spits at Dinah. "It's all yours now. And apologies if it stinks."

There—was that tantrum worth it? I want to ask Dinah but don't. Emotions are running high and I am too tired to engage with her. I wish we had more to keep us all busy.

Supper is minced beef, eggs and spinach. It's hot and burns

my tongue because I'm too hungry to wait. Fern ladles second helpings into my bowl. Harrio bursts her eggs open with her fork. She takes two bites and asks Grey if she can lie down.

Grey shakes her head. "You need to finish for once tonight. You need fuel."

"Fuck fuel," Harrio says, pushing her plate away.

"Language!" Fern groans at her.

"Sorry." Harrio places her forehead on the table.

Elspeth and Dinah have eaten their seconds before I can finish mine. The roof of my mouth is metallic and peeling. I am horrible at waiting.

I haven't received any letters from my mother, Gram Evelyn or Kassia. I miss them. Harrio, Elspeth and Dinah quarrel all over the place, argue about the heat, argue about which one is fattest, which Match is the best looking. They are making me sick.

HARRIO AND I SHARE THE MEDIC TENT. SHE TAKES THE time slot right after me. Mine at six, hers at seven. Grey stays put and waits for her. Each time I leave the medic tent, a little sticky and tired, overwhelmed by all of Grey's questions, Harrio points toward the lake and the lifting sun as she passes me and mutters, "Another blistered day in Hell."

I always pretend she's saying "blissful" although she's right. It does feel blistered. I miss normalcy. Harrio and I get along fine. Dinah and she do most of the time, except when it comes to sharing the water closet. Elspeth, on the other hand, is a real nut.

Elspeth says she has strict parents. Her Father agrees with Feles that removing lust and hysteria from society is just and right.

He used to design roads in Main Stream. Now, Elspeth brags, He will help with Feles's expansion goals for the plant. He'll make the plant and our Trail look more modern, less pathetic, less Amish and hillbilly, as she puts it. This would be more interesting to me if I could walk and feel and see the roads He once designed.

"Shut up, Elspeth," Harrio says from her bed one night, interrupting Elspeth's latest boasts about her old church, her Father's spiritual and career achievements. "I thought you said you hate your Father."

"I do," Elspeth says back. "That doesn't mean He isn't accomplished."

"Well, you and I, we have to try to move on. No more Main Stream. No more."

"Fine," Elspeth says. "It's just, I miss home all the time."

I know by the way Harrio slaps her pillow over her ears and tells us all that it's time to rest that she misses her home, too. She falls asleep first every single night. I am so envious. How Harrio loves her sleep. It seems to find her so easily.

I AM NOT SURPRISED WHEN I AM ASSIGNED TO BE A laundress—I am awful at sewing, worse at cooking, have no experience growing or caring for plants or crops. Laundering seems simple, relaxing enough.

The job announcements go on for what feels like hours. We're sitting on blankets in the morning frost, a pleasant blazing bonfire behind us. Lion reads out our names and positions from the balcony of the Domicile. Some girls clap and stand when they hear their positions. Most of us don't. Dinah gets seamstress. Elspeth is assigned to working in the Domicile, cooking.

Mamie gets hen feeder. There are chickens in the Yard that lay daily eggs. She must feed them and collect eggs, feed them and collect eggs. Rake the coop and hay. Tend to the few goats and piglets there as well. Girls snicker when Lion assigns the outdoor farming-type positions. Rumours spread that they are for the girls in the poorest favour. The girls with low-class Fathers. Flora gets hen feeder too. I've barely seen her since the shuttle bus. Her skin looks brighter, like her anemia is under control.

Harrio is a laundress like me and she is angry about it. She wanted to be a seeder, even if it made girls laugh at her. To plant and stay outdoors, tend the crops and be the reason we're all fed and full and healthy. Harrio is stuck with laundress because we're both stuck with Grey for a midwife.

"My mother was a laundress," I tell her. "That's probably why they gave it to me."

Harrio is sitting beside Dinah and me on the grass, digging the toes of her boots into the dirt, deeper and deeper. "I hate the smell of bleach," she says. "My sister burned her arm with it once."

I don't ask her anything about this. She's never talked of her sister before, not in all the times I've talked about Kass.

"Stop messing your shoes up," Dinah scolds her. "You'll have to clean them yourself now. That's your job."

Harrio stops but the tips of her white boots are smothered in mud. She presses her hands on the soles, then rubs her dirty hands against her coat, staining it, as if to tell Dinah she doesn't care, as if to startle everyone here with her unhappiness.

"Work begins tomorrow," Lion yells, dismissing us once the last girl receives her position. I am glad we're finished. As we walk to eat our afternoon meal, drops of rain slap my wrist, the back of my neck.

◇◇◇

THE SAME EVENING AFTER SUPPER, HARRIO AND I WALK back from the Domicile with our ration of fresh firewood. She's high on her DociGen, but I hid mine in my apron hem again, as I do every night. We pull the logs in a yellow wagon but it's still awkward and heavy as it rolls along the rugged shoreline. Harrio wanted to stroll along the lake. She wanted quiet away from the other girls.

"Sable, I woke with blood clots in my underwear today." She says it so calmly and normally that she might be describing a silly dream or an old family recipe.

I stop walking, clutch her arm. "You need to tell Grey."

She shakes her head. "I won't, and you won't either. I cleaned myself and changed before my tent time. But I need more under-wear. I've buried the dirty ones."

I have one extra pair in my drawer and agree to give them to her. "You're lucky we're laundresses or I wouldn't have any to spare. We can use the washing hut as much as we need. That's the good thing. They'll give us keys tomorrow."

Harrio clutches my shoulder and I feel her fingernails scratch. I think she wants me to stop prattling on. It's what I do when I am nervous. I can tell she's scared and trying to pretend she's not.

There's a flock of geese in the middle of the water. I can only make out a few of their twitching heads and rested wings. But their calls are incredible, trumpet-like, full of gusto, wildness.

"How many do you think there are out there, Sable?"

We try to count the silvery bodies, black beaks, but we lose track. They're swimming in small circles and bobbing down under the water. I give up at twenty.

We hear footsteps behind us. It's Grey. She carries clean linens to make up our beds. She has a small battery-powered flashlight around her neck and her face glows ghostly. "Girls, bed. Your work starts tomorrow. You need rest."

We follow her quietly. After Grey tucks each sheet into its rightful place, stuffs our pillows into fresh cases, Harrio lies down and falls asleep, without speaking to her child or saying good night to me as she normally does. I toss my extra underwear on her bed. I listen to Dinah sleeping above me. My chest rises and falls as I breathe along with her. It makes me homesick and I wish I could talk to her.

Miscarriages are inexcusable. They open up many undesirable doors. What is wrong with the woman? What did she do to provoke this? How will her Match forgive her? No one even thinks about the grief we would feel to lose our babies inside us. I barely know Harrio but I worry for her. Spotting and bleeding are your body admitting that it's failing.

GREY AND FERN AND THE OTHER MIDWIVES LEAD GROUP exercises before we walk out into the woods toward the Ablutionary, the washing shed. We lie on the lawn looking up and deep-breathing, feeling our pelvises, the weight of us. We march in place, bend to try to touch our toes, which most of can't do anymore. Unswallowed pills rattle in the hem of my apron. I will bury them soon somewhere in the Yard.

After exercises, we walk past the less desirable cottages. To me, they're fantastic. They are their own wooden worlds. They're quiet. The roofs are mossy and smell a little rotten and pungent. They are smaller than ours and built side by side, with black mesh windows, no stoves. Grey says these are the older cottages, where my mother would've stayed. She says she likes to think of all the mothers and girls who have slept here. These cottages have no heat and this makes me envious. I am sick, sick, sick of night-sweating. With the fire and body heat and my hormones and extra flesh, it's all too hot. I now find myself looking forward to washing my nightclothes, my underwear, ridding them of the reek of sweat.

The Ablutionary looks like an old church from a Lessons textbook. It has a domed roof. A middle-aged midwife asks us to line up in front of the wooden doors. She presents us each with a small brass key. "My name is Claudia. I've worked guiding the laundresses at Ceres for over a decade. Laundresses are very important. The clothes you wear shield and hold your child, the clothes you wear say who you are, what kind of woman you are. Stained dresses, unstarched headscarves, damp, crinkled socks—we don't tolerate that at Ceres because we don't want you to tolerate that in your own lives. Once a week, all the laundry from the Trail and the plant will arrive here. It's your duty to clean for The Den. You'll take extra care of Feles's and the Men's things, won't you." We all nod. Of course. We'd be foolish not to. "The Ablutionary will be unlocked in the afternoons," she continues. "You have keys in case you need to work harder, complete a task, put in extra work."

Claudia files us into the dark space. It smells of both dirt and soap. Grey pulls a cord by the door and the room comes alive with light. It's a large room of rows. A row of cabinetry, a row of clotheslines. Its finest, most ornate feature is a large circular stone sink, fountain-like, in the back of the room. Little faucets surround the basin, sprout from the mouths of carved stone statues of women. I can see the details of their hair and eyes from the doorway, the dark protrusions of their nipples in stone, the chipping of their faces over time. Grey circles the room with a broom, swatting flies and lowering cobwebs.

"Not many people have been in here since last birthing season except a few midwives to wash your sheets and clothes. As you know, The Den's laundry is done by women in the home the rest of the year. Your mothers and sisters will be excited about their break. Time for you to learn what's right and how to contribute," Claudia explains. "Your first task is to clean it."

Claudia hands us each blue medical masks to wear so the bleach won't affect us too badly. I slip mine over my mouth and nose. Claudia then gives out DociGens. She watches us swallow. I jam mine in between my index and middle finger, then cup my hand to my mouth, only pretending to take it.

Some of the girls groan that we have a lot of work ahead, but I know better. It takes half an hour for the DociGens to take effect. They'll be scrubbing and polishing in bliss very soon.

The midwives file out and say it's time for their supper and baths and they'll be back once we have our new workplace sparkling and bright. I am not surprised that Grey stays behind and follows Harrio and me to the sink. Harrio begins with a cloth and a bottle of vinegar, wiping the chest of one of the stone women until I imagine I see her stone organs inside shine through her skin.

I clean while noticing other girls' DociGens kicking in: they begin to hum and sway happily while they work. I smile and pretend I am in their world. Harrio's eyes look less dilated, less glossy than they usually do when she's on DociGens. She continues to scrub each statue with care. I have a wire brush and I am taking the green mildew off around the edges of the large basin. It's oddly satisfying but not blissful, meaningful work. The green grout rinses away when the women's mouths open, producing a stream of lukewarm water. Harrio splashes the water on her face.

I need to get rid of Grey so I can speak with Harrio privately. I ask Grey to fetch us tea, tell her I am cold. She goes up a narrow staircase to a small loft where there is seating, a table, a kettle and cups. Harrio and I are finally alone but for one girl beside us. The girl has long braids and a blue apron. She begins to spray vinegar on the small drains under each stone woman. She hums. She is enchanted. She is content.

Harrio won't make eye contact with me. "I didn't forget," I whisper. "I haven't forgotten what you told me. The blood." She shushes me and digs her nails into my arm. I get a good look into her eyes. "You didn't take your DociGen, Harrio."

She looks wildly at me, as if I am challenging her. "You never take yours," she says. "I've watched you, Sable. I just wanted to know why you don't. They feel good."

"They do," I say. "But I want to be myself. I don't want to let them win."

"Me too," she says. "I decided I want that, too."

Grey returns with a searing cup that smells like licorice. I thank her. Harrio and I pass the cup back and forth, slipping off our masks to take sips. We pretend to be high and giddy in front of Grey. It's exhausting. The Ablutionary smells pleasant and clean after an hour or so. The girls, drifting and happy, sit on the cool floor tiles, admire their work, stroke their bellies. Harrio and I join them.

Before long, Claudia re-enters in her nightclothes and rubber boots. I can see her breasts through the sheer fabric of her nightgown. She looks ghostly, but the soft sagging of her chin is humanizing. She circles the room and drags her index finger along the surfaces. She's beaming at us. She looks impressed. Once no speck of dirt has shown up on her hands, she dismisses us. She rings a small brass bell and we walk home through the path in the forest.

Harrio is wincing as she walks. She looks as if her stomach is cramping. "Something's not right," she says.

I place a finger to my lips, gesture toward Grey, behind us, listening. "Probably just supper."

"You're right, yes." Harrio steadies her voice. "We don't eat much trout where I'm from. Must've pickled me up."

"I can help," offers Grey, speeding up to match our pace. "I make this tonic with lemongrass, dried sage. Really settles the stomach, cools the brain. I can prepare it and bring it tomorrow, Harrio."

Harrio smiles at Grey and nods. Harrio squeezes my hand. Her steps are awkward and her heels drag. I've never been in the kind of pain that affects your walking. I'm scared for her.

In our cottage, Grey pours us water and leaves for the night. The warmth of our plastered smiles can finally fade. It feels good to be honest.

"Sable, I knew this would happen to me. I'm not good."

I shush Harrio and help her into her bed. Elspeth and Dinah are snoring, in a pleasant state of DociGen-induced sleep, tired from their first day at their work.

Harrio cries in bed, smothers her head with the pillow to stifle her voice. I cannot help her. She doesn't want my help. "If you lose it," I say, "we need to tell Grey."

I give her the blanket from my bed, layer it on hers. "Use it for any more blood," I whisper. "We're laundresses now. We can wash our sheets whenever we please. Don't wake Elspeth or Dinah.

They'll just make it worse. Do you have anything else that can soak up blood?" I go to Harrio's dresser.

"That's mine, Sable. Don't touch anything. Stop it."

I don't listen. I open her drawer. There are four face cloths folded neatly, but what catches my attention is a long-bladed knife lying beside them. "Harrio, what is this? You're not allowed a knife," I hiss at her.

"I wanted Him." She cries. "I know I'm not going to have Him."

I sit at the edge of her bed and squeeze her hand. "Did your sister have trouble?"

"My mother," she says. "Her last child."

"The knife . . ."

"My sister made me bring it here. She says I'm better off dead than losing. We don't see my mum anymore. My Father wouldn't let her join The Den with us, says she's only half a woman, that she's a witch, that she didn't raise me well enough. I want to be back in my life. Or dead. More than here."

"Is she alive, your mum?" I close the drawer, think of what she said about her sister spilling bleach on her arm. Was it her Father? Did He hurt the girls like Men I know on our Trail?

"I don't know," Harrio says. "He wouldn't tell us."

I hold her head up so she can sip water. It drips down her chin. She manages to swallow a little. "Your sister is wrong. You're never better off dead," I say, though I am not sure.

I leave Harrio alone so she can try to sleep. I read my atlas in the dark. I pretend there is a letter from Kass slipped inside. How she'd write that everything is the same at home, pleasant, ordinary, that there's nothing new to tell me. I don't believe that the girls at Lessons have stopped teasing her. I don't believe she loves herself. I hear an angelic, entranced Dinah sleeping, and wonder why women have to hold so many secrets in.

EARLY IN THE MORNING, BEFORE MY TENT APPOINT-ment, I take Harrio's knife under my dress. I walk in the fog to the lake. I bury it by the dock, deep beneath grainy wet sand. I push lake weeds over it. Their slick algae feel like the body hair of a Man. I won't let Harrio hurt herself. She fell asleep late in the night. This morning I folded her stained blankets under her bed, covered her body with my bedsheet. The blood is undetectable. I don't know what to do now. After I bury the knife, my stomach churns. Grey startles me by calling from the tent, says I am late for my appointment.

In my medic tent with Grey, she measures my breaths. She is leading me through some pelvic stretches. The shimmery, high-pitched music on the radio sounds like someone playing glasses of water. It makes me have to pee. I still smell the rust of the knife, feel the weight of burying it.

I sigh heavily. "I'm sorry, Grey, but I don't feel like moving today."

"Do you feel sick, Sable? Harrio has some kind of flu too. May Lynx heal her."

I feel anxiety in my stomach and knees. "Maybe. Maybe that's what I have."

I think of the knife. I think of Harrio. I think of Harrio's blood. I think about what I have stopped her from doing.

My appointment ends and I see Mamie outside my medic tent. I open the fabric curtains and see her dumb, beaming face I love so much. It's a relief to see her. Mamie hasn't made any friends in her cottage. From behind her back she pulls out a pink apron. "A girl, Sable. I am having a girl. My middy, Ollie, says it's for sure!" Mamie is crying big and bright. I do the same and hug her. Our bellies are touching. Our girls must already love each other. Deep down, I am brined with worry. I need to go see Harrio, need to help her hide her loss. There is no good finish for a woman who loses. There are only consequences, isolation, sadness.

"My clothes keep getting tighter," Mamie says, wiping her eyes. She fiddles with the waistline of her linen pants and apron. "It's starting to feel like I've swallowed rocks or something."

My belly has little stretch marks, veiny but elegant like the yarn embroidering my mother's beloved kitchen tapestry. The tapestry is of a Man playing guitar. The music notes are blue. The notes leave the guitar and circle back into the Man's mouth. The stitched music notes resemble my veins, now more raised than ever before from pregnancy.

Mamie walks to the barn with a heavy sack of chicken feed in her arms. I hear her blissfully make clicking sounds, calling to the hens, her voice liquid-smooth, nurturing. I return to my cottage.

"IT ISN'T RIGHT." HARRIO HUGS HER ARMS AROUND HER-self. She's wincing again.

"You could be bleeding internally," I say. "My mother taught me that. You could be. You're clotting so much. And the cramps." There are clots of blood on the sheet I gave her. She's sweating. I pour her water. "Grey is coming. You'll need to tell her or tidy yourself."

It's just the two of us in the cottage. Dinah is in her medic tent and I don't know where Elspeth is. "I'm so sorry," I tell her.

The cobweb has returned to the corner of her bed frame. The lights are off and the dark is boiling with heat. A small lick of light leaks through our window, falls on the beds and Harrio and me.

"Don't touch me," she says. "I don't deserve anything."

"We need to tell Grey. You could get infected. You need medicine. You need help."

The door opens. It's Dinah. She cusses that it's always dark in here and that we're loons for keeping the lights off. "My appointment was so weird today, Sable. My middy, that dumb Fern, says I need fucking iron pills, but they make me so constipated."

She flicks the light on. Then she sees us, really sees us. "Sable, what's wrong with her? Is that blood?" She points to Harrio, sweating and moaning into her pillow, the stains on the sheets.

"She's losing," I say. I begin to cry. "Or she's lost. We told Grey it was a flu. She'll be back any minute with tonic and towels. I—I didn't think she'd actually lose it. I don't know what I thought."

Dinah is stunned and rubs her temples like she has a headache. "You're cursed. You're going to ruin yourself," she says. I don't know if she's speaking to Harrio or me and I don't care. She leaves the cottage, leaves the door wide open.

A cool breeze brings my body back to feeling. I am on my knees on the floor, my hand lightly on Harrio's foot. She is twitching and hurting. "Kill me before Grey comes. Sable, kill me. Please, kill me."

I see Grey's figure through the doorway, the smallness of her, her quick strides, walking through the mud and grass. My tears blur her out. Then I hear her in the room. I speak but I don't know what I say.

Then I am running. I run. A pile of bloody blankets and sheets in my arms. I run them into the woods. I run them to the Ablutionary, throw them in the basin. All eyes on me. The stone women's mouths open and rinse away Harrio, rinse away her future.

I scrub my hardest but nothing is working. No one is near me. Everyone has abandoned their washing. I feel watched. There must be others who lost or will lose. They are normally kept quiet, spirited away, sent home or made into midwives, tested and prodded, studied for their failure by Feles.

The sleeves of my brown dress are now red, a rusty, brownish red. It is obvious and gross. It stinks of metal. My hands have blood in the knuckles and cuticles. It isn't coming out. It's fading but still hauntingly present. Where will Harrio go? Will Lion take her away? Will her Father harm her?

All of a sudden I am in a bedroom, the walls the colour of the stained sheets. Harrio is in the centre. There is no bed. She is naked. The windows are barred. There are pretty pictures of cities on the walls, smiling Men. Wind blows under a doorway. The photos blow to the ground, then float in whispering shapes around her. Harrio screams. She holds a knife to her stomach.

I realize I am screaming in the Ablutionary. A girl I have never seen before clutches my shoulders, tells me to stop. "Lemon juice." The girl presents a white pitcher with a sour-smelling cleanness inside. She pours it over the sheets slowly, runs water over them.

It helps. It helps a little. But the stain is still there. This day still stained. The girl helps me wring, pin the sheets up on the line. "Hey, it's okay," she says. "Undress. I'll wash your clothes. They're bloody. You need to take them off, okay?"

There are so many eyes on me. No one has been speaking. No one is high on their DociGens right now. This is real. They see it as real. I nod.

"You have to tell me," the girl says. "Was it you who bled? Did you miscarry?"

I shake my head. I remove my clothes. I stand naked in the middle of the Ablutionary, behind Harrio's sheets. They shield me. I stand there for what feels like forever. The girl scrubs my clothes with the lemon juice.

"I'm sorry," she says. "For what you've seen."

I thank her. I thank her for helping and not just staring.

"Of course," she says. She holds my dress under a large heated fan. She asks another girl to help hold the left sleeve. My dress waves back to me like a flag. I concentrate on the veins on my belly, try to hear the music stitched into my mother's tapestry, try to hear home.

WHEN MY DRESS IS DRY, THE GIRLS TOSS IT BY MY SIDE and get back to their work. Grey retrieves me and wraps a towel around me and we walk together back to my cottage. The lights are off. We're at the kitchen table. She slips a pill into my mouth. "Sable, be at ease." She kisses my forehead. "Breathe."

I spit the pill into my hand. I almost took it. I almost wasn't paying attention. "Where is she?"

Grey stares down at her shoes and her face turns red. I am so angry. I go to the sink, throw a bar of soap at Grey's cheek. I throw my shoe. I throw a glass of water, full. The glass breaks at her feet and she shrieks.

"Sable, she's in the Domicile. We had to tell them."

"What she did was not her fault. It isn't wrong. You need to believe it wasn't wrong, Grey."

Grey collects herself and gets a broom, sweeps the glass around us.

"Sit on the bed. Or you'll cut your feet," she says. "He knows you knew, tried to protect her. And guess what I know? I know you aren't taking your DociGens. I know you aren't feeling the need to serve. I know you're fighting."

I listen to Grey, sit on the bed. Her voice is calm. "When you ran to the Ablutionary, I stayed with Harrio. She didn't want me. She was going through her drawer over and over, cursing you."

I cross my legs and catch my breath. "You're so observant, Grey. If you're so fucking observant why couldn't you see it coming? Stop her from losing?"

Grey's face tightens. "I've never done this before. I didn't know what I was supposed to see." Grey drops the broom, steadies her shaking hands against the table. She's swallowing back tears. She coughs. "Because when I lost mine, it looked different. They all look different. They brought me to Ceres. Away from everyone. My mother. I lost my mother . . . But I'm here. I try to be here for you. You won't let me. And Harrio, Dinah, you all hate me. Why?"

I feel horrible. I go to Grey's side. I squeeze her waist from behind, wrap my arms around her. She is so soft. She's so young. "I'm sorry. I didn't know. Do I know your mother?"

"Helena."

"Yes, I do know her. She's lovely. She sews with my mother."

We both stare into the sink, that black hole leading water and the insides of us under and out of our worlds. Water keeps us alive. But it's also water, power, that ruins us.

CHAPTER 12

It's May. This month, we're told to warm to thoughts of Ceres, whom this Yard was named for. A Roman goddess, she is brightly connected with May and fertility for fields, herds and bodies of water. Feles chose her for this Yard because she represents all life—life of the field and life of the family. Dinah and Elspeth bid her spirit good night each night as instructed before we go to sleep, as if they think she is near, as if the gaps in them hold her music, her power.

We're given double doses of blood capsules and more servings of fresh vegetables. Fern announced from Lion's balcony on the evening of May 1 that double the amount will allow our babies to hear us better, that they will become more disciplined in their own growth.

This month, they encourage all the girls to sing at any point during the day. Hymns of The Den, songs written for Lynx. One song for Ceres is a harvest song, personifying each ear of wheat as a small girl.

But me, I am not celebrating. I am not full of joy and harvest. My girl and I, we slip through the cracks. I slip. I am unseen and breaking. My stomach hurts often. My fingernails are cracked. My blood capsules keep me strong but everything else feels off.

I keep dreaming I kill Harrio. I dream she's lying on Elspeth's top bunk and I'm below. I take a knife and slide it between the bed slats. She screams. I stab again. Her blood rains down on my arms and face and legs, soaks the sheets. It's not the blood that horrifies me. It's that before I wake from the dream, each time, I always hear her tell me *Thank you.*

Our suppers are now consumed outdoors. Lion has put a stone statue of Ceres in the centre of the field where the bonfires are held. The statue isn't large. She stands only a few inches taller than most of us girls. She holds a stone child in her arms. The child has no face. The robe she wears cloaks the baby's body too. She stares down at her child with eyes widened with bliss. Her mouth is open as if she's singing to Him. She wears a laurel crown. It's not until I get really close to her that I notice her left ear is broken off and there's a crack on her cheek.

The midwives set up our dinners before heading to their quarters. The lineups for supper are painfully long but I don't mind. It's nice to get fresh air, to eat so near where food comes from. I love feeling the earth as I sit and eat. Some girls sit on blankets but I don't mind my clothes getting dirty. If any midwives caught me, they'd scold me, but there are too many of us and I am not afraid of them. I love seeing my belly look like a mountain against a backdrop of stars.

Dinah joins me under a poplar tree. She's high on her DociGen. She asks if I need a glass of water. I shake my head. I keep my eyes narrowed at mealtimes. If I am seen without dilated pupils, I will be made to answer for it. Dinah pushes a forkful of her corn to my mouth. "Sable, you've thinned."

I shake my head. "How could I? None of us are thin, Dinah." I accept the mouthful anyway. I love the buttery sweetness of corn, even canned corn.

"It's in your face, Sable. It's your face that's thinning."

No one has mentioned Harrio's name. They let her be erased. It's been a week now. I put my plate down on the grass. I reach for Dinah's skirt. "Do you wonder where they took her?"

Dinah stares at me, then almost through me. She gestures over to Mamie, chanting with a group of girls in the line for food. They kneel down and face Ceres. "Mamie seems so happy here," Dinah says.

I leave my plate beside Dinah, the meat and sauce I can no longer stomach. I walk to the middy quarters, though we're not supposed to disturb them during this hour. Their reward in May is an extra piece of fruit after supper, and an extra hour of quiet while we eat. I walk there under the lowering sun to find Grey.

"Sable, where are you going?" Mamie calls. Pleasant, naive, always hungry Mamie. She is buttering a slice of bread and helping herself to wilted greens from a glass bowl when I turn around. I don't answer her. I let her eat in peace. She deserves not to worry. She deserves to forget Harrio. She deserves to forget me.

I WALK BEYOND MAMIE'S AND THE POORER GIRLS' COT-tages to the middy lodge. I knock on the greened copper door of the red house. It's four floors high. Only the first floor has windows. Dead ivy covers them. But the garden is beautifully kept. Midwives live sustainably off their own potatoes, corn and root vegetables. They seldom eat meat. The meat is reserved for women who can conceive. We're in greater need of the protein, the iron, the fat. Bright pea plants lace up the sides of wood lattice panels.

The front cobblestones look well swept. Potatoes rest in freshly churned earth. But it's gloomy here. You can't see the lake. I get why Grey says she doesn't care for it. Maybe forests frighten her. Maybe they've done her wrong before.

No one answers my knock so I try again. I hear a voice, an older voice. It sounds like Claudia, the washing-hut midwife. "There's a girl out there. They can't be here."

Then I see Fern. She bangs her hand on a window. I see her through the unwashed glass and ivy brambles. "Sable, we're bathing. We're eating. You need to leave," she says.

"I need Grey. Please. I need to speak with her."

Fern hits the window again with her palm, as if I'm an unwelcome fly and she's squashing me. I flinch even though we're far apart. "I'll get her. But don't make this routine. Or other girls will do it too."

I nod. A few moments pass and the air grows chillier. I stick my hands in my apron pockets, feel the protrusion of my stomach where it used to be flat. It's kind of amazing. I don't care if I ever look like I once did. I don't care. Grey exits the front door. Her hair is draped in a towel. She holds a chunk of bread.

"I made this yesterday evening with Fern. Would you like to try it?"

"I've had my calories today. You enjoy it."

Grey takes a large bite. Bathwater drips onto her shoulders, dyeing her dress darker.

"It's nice to see you comfortable," I say. "What does the building look like on the inside?"

Grey continues to chew. Her eyes wander to the forest. She points. "Do you see that, there by the cedar?"

I turn. I do see it. A rabbit perches in peace, unmoving. Its ears are perked as if trying to hear a message. Its body is long, dirtied with soil.

"I used to catch them. With my Father. He'd take me with Him even though it wasn't permitted. My mother prepared them in broth. With potatoes and leeks and garlic." We look at the rabbit. "I mean, such a wonderful animal to watch. But such dark, beautiful meat."

I touch the crook of her elbow. "I want to know what happened to Harrio. Can you live without knowing?"

The rabbit leaps into the brush but Grey still watches the place where it rested. "I think Lion's wanting to speak with you. I heard from another midwife. Maybe you can ask Him then. But Sable, He doesn't owe you anything. He doesn't owe it to us to say anything."

My baby girl has begun to kick. The kicks always start slow and resemble the feeling of my stomach digesting. Then they grow firmer, precise. I love her so much already. I love her so much.

Elspeth has taken up Harrio's bed, migrates down to her bunk when the top mattress is too hot. Up and down she climbs and I am full of hatred. She has so many letters. She's always staying up reading and giggling aloud to make us feel inferior for not receiving any. She says all the girls in the Domicile have gotten some and that they are more favoured.

And no one really sees Lion but the girls who work inside the Domicile. The ones who sweep and dust and care for His house. The ones like Elspeth. The ones who help prepare the bread, divvy out drinking water and tea for every meal. The ones who apparently get more letters and are loved more than us.

There is something else different about those girls, but no one says anything about it. There is a heaviness like they're hurting. Like they're in pain. Their hands jammed in their pockets. The way they stare at the ground, the way they walk after their evening DociGens, collecting stray grass from the walkway, weeding plants that no one asked them to.

Each day in the Ablutionary, we laundresses scrub the linens and outfits of different girls here, hang to dry, hang to dry. I have grown used to the sopping music of clothes hanging on lines. The familiar fabrics and colours—all blues and pinks and browns. The Arrival dresses of younger girls. I imagine I am cleaning Kassia's dress every time I wash one with a pink sleeve like hers.

The girl who helped me scrub Harrio's blood with lemon juice doesn't come near me now. If I am washing dresses and slacks under the fountain, she goes to the steam boards and presses headscarves. If I go up to the loft for tea, she'll instantly descend the stairs and hang socks to dry by the front doors.

Dinah tells me one night, when she has adjusted to her DociGen, that there is a rumour going around that I am dangerous, that I hurt Harrio. Or, she says, that I am cursed and miscarriages happen in my presence.

"Who told you this?"

"Elspeth. You know her. She likes to brew storms. She's bored." Dinah lies on the braided rug and strokes her hand up the table leg. It gives her a splinter and she tries to pick it out with her sharpest fingernail. "It doesn't matter who started it. It matters that girls are afraid of you."

I couldn't care less if they are.

"They think you're too selfish, that you don't care enough about your baby."

"I love her. More than anything."

"I know," Dinah says. "I believe you."

She stands and spills water from her water bottle onto her palms, then rubs her face, exhales. In the sewing shed, Dinah replaces buttons on shirts and sweaters, patches trousers for all members of our Trail. Sometimes the midwives make her stitch initials or beads onto plain sheets as a test to see how skilled she is at her job. She is quick and talented. I've heard she gets her work done first. "Ice soothes them. My fingers are stiff as all hell, Sable. They feel like wood."

I nod. I can relate. My hands are so dry from bleach and washing soap they could flake off.

"Hard work is shaping us," Dinah says in a satisfied tone. She lies down in her bed. Soon, I hear her nod off to sleep, joining in the chorus of Elspeth's snores.

But I haven't slept well since Harrio was removed. Some nights, I picture her child as a ghost in the room, newborn, in the basket on the table. The basket is actually filled with bread and fruit and I know this, but at night, my mind tricks me into seeing otherwise.

I DON'T BELIEVE WHAT DINAH TOLD ME ABOUT THE rumours until my next shower. I go to bathe in the morning after my medic tent, before working in the Ablutionary. Before, the water girls barely seemed to care who I was, would say good morning, giggle as they always did at seeing naked bodies day in and day out. They would give me a bar of soap, fill the sack of water above me.

Today, one of them, a girl named Cynthia whom I've known since I was a small girl, put freezing-cold water into the sack. When I pull the cord, the rush of icy liquid chills my spine and I jump, almost slip on the cement floor. I look up at her. She's on the stepladder, staring at the clouds, pretending she has no idea the water isn't hot. "Cynth, hey, it's freezing," I tell her. She doesn't make eye contact with me. She doesn't say a word. She sticks the end of one her braids in her mouth and hums a song for Ceres.

"Excuse me," I say to the girl on the ladder beside her. A Main Stream–born girl. "I didn't receive any soap."

"We're out, Sable," she snaps. I didn't know she knew my name. "Lion says you only get ten minutes today." I know she's lying. Lion would never go out of His way to tell her that.

"It's fine," I say. "I only need ten minutes. Soap?"

She shakes her head.

"Fine." I pull the cord again, rub a bit of icy water under my armpits, the soles of my feet, my crotch, then march toward the shelves of towels beside the shower stall. I yank one from the bottom of the pile so the rest spill to the sopping wet floor.

Cynthia still doesn't look at me. Now they've run out of towels. Now they have a mess to clean up.

The other girl says, "Aren't you a laundress?"

I realize I've only given my own girls more work to do by spoiling the towels. I am just so bitter they are shunning me, treating me differently. Because I watched Harrio miscarry, held her hand.

Finally, Cynthia pipes up. "Allie, make sure Sable doesn't take more than one towel. She's known to steal. And she's violent. She kicked a Boy on our Trail, you know."

"Fuck, just leave it," I mutter at them. I rub my belly. "Can't you see? I'm just like you. You don't need to be like this."

Dinah was right about the rumours. Elspeth did help spread them. She told them that I protected Harrio. Other girls judged me before the Yard because I hurt Caleb—this has just added kindling to their stories. I have to embrace their hate, their heat. The girls are all losing it here—addicted to their pills—and their minds are bending and not fully theirs. But all the same, I am still bitter and hurt.

I walk away with my towel under my arms as a dress, my apron over my shoulder. I walk away thinking of Harrio, Dinah, Mamie, Grey—women who do care for me.

Lion has summoned me to meet with Him tonight. I wish I had gotten to bathe properly. I feel coated with dust and dirt. I wish I felt cleaner, more confident. Grey walks me to the Domicile porch after supper. "You're not going to give me a DociGen now?"

Grey says He's requested that I take it afterwards. "He wants you clear-headed, to hear your thoughts."

I wonder what He wants from me. But I know what I want from Him—answers about Harrio. I want to know if she's okay and comfortable, where she is now and where they will send her.

"There must be others who lost, Grey. This season."

Grey puts a hand on my shoulder. "Don't ask for numbers, for names. If anyone else has miscarried in their second term here, it'll be hidden. Even the midwives aren't allowed to talk about it. This is your one chance to ask about your friend."

"She was barely my friend," I say. "She was just a girl. A funny, strong, kind girl. Grey?"

"Yes?"

"Have you heard other midwives mention me? That other girls don't like me?"

Grey pulls a cord to ring the doorbell. "You go in now. Fourth floor."

"How long did the pain last?" I turn to Grey from the top step.

"Sable, after a miscarriage, I can't even say. There are so many kinds of pain."

LION IS SEATED AT A LARGE DESK. BLACK, THICK CURTAINS block the starry night sky. His back is hunched. He sips from a glass of brown liquid. He turns when I enter the room.

"Sable. I hope you're well." He stares at my protruding belly.

"I am." I nod.

His face is splotched, alcohol-induced red. His breath reeks as He comes closer. It makes me nervous and, strangely, makes me miss my Father. "You enjoy being a laundress?"

I know the answer I am supposed to say. How could I truly enjoy it? How am I expected to be satisfied, stimulated solely by the fucking smell of soap? With the feeling of scrubbing fabric until broth and blood are rinsed away? As if the messes never happened. Laundering is like erasing memories. I try to find power in this.

"I like it very much," I say. My belly tenses. My girl kicks me hard. My ankles are sore from the day. "May I sit?"

"Yes, please."

There are two large black couches. A vast library of books takes up three walls. "What are you reading?" I feel bold.

"Doesn't concern you," He says. He sits across from me on the other couch.

I stare at the floor, embarrassed.

"*The Life of Johnny Reb*. Civil war. Fallen states. True accounts. I could read war all day. Main Stream adores war. It's a weakness. My Father and Brother sought so much peace."

Somehow I see war on His face, war in His eyes, war on His tongue now. A flaming. My mouth dries up and I'm not sure what I'm even doing here.

"Sable, you are making a storm of calm land. You need to stop. You tried to cover up a miscarriage. You know that's an illegal act. You know it's unfaithful to the Family Body."

I stare toward the curtains. I'm sitting on my hands and I feel the leather make small imprints in my palms. I want so badly to open the curtains, see a flicker of sky and light. Watch Mamie with the chickens across the grass. Watch her care for them in the confines of soft hay and fences, watch her mouth click and croon.

"You know who I am. I kicked your Son." I hang my head in appropriate shame.

"But you've been cleansed of that experience, forgiven. Why act out more here? Are you that uncontrollable? Stupid." Lion spits on His palm and laughs at me. I hate being reminded of the spitting. I've tried to block it out. My jaw tenses.

Lion refills His drink from a large crystal pitcher. To the top, no ice. He takes a small sip and wipes a layer of sweat from His forehead.

"I saw the signs of her miscarriage, yes," I said, "but she told me she was just ill. A flu."

I find myself lying. I find myself being a coward. There is a glass table between us. Roses rest in a vase. A leather-bound journal and a steel cowbell lie on the corner closest to Lion's resting elbows. He leans low, His legs spread open. His navy suit is clean. I recognize it. "I washed that suit for you. Yesterday."

"Birth Yards are meant for community, not friendships. Understand?"

I nod. But I don't understand.

"I understand you've come here with good friends and it seems you're the type of woman others confide in. This is dangerous for you. And I know you can tell. Harrio has been sent back to Main Stream. Away from her family. She will not be permitted to speak with them again. Her Father doesn't want her in The Den now. She was healthy enough to go."

This is the answer I expected to hear. I do not believe Him. He says it too plainly, too rehearsed. "But what will she do there? How will she have money? Where will she live?"

"I don't think you understand the severity of losing a Man's baby. Losing His legacy. You have one job. You have plenty of people sacrificing their time and knowledge to help sustain you." He takes another sip. "I have devoted my whole life to women, to Ceres. It makes me look bad when miscarriages happen. You know what a reputation means to Men? Women, even?"

I nod.

"Like when you were labelled as a rebel, uncoachable, unbridled. When you kicked Caleb, my Son, instead of that slut girl He was with."

I feel myself turn hot. The world starts to blur. "Ambrose forgives me for it too."

"Sable, everything here needs to be faultless. This is a warning to you. Be good. Honour The Den. Me."

"Yes, Sir."

There is a knock on the door. A blond, freckled girl enters. She is in a robe, nothing else. Her fat belly looks glorious on her. She doesn't look me in the eye. I've seen her in the Yard at night. I've seen her wade in the lake with others who work in the Domicile. Lion shoots her a look. The door closes and we are alone again.

"Thank you for coming to speak with me. I'm afraid it's getting late now. Report to Grey for your DociGen."

"Yes, I look forward to it." I realize how obvious and bad at lying to Him I am compared to when I lie to Grey. Thankfully He doesn't know me well enough to know this.

"I've spoken to Grey about Harrio's losing. That moronic woman. I believe she didn't know it was more than a flu."

"Right," I say. "Grey said it was the flu."

"You know, blood capsules were my creation." He stands up to show me to the door. "They help prevent anemia, and they pass on the psychological strength of past breeders. It's remarkable. Sable, you can be remarkable too. Do your part. Or hurt will come to you. Your fetus is your friend."

I thank Him for His time. He thinks He's scared me more than He has and I will let Him feel that way.

"Before you go." Lion goes to His desk, opens a drawer stuffed with envelopes. He sorts through them and hands me a small brown envelope with my name scribbled on the front. "Obedience, at all times," He says. "Clear?"

"Praise Feles," I say.

I leave down the stairs, passing the blond girl in the robe, waiting in the hallway. But all the other girls have been excused for the day. I can't think of this. I can't think of anything. I run home to my cottage. I run home to Dinah. She stays beside me and I wait for her to fall asleep first. I grab the envelope from my apron pocket where it's hanging on the coat rack. It's my time to be with Ambrose. It's my time to remember Him. I am so over-wrought and excited and confused. Were there others from Him? When did He write this? Is Lion withholding our letters?

I open the letter.

Sable, I miss you.
Happy we are having a girl.
Your mother visited mine last week.
They were crying. They miss you.
Mostly they're really excited.
I have been learning how to stitch wounds. I passed the testing at the plant. I was so nervous my hands shook. I hope you are staying calmer than me.
In Feles's love,
Ambrose

My hands feel pleasantly numb. I fall asleep with the letter on my chest.

"YOUR FETUS IS YOUR FRIEND? HE SAID THAT? WHAT kind of moonshine advice is that?" Dinah is awake early. I'm hav-ing a cup of tea with her before my medic tent appointment.

"I don't know. Do you notice that there aren't many friend-ships here? Between the other girls?"

"I guess not that many."

"Do you think the DociGens cause that?"

Dinah takes a slurp of cream from a pitcher. "DociGens help distance, I think. I don't know. They're not Reposeries. I miss those."

"Hey, are you worried?"

Dinah takes another sip. Cream clouds her upper lip. She wipes her mouth with her sleeve. She touches her stomach and her jaw tenses. "About?" She jerks her head over to the sleeping or pretending-to-sleep Elspeth and her eyes widen, warning me not to mention anything I shouldn't. About Garrison. About her adultery toward The Den.

I have my answer. She's terrified.

"Nothing," I say. I change my tone. "Just shitting ourselves while we deliver."

"Don't be gross, Sable! I don't do that."

"Ever? I'm sure I've smelled it." I go to the water closet. Dinah laughs and screams at me to stop. I haven't heard her laugh this hard since we were home.

"Mm-hmm." I take an exaggerated whiff. "Fresh."

"Yes. Okay. If I poop while I give birth." She uses a facetious tone, presses the back of her hand to her forehead dramatically. "I think about it often. It keeps me up at night sometimes. Then I can't go. My bowels freeze up."

I picture Dinah in the birthing tent. I picture her excreting into a midwife's hand. I can't control my laughter.

"Well, I hope you shit all over Grey!" she says.

I hook my arm through hers. "Grey is a saint. I could never."

Elspeth is awake now. "You whores get out of here or I'll tell Fern you're keeping me from sleep."

Dinah lifts her middle finger at Elspeth. She walks me to my medic tent. Every step in the oozing brown mud only makes us laugh harder.

"I'm doing a terrible job," I say. "My fetus can't be my only friend."

Grey opens the linen curtains of the tent for me, says a quiet good morning to Dinah. I kiss Dinah's hand and she saunters back toward the cottage. "She's in a good mood," I tell Grey.

"I can tell. How are you feeling, Sable?"

I lie down on the stretcher. It feels good to be on a slight angle, blood rushing to my head. The pendant light clipped to the centre of the tent dangles down. Its tassels rustle with the wind. "Physically?"

"Whatever. All aspects of your health."

"Well, I've noticed my hands growing puffier. My ankles too."

Grey puts her cold hands on my ankles, peels down my stockings. "Edema. Very normal, Sable."

"I'm hungrier. I feel my body thickening."

"That's good. You didn't eat enough when you first arrived. Insomnia? You seem to fall asleep fine whenever I'm there."

"Because I don't want to talk to you." That's not true. Grey comforts me more than anyone.

Grey bites her lip. "Understandable."

"You don't really think Lion sees me as a threat, do you?"

"I think He admires your spirit, fears your independence."

"I'm not really independent. I just think our bodies are ours."

"You'll need to get a needle today."

"Fine." I roll up my sleeve and offer my arm to Grey. This will be the fourth needle I've gotten since arriving here. "They don't hurt me."

"You're brave. Harrio kicked me when she had her first done."

"Let's not talk about her, Grey." Grey nods. She ties a thick band around my arm and squeezes it. Blood pressure's fine.

"I am surprised. I'm so angry all the time," I say, rolling my eyes.

She runs her hands along my stomach for a while. "Her size feels healthy from what I can feel."

I nod. "I feel her move but not that often."

"Lion might separate us," Grey says, searching for my vein. "He thinks we're a bad fit after what happened to Harrio. And He wants you to be focused."

Grey injects fluid into my arm. I watch. I am focused.

"Ambrose wrote me. Did you know? Lion has letters in His desk. Ambrose knows we're having a girl! And I was convinced He didn't care."

Grey sticks a piece of cotton where the needle was. She dabs. I see the littlest bit of blood. She seems underwhelmed by my news. "Well, I'm glad you heard from Him."

Grey rubs my ankles for a while and puts a hot cloth on my forehead, tells me to rest. Then we do deep breathing and I stand, swing my arms, lift my legs. As if we're hiking. Grey counts to ten and back down again, ten and back down again. I feel my girl kick.

"She's going to be as restless as me."

"Let's hope so," says Grey. "You bring joy, Sable."

I don't think I bring joy. I think I'm a good friend, but I think I'm too cynical to really bring joy. But I thank Grey, wonder when the last time was she brought herself a sense of joy.

The heartbeat of my girl fills the tent. It is both the most beautiful sound I have ever heard and the scariest. "She sounds louder."

"She's getting bigger, that's all."

"She brings me joy already," I say, and it occurs to me that she will one day be outside my body, born into this same life.

I LIE IN THE DARK IN THE FIELD OUTSIDE THE DOMICILE as the other girls sing and work, high on their DociGens. I hear Ceres's name tossed in the wind through song and stories. Everyone seems thrilled to be able to glorify and praise a woman. The midwives are eating around a fire. I am on the other side of the chain-link fence from Mamie. I watch her shovel and scrape out manure and dirt from the wooden coop. She doesn't see me at first but I like being close to her. I hope my absence from laundering goes unnoticed. Lion's windows are shut and the lights are dimmed. His passion for birth, our gift of life, runs so deep, He forgets we're people and not factories. Factories made of flesh.

"Sable," Mamie says, looking up from her work. "What're you doing here so late?"

I shrug. "Do you ever hear anything from up there?" I point to the Domicile. "There are so many people in and out all the time."

Mamie stops shovelling and walks toward the fence. She reaches her fingers through the metal to grip mine. "Recently. Screams. But not like horror, murder ones. Quieter."

The chicken coop is below the highest window, Lion's window, usually left open. She said the screaming at first sounded much more dreadful, then became relaxed, a cooing, a giving up. "It faded. And a little while after the window was shut by a shadow I couldn't see in the dark. I haven't heard it since. So I'm not sure. Maybe I was just too high. Maybe it was my head."

Mamie knows the DociGens are against us but she loves the solace. She is addicted. "Do they ever affect you like that, Sable? DociGens."

I stare into my friend's dilated eyes, stare at her hopelessness, her hands and cheeks dirty from work.

"Sometimes," I lie to her.

"You know, if you don't take them, Sable," Mamie says, squinting at me, studying me, "Ambrose won't want you. You'll be bad at servitude and He'll notice. And it could affect her health." Mamie stares down at my belly.

"I take them, Mamie. Don't worry." I have buried my DociGens by my medic tent twice in the middle of the night. They continue to collect in the hem of my apron each day.

"I miss Harrio, Mamie. She reminded me of my Gram. She was really strong."

I miss Harrio dreadfully. I often picture us giving birth. We're next to each other. Her labour is first. Grey with gored-up hands and fretful brows motivating, whispering. Harrio's scream blood-curdling until they give her an epidural, DociGens, Reposeries. Then she says she's floating and delighted. Euphoria claims her. I watch, rejecting my own pelvic pain and burning body, as she greets her Son for the first time, as Grey wipes the mucus and blood off His blue body, places Him in Harrio's arms. Her life forever changed.

Mamie lets go of my hand through the fence. "You have enough friends, Sable." Mamie takes a hose to the coop floor. The water rushes and sprays to cleanse the wooden boards of all feed, all feathers, all droppings, all remnants of life.

◇◇◇

THE NEXT DAY IS A SHOWER DAY, BUT I NEED TO AVOID my shower tomorrow because the girls are so cruel and strange around me.

I grab myself a leftover bucket of water, soapy and cold. I lift it over my head. My arms ache as I tip it over me. I like showering alone because the girls aren't looking at me from above, examining my sex, my belly, my mannerisms. They shame and gossip about bodies, about their superiority, from above us.

I rinse under my arms, around my belly button. It used to be so concave and now sticks out ugly, a loose button. I swallow some water, swish it in my mouth and spit on the cement. I don't have a towel. There aren't any left in the cubbies. When I feel clean enough, I put my clothes back on my wet frame, make my way back to my cottage. The evening heat dries me only a little, comforts me even less. But now I can avoid my shower tomorrow. I can go to my medic tent, back to sleep, until it's time to clean towels and sheets in the Ablutionary. Monotonous, predictable days. In some ways, even less comforting.

Two girls sit together on the gravel by the lake. Their shirts lifted, they rub their stomachs. I lighten my footsteps. I don't want to interrupt any sense of peace any girl has found here.

PART III

THE
FREE
SEASON

CHAPTER 13

CERES'S REIGN HAS PASSED AND ALL SONG HAS worn thin. Things have gotten quieter, our bodies swollen, breasts tender, everything more irritable. We're given a new drink for the morning, to replace our regular water and herbal tea. A gift from Feles. Along with our blood capsules, we're to drink this murky cup of brown water. It tastes godawful.

"It's for luck," Fern says to us, ladling second helpings from a pot on the stove into our mugs.

Dinah clutches her stomach. "I can't drink any more of it."

"I will," says Elspeth, inhaling the odorous liquid steaming on the stove and scrunching up her face. "If you tell us what's in it."

Fern taps her foot on the ground, irritated. "Just drink it. It's good for your babies."

Midwives are trained to think every idea that pops into Feles's head is good for our babies—blood capsules, DociGens and now this vomit-tasting tea. I slide my half-full cup away. "I'm finished." I walk out the door and don't look back.

Elspeth slow-claps behind me. "She's got the courage of a Man, that one. Only, she's totally senseless."

I try not to gag as I smell the liquid being brewed in every cottage I pass. As with all new things, we must adapt. And go to them blind. No questions. I ache for home. I ache for a life that isn't this.

GREY FINDS ME IN THE ABLUTIONARY LATER IN THE afternoon. She approaches me by the large basin, striding across the wet floor. She looks displeased. "Fern told me you walked out on her. You can't do that, Sable."

"She was being condescending and forcing us to drink that gross stuff. Midwives are supposed to serve us, aren't you. And you're not even good at that."

Grey fiddles with a button on her plaid blouse. She looks unkempt, her hair greasy and her skin chalky. "It's a mutual relationship. Or it's supposed to be. Sorry, I'm too tired to even be angry. Lion has kept us up prepping for birthing. It's exhausting. We run scenarios and practise in case the baby's breech. We learn what to say to encourage the mother. We learn blessings from Feles to say aloud too." Grey yawns. "Maybe I'm not cut out for this."

"I'm sorry. You're doing just fine," I tell her. And I mean it. I feel guilty. None of this is Grey's fault.

Gram Evelyn says midwifery was once an honourable profession, a calling, not a punishment, not a means of isolation to cause pain. There's nothing I can do for Grey. I keep lathering towels in soapy water and wringing them out over the basin. Because none of the girls like being near me, no one is in earshot.

"Grey, is the tea . . . blood?"

Grey nods. "His hair. His blood."

I nod back, bite my lower lip. I'm supposed to be excited. We get to ingest a Man who loves us. Protects us. Keeps us. Feles's hair. Feles's blood.

Grey continues. "It's not a secret. You should all be honoured. And Sable, you particularly need to obey. Be grateful."

"Okay." I nod again, wringing out the last hand towel, watching some of its blue dye mix with clear water. "I am."

I think of Feles sending us locks of His long grey hair, vials of blood, how this will be used to nourish us, nourish our babies. I think of my daughter. I want her to want more than the blood of a Man, the sex of a Man, the honour of a Man. I wish I could say this aloud. I wish I could speak my mind.

I CONTINUE WATCHING MAMIE WORK IN THE EVENINGS when I am supposed to be in the Ablutionary, helping to wash the plant workers' clothes. I don't want to work because it's warm out and I miss being with Mamie whenever we wanted. I like to watch her working in the chicken coop, high on her DociGen. None of the girls in the Ablutionary have complained about my absences, my lack of effort and community. They don't want to be near me because Lion doesn't like me and they are afraid of me, so it seems we have a silent agreement. I do choose to work sometimes, but on nights I don't, no one says a word to the midwives. Even Grey has given me more time alone than usual.

But tonight, at dusk, Mamie isn't at her post. Flora's there, collecting eggs in the coop. She sees me so I wave. She waves back with her free hand but averts her eyes from mine quickly after that. I remember our conversation on the shuttle bus. I remember how much she seemed to like her Match. I hope she has been allowed to read letters from home. I hope her baby is fine.

"Flora, where's Mamie?" I ask.

"She was called to the Domicile," she whispers. "You can't be here. You're here too much, Sable. Lion can see us."

"I just want to see my friend."

Flora approaches the fence, feeds her headscarf through the chain links. "Take it," she says. "It's dirty."

I don't want to but I take it. She goes back to her work without another word.

I clutch the dirty scarf. It has sweat stains around the hairline. Flora is right. It's filthy. I know she wants me to take it to the Ablutionary. She's afraid of me too and wants me to get to work. Fine.

On my way to the forest, I walk along the front lawn of the Domicile. I pass under Lion's balcony, wait and listen. There are girls sweeping the front steps beside me, pulling weeds and spraying plants. They stare, as if wondering why I am out walking and not working. I hold up the scarf, indicate I'm off to do laundry. But I stay another minute because I hear Mamie's voice through the open window of Lion's room.

One of the midwives comes to the edge of the stoop. "Please, see to your work. You're Grey's girl? I'll tell her you're slacking."

I nod. I have to pretend I love work, my service. I wonder why Mamie is with Lion. I am afraid and my stomach coils up, my pulse quickens. I walk quickly to the Ablutionary. When I open the doors, no one notices me. They're focused and quiet. I add the scarf to the pile of dirty garments by the sink. I begin to help rinse socks under the stone faucets.

Washing brown socks is the most satisfying. The scent of soap is the indicator of clean. Colour plays no role. You can't tell unless they smell nice that you are finished. I rub the toes and heel of one, try to guess whose it is. It's a stupid game because we all have the same socks. I pretend they belong to Cynthia from the shower huts. I want to spit on them.

I leave the white socks to the other girls on their DociGens. They're more dedicated and precise. They scrub the clothes with small brushes. They wear white masks over their mouths for the bleach. A girl appears beside me and washes her hands. She says hello to me. Surprised, I say hello back. She hums to herself while she works out the dirt under her fingernails. Her apron is blue so she's having a Boy. She looks so comfortable with her body. I long to be like that—accepting of the way things are, content to serve.

I want to recite poems or words from Lessons to pass the time, but they're too far away in my mind. The back closet of it. There's a pile for socks with holes, broken stitches. They'll be sent to the seamstresses soon. They'll be passed on to Dinah.

DINAH IS ENVIOUS OF THE LETTER I RECEIVED FROM Ambrose. I catch her reading it one night.

"My mother hates me," she says when I snatch it back. "She hasn't sent anything. Let alone Colin. They're probably all happy to be rid of me for a while. Peace and quiet. Fuck them. I bet Meadow has letters from Him. I bet He sends her fucking fruit baskets."

"Colin wants you," I say, thinking of Lion's drawer of letters.

Her eyes are dilated. She's high. "I want Him too, Sable. Well, I wanted Garrison but now this is what I want. But you know, Colin wants Meadow more. I bet He does."

I don't have answers for her. I reach my hand out and squeeze one of hers. And she lets me. Maybe Dinah taking drugs is a good thing. The thought brings me a bit of warmth although I don't actually mean it.

"It's not even that good of a letter, Dinah," I say. "The idea that He must think I'm having some kind of stimulating, transformative experience here hurts. It's false."

"You're a brat, Sable. At least you heard from someone." Dinah ties back her hair and climbs up to her bunk.

She's right. I am acting spoiled. I tuck the letter into the atlas under my mattress. I never spend time looking at my atlas unless I am alone, for fear Elspeth will tell and it will be confiscated and I will be punished. One stupid letter is enviable to Dinah. And going home will be no different. It pains me that Kass will go through her Birth Yard, too. But if Kass were to miscarry, I'd come for her. I'd never let her be away forever, taken away, exiled to be a midwife.

I wish I had heard from Kass and my mother by now. I wonder if Dinah's mother has written and if the letters are being withheld. I go comfort Dinah, tell her over and over that her mother loves her, is thinking of her. I realize after a while rubbing her back, squeezing her hands, that I am mostly telling myself.

I HAVEN'T SEEN LION ANYWHERE SINCE OUR MEETING. I have barely seen anyone. I wake, go to the tent for my exercises and meditation, then straight to see Mamie. Sometimes I go to the Ablutionary. I work there isolated from everyone and no one bothers me. We're all becoming thicker and more ill-humoured. I only feel good when I am with Grey doing exercises in the tent and talking to her about my daughter.

Mamie has received countless letters from Isaac, has been permitted to read them, and I am hurt I haven't gotten more. I still haven't asked Mamie what she was discussing with Lion in the Domicile. I am scared to ask her because I don't want her to be punished for gossiping.

It's the weekly cleaning of our cottage. Elspeth is kneeling on the floor scouring a soup stain. I am on my bed, finished with my tasks. "Lazy bitch," she says to me. I give her a look and turn away. She drops her rag and stomps over, lunging to grab my throat.

"Look at me, Sable!" she screams. She squeezes tightly and forces me to look at her.

She's on top of me on my mattress, her knees trapping my thighs, her hair dangling down on my shoulders and her hand gripping angrily. She has noticed my eyes. I claw at her hand to make it let go.

"Elspeth," Dinah yells, tossing her broom to the ground. "Are you fucking crazy? Don't touch her. Stop touching her." Dinah runs to help me. She grabs Elspeth by her apron and yanks her back. "It's the drugs. You're fine. Leave Sable alone."

Elspeth does what she says, lets me go. Then they both continue on with their work. Elspeth speaks after a few minutes of quiet. "I just don't know why you aren't taking your medicine. It isn't fair. You think you're better than us."

"I am, though. I am taking it," I say, holding back tears. I miss Harrio. I wish she were here to stick up for me. She hated

Elspeth. She would protect me. I go to the water closet. There are red finger marks on my neck. I splash cold water on my face. The coolness calms me. I feel no pain. I am sober and strong. I serve only myself. I lock the water-closet door and fall asleep on the floor using spare towels to keep me warm. Once Elspeth and Dinah are sleeping off their DociGens, I will return to my bed, return to the normalcy I'm supposed to accept.

I think of Elspeth, so capable of violence, and how this is punished in women. She hasn't set foot on our Trail. She hasn't even seen The Den. I don't think she knows how much of herself she's about to continue to lose. I may hate her but I also pity her.

Lion has us assemble on the field outside the Domicile. There is still washing to be done and dinner to be eaten, but He insists we gather. My shirt is damp with sweat because the Ablutionary is so hot. I am not alone. The other laundresses have sweat shining on their necks and cheeks, dark marks under their armpits. The seamstresses gather, the planters, the water girls, the Domicile workers, the animal feeders, the seeders, the midwives, everyone.

"This morning," Lion says, then clears His throat, "I sent some of the seeders to weed between the cottages, tidy the grounds, plant some grass seed where needed."

"Where is He going with this?" Dinah whispers. My baby kicks. I rub my stomach and comfort her. I place Dinah's hand on my belly so she can feel, too.

"Sable," Grey hisses. "What did Lion say about friendship? Touching each other?"

Dinah pulls her hand away.

"The girls found these." Lion holds out His palm and drops handfuls of dirt-covered DociGens from the balcony onto the grass. They rain down and I feel another movement in my stomach, but it isn't my baby. It's fear.

"Whoever isn't taking her medicine, whoever it is, I am watching. You are betraying Feles and The Den. I will find you and you will be punished."

We all bow our heads as He says, "Praise Feles. Praise Him and The Den."

I feel the need to vomit but I hold it back. He has no way to know it was me unless He wants to check everyone's pupils and work ethic day in and day out. I want to call His bluff. He isn't really watching. I feel the pills rattling in the hem of my apron.

Elspeth glares at me as I pass her on my way back to the Ablutionary. I wonder if she tipped Lion off. I don't know whom to trust. What she doesn't know is that the only thing on my mind isn't loyalty and compliance—it's where to hide my DociGens now. I need somewhere new.

MAMIE BANGS ON OUR DOOR ONE AFTERNOON. I TELL her to come in. My feet are swollen and I don't feel like moving. My veins are puffy blue bodies of water lacing in and out of each other. My ankles, expanded and thick. I'm elevating them on a kitchen chair.

"Sable," Mamie says, rushing to my side. "You won't believe what they made me do." My friend looks distraught, her breathing shallow. There is blood on her apron.

"What happened?" I lower my feet and face her. I place my hand on her protruded stomach to help guide her breathing down, reminding her to be calm.

"Lion made me kill a chicken. It was a hen that no longer laid eggs, and some of the favoured midwives requested it for their dinner. Lion agreed to it only if I did it. We've never killed them. Only collected eggs, befriended them in some strange way. And the thing screamed so loud. It was scary, Sable."

Mamie shudders at the memory. I hate how Lion is intimidating us, likes to make us feel small when, physically, we are the fullest and biggest we've ever been.

Mamie asks me to walk with her to the lake. I agree because she is so upset, but we take a while to get there because of my swollen ankles. We sit by the shoreline and I stretch out my legs. Mamie dips her soiled apron into the water. She says Lion watched her and laughed, watched the corpse run wild, make tracks in the mud like a ghost.

"How did you kill it?" I ask.

Mamie kneels in the lake. She rests her elbows on the bulging curve of her stomach, dips her face down into the surface of the water. "Sable, this is so nice. You need to try this."

I follow suit. We dip our faces in. I watch lake weed and minnows in their little worlds, their infinite, endless Yard. I surface and feel the sun beat against my scalp.

"How did you kill it, Mamie?"

"My middy, Ollie, told me what to do. The broomstick method, it's called. She brought a broom from her lodge. It had hair and dirt clinging to the bottom. She laughed at me for rinsing it in a puddle. I thought even a chicken doesn't deserve to be soiled before dying. I put the chicken in an empty trough. It was hard to keep it pinned down. Feathers flying everywhere."

She splashes water on her face and at me. The soft lake floor feels so good on my tired legs. The lake weeds tickle, like soft, pleasant fingers.

"I put the broomstick behind the chicken's head and stepped down. I held the legs. Nothing happened except it screamed and screamed, and Ollie was yelling at me to press harder. So I stomped on the handle. Its neck snapped." Mamie snaps her fingers and a squirt of water hits my face. I cringe. "The sound was so meaty and thick. Then it leapt out of the trough. It was dead but it ran all over the yard, with its head flopping. The other chickens screamed alongside the one I killed, too, like they knew what I did."

"That must have been awful, to kill something."

"It was barren. It didn't matter," Mamie says, and she stands and flaps her arms toward the sun. "Sable, did you mention me? To Lion? It's just . . . He asked me about you, at the Domicile one night. And now this. What does He want from me?"

"I have no idea," I say, "and no, I didn't mention your name. But He knows a lot about me. He thinks I shouldn't have friendships. He thinks I am unbridled. He probably thinks we're too good of friends and that girl friendships are threatening."

Mamie says Lion asked her many questions that night. He did not touch her, but she was there a long while. She says the DociGens have fogged her world; it isn't clear what was discussed and what wasn't. I do not press further.

GREY PUSHES BLUE GEL AROUND ON MY STOMACH IN THE medic tent. It's six in the morning, still fresh and dark outside. I face a screen—the little television plugged in only when it's time for ultrasounds. I can see my girl's fingers today. On her left hand. They're spread out into little sticks. They curl and move slowly.

"Grey."

Grey lifts her probe for a moment from my stomach. "Sorry, I know the gel is quite cold."

"It's not that. Does Lion hate me?"

Grey shrugs. She lifts the probe again and wipes it with a cloth. She then wipes my stomach. "He was warned to be wary of you, Sable. You hurt His Son. That's no easy thing to forgive."

"You mean I defended a young girl about to be hurt."

Grey ignores me. "I also think Lion has seen a lot of sorrow. He's not the favoured Son. That would harden anyone."

"How many Matches has He had? Does He have more than one?"

Grey's cheeks flame red and she tells me something Fern told her. Lion once got a midwife pregnant. One who had been declared barren but was able to conceive. He had to abort the baby Himself in the Domicile because Feles deemed the child illegitimate to The Den. Fern said she heard the screams. Fern didn't see the midwife again after that.

"Yes," I say, disturbed and enraged by her story. "I suppose that would very much harden someone."

I DREAM THE PREGNANT MIDWIFE IS GREY. I DREAM that Grey's baby is being aborted in Lion's room. She is splayed on His tea table. He holds a long skewer, a rusted fireplace poker of some kind. She's unable to scream. Her lips are twitching. She's afraid. She's clutching her belly. Lion says nothing.

I wake, sweating profusely. I tap on our window, hoping Grey is nearby and not in the midwifery quarters. Sometimes she sleeps outside our cottage. I think she likes to be separate from the other midwives, but she tells me it's in case I ever need her. She only started doing this after Harrio's miscarriage. She sees me through the dirty glass and comes inside. "Sable, are you all right?"

I beg Grey to let me wade in the water, let me leap off the dock and feel the calmness of water. She does not permit it, but says I can watch the lake and I can sit with her until morning. The lake is so still. The moon gives no light to the water tonight. I can't see across to other land, the lush forests. For now, I can't drift off and imagine elsewhere. I'm stuck with myself. I'm stuck here.

CHAPTER 14

THE HEAT HAS AFFECTED THE FOOD IN THE fields. Everything is scorched dry—corn, fruit, herbs. We are eating potatoes from the Domicile cellar until a truck can come deliver extra provisions from Feles's Main Stream connections, most likely a willing nearby farm. It's blistering hot. In May, we could walk barefoot on the grass, and now it burns and the blades are yellow and poke into our heels, leaving small razor cuts.

I am lucky to be a laundress. We have all agreed to wash everything with cold water, even to speak quietly to conserve energy. The relief is gorgeous. Dinah almost fainted in the seamstress shed from the heat off the sewing machines, the steam off the ironing boards.

Now Mamie comes to me outside the Ablutionary instead of me going to the coop, so I can give her cool cloths for her to moisten her stomach and face after her work. The heat has made me love the Ablutionary, forget how much I feel like an alien there, forget how much the other girls enjoy avoiding me. Mamie says one night she grew so hungry, she put a scoop of chicken feed into her mouth. The crunch of the seeds was satisfying but the thought of swallowing them bruised her pride. She spat them on the ground and did not explain herself as Flora watched.

Grey allows us to sleep with our cottage door open for better air circulation, though I doubt this is helping. The heat of the land and lack of good food infuse the way I think, muddle my sense of clarity. I keep burying my pills. I've chosen a new spot near the lake under a firm rock by the shore. DociGens cause great thirst and I know this way I am more comfortable, less manic.

Some of the girls scream and fight in their cottages over water. They are rationing our water because of the drought. Lion must be stressed. I wonder if He'll sleep and ignore us until the emergency food supply arrives. Maybe it will be my Father to deliver us provisions. Maybe I will see Him again. Maybe He will save us.

Elspeth and Dinah and I all stink. We haven't bathed and I wish so badly we were allowed to swim in the lake. They still won't let us even with these circumstances. Our feet are raw and gross so we wade all the dirt away. But I wish I could wash my entire body in the lake. We rub dry soap under our arms before sleep but it doesn't rinse away the odour fully. But we find time to laugh about the stink because that's easier than losing a sense of pride.

Elspeth thinks Lion doesn't find her attractive and that's why He shows no interest in her, why they've barely spoken. She says He hasn't been leaving His room in the heat, that the Domicile is unbearably hot and the walls are dripping with condensation.

One evening, Elspeth brings paper napkins home to share. We fold the paper into fans. We wave hot air at ourselves and it slowly cools our bodies down. This is the nicest thing Elspeth has ever done for Dinah and me. Of course, her fan is the largest.

She's lying in Harrio's bed with just a T-shirt on, her large belly moist, her arms plump and luminous with sweat. She fans her sex and erupts with laughter.

"Erotic," Dinah jokes. She's splayed out on the floor on her side. She's moved all the furniture against the stove. "Maybe we'll lose some weight." She rubs her fat stomach.

I worry about my girl shrivelling up inside me from lack of water. I know it's impossible but I can't get the gruesome thought out of my head. "Thank you, Elspeth, for the fan," I say. "I'm surprised. I thought you hated me."

"Really? I thought she was just scared of you," Dinah says. She's good at getting a rise out of Elspeth.

Elspeth crosses her arms. "I'm not scared of you, Sable." She sucks the corner of her fan. The paper turns wet and wilts. "You're not as special as people say. You're ordinary."

"Thank you, Elspeth." I truly enjoy that she thinks I am bland, normal. I flap my fan faster to dry the sticky curls against my forehead and neck.

"Sable is free-minded. Definitely not ordinary around here," Dinah says. Our pendant light flickers out and we know it's time to sleep, or attempt sleep.

"Remember Mildred, from the shuttle bus?" Elspeth asks.

"Your friend, yes?"

"Well, we aren't friends exactly," Elspeth says with a slight laugh in her voice. Dinah is still on the floor. I am resting on top of my mattress, coverless.

"Her Father knows Lion very well, that's all. He runs the pharmaceutical company in Main Stream that makes most of your drugs. He's mad rich. He's pumping The Den with money apparently. So, when we were conceiving our offspring with new Den members, I got to know her."

"What's her work position here, you snake?" Dinah squeaks her heel across the floor.

"She's in the Domicile with me. Upstairs."

"Does she tend to Lion?" I ask. I feel my breath grow short. I give up on my fan. It's too hot. I drop it on the floor.

"Most definitely. Almost every night."

"Does she seem all right?" I feel dumb to even ask this.

"I don't know, Sable. All I know is she steals letters when He's sleeping. That's how I have so many now. She passes them out for favours. That's how I've gotten so much information from my Match. My Father too. I can help you. I can ask Mildred. I'll call in my favour later on, though. You will have to pay me back. You'll owe me."

I click my tongue in the dark. "Two good deeds in one hour. Thank you, Elspeth."

"Sable, just because I don't want to be friends doesn't make me a total prick."

Grey comes to the door, asks why we are still talking and if we'd like the door closed. Dinah sits up. I see her shadow in the dark. "Open is fine, Grey. Please keep it open."

ELSPETH BRINGS BACK TWO LETTERS FOR ME THE NEXT afternoon. One is from Ambrose. I am so happy He's thinking of me. The other is a green envelope from Gram's Elder home. I wish my Father would write.

"Mildred says this is the last time she's helping me. Good thing I got a whole heap of letters. I'm even reading some of the other girls'. Mushy hogwash from some of these Matches. The Men on your Trail would get beat up in Main Stream."

"I doubt that," I say. "They're all raised to be tough."

"I think that it's sweet they're showing care," Dinah says, wiping her face with a slightly dampened towel in the water closet. She has gotten very greasy skin and spends more time than ever fussing over it, patting it, wiping it. "And you shouldn't read other people's letters, Elspeth. If you're caught—"

"I won't be. And I'll just burn them after. Or bury them with that crazy DociGen girl's pills." Elspeth tears open a pink envelope and raises her eyebrows at me. I feel my face redden. She's forgotten that she attacked me, accused me. Or she refuses to acknowledge it. I won't acknowledge it. "And besides, no one sends any money. You Den pioneers don't believe in it. So then, it's not theft."

"You're one of us now. You're a pioneer too." There is humour in my voice so she doesn't get angry, but I wish I could sting her with my words. She can be so arrogant.

I open the first letter.

Sable, I haven't heard from you or your letters haven't reached me. I hope you are okay. The land's scorched here. I am dying to see our girl soon, and you, her mother, come home. Be safe. We've heard some girls have lost. Do not lose, for Feles. Do not lose, for me. Love, Ambrose

I am not angry at Him, but I am sad He thinks if I lost it would be more about Him than me, than *us*. And I did write Him back. Maybe He never received it, but I did. I wrote Him. He says some girls have lost—not some girls lost and were sent away. Where is Harrio? Where is she?

I leave for my medic tent. It's afternoon so it's not my time slot, but I am hoping there is a lull and I can have privacy. There isn't. Flora is in the tent. She sits up from her stretcher when I enter. Her midwife sticks her hands on her hips and says I am rude for interrupting them.

Flora sighs. "Sable, can you please leave us alone? Why are you always in my space?"

I feel embarrassed. "Right. I'm sorry for interrupting."

I walk toward the Ablutionary. Flora probably thinks I am stalking her, endangering her, and I don't want to scare her like that. She's kind of pathetic, dim. There are dense fir trees behind the Ablutionary. There's never anyone around. They reek of rotten citrus and remind me of the furniture at home. I crouch under their arms into a circle of dead needles and littered cones. I sit and open, soak in the words of my Gram.

> *Sable,*
> *I am sorry for not writing.*
> *My migraines have been terribly burning.*
> *Afterols starting to really dig in.*
> *I'm feeling the pressures of time and grace.*
> *If you are reading, I hope you are safe.*
> *I hope there is fire and lots of life.*
> *I hope you aren't homesick or need us.*
> *I cannot wait to meet your girl.*
> *Mostly, I cannot wait for your life to start.*
> *In Feles's arms,*
> *Gram*

Her letter feels scrawled with worry. Elders aren't permitted to receive letters so I cannot write back. Feles limits what they experience from outside the Trail, Birth Yards included. I wish Gram was permitted to live with us again but it was only agreed upon for the Gathering Season. She's allowed to join us for supper at my parents' invitation, but she isn't free to roam. Her words seem empty and tired. I want to tell her I am not yet empty and tired, that we need to hold on.

Even though Elspeth is terrible, she brought my Gram to me. I roll up the letters into the hem of my apron with my DociGens. I take a moment and spend time with my Gram, my mother, our roots. I sit in the trees for some time. It begins to rain, but the drops cling to the sap and branches that form a roof over my head. Rain. Finally. We will eat. The sky's honouring us, our life.

THE EMERGENCY SUPPLIES ARRIVE WHILE WE'RE WORKing. I don't see if the shipment was brought in from a farm or if it was my Father or if it was someone from Main Stream. It's a mysterious offering to most of us. There are hundreds of crates of fresh food and jugs of water on the porch of the Domicile. On our walk home, we see Lion counting it all in the restorative rain. He hands crates to the Domicile girls to carry into the kitchen. The rain has brought relief. The abundance of food has brought joy.

Lion walks cottage to cottage in the night to deliver pitchers of water and fruit. At first, we all expect Grey or another midwife. The light flickers on as if it knows His presence, His voice. It's strange to see Him in our space. We stand when He enters. He places water and food on the table. Dinah and Elspeth thank Him in unison. I nod and smile. I am still half asleep. I was dreaming again of Harrio and can't erase her face from my mind.

"Elspeth. Sable." Lion nods at us. "And you are?"

"Dinah." Dinah bows to Lion.

"Oh yes, I know your mother." He nods at Dinah. "The rain finally found us. Are you all feeling well?" Lion starts taking apples out of His basket.

"Yes," Elspeth snorts. "Just sick of potatoes."

Lion smirks. "Elspeth, isn't your Father from the east, where they grow potatoes? Shouldn't you be used to them?"

Elspeth shakes her head. "No, Sir. We came from a town nearer by."

"You're my last stop of the evening. Can I slice you some fruit?" Lion asks.

I look to Elspeth. She's swooning around Him. She thought He didn't know her name and now that she knows He does, we'll never hear the end of it. "Yes, Sir," she gushes. "That's very kind."

Lion places the apples on our wooden cutting board. Dinah reaches into the cutlery drawer to assist Him.

"No, I'm fine. I've brought my own," He says. He pulls out a knife from His coat pocket. It's trimmed with rust. It's caked with dirt. Harrio's knife. Lion is holding Harrio's knife. I feel nauseous but must uphold my innocence. I keep my posture straight and confident.

I speak to Lion directly. "My girl must love apples. I crave them often."

Lion hands me two slices. I take a bite. The skin around the outside is very tough but the inside is fleshy and granular, the way I like it. But it sticks in my throat and I cough until I am red in the face.

Lion hands slices to Dinah and Elspeth. We eat and thank Him. He rinses the knife, sticks it back in His pocket. "You haven't seen this knife before, have you?"

We all shake our heads. I am the only one lying.

"The handle has a mark I've never seen. So I guess it's from Main Stream, not forged in The Den."

Elspeth nods dumbly. "Looks expensive."

"I doubt that it is. I found it." Lion looks at me, then around the kitchen. My heart is pounding like a hammer on steel. I keep telling myself I've done nothing wrong. I feel the weight of the DociGens in my apron hanging on the back of the door. I sit on the bed. Dinah looks at me strangely. She can tell I'm not okay.

Lions smiles widely. "This rain will be good. We can all be clean again."

We say good night and He leaves. Elspeth locks the door to the water closet. I hear her inside retching, vomiting. She wasn't the only one nervous. I turn toward her bed. The stolen letters lie there, obvious and exposed.

I bang on the door. "I don't think He noticed."

"Shut up, Sable," Elspeth growls at me. "Go to sleep."

Dinah wipes her arms and face with a cloth at the kitchen sink. "You two haven't been around Men for too long. You're all bloody loopy."

I shoot her a look of judgment, of knowing, that always pierces her and helps her remember her own secret, her own problems. "Sable," she says, "I don't know what's eating you up inside, but you're fine. We're all fine. I promise."

◇◇◇

I'VE MADE IT WEEKS WITHOUT TELLING GREY OR ANY-one about the knife. I feel heartburn and spasms in my belly often, and I hope that has more to do with being with child than being plagued with fear and anxiety. I write my mother telling her I am fine. I write Kass telling her I am fine. I look in the mirror and tell myself I am fine. One day, I'll tell Grey I am not.

We've had luscious meals, shiny, meaty fruits and vegetables. Rich, sweet milk. Grey tells me the dairy farmer who supplies us told her good rain brings out the cream and joy in His cows. I cannot take my mind from the knife. I picture Lion killing me with it, stabbing my gut, prying out my girl, ending us. These dreams ruin me some nights.

Dinah says you can't get nightmares on DociGens. "You're just haunting your own mind, Sable. You can control your thoughts, you know. You could afford to learn how."

So I pretend I am lying about my dreams, tell her I am home-sick and just need attention. She is satisfied with this answer.

Dinah lets me walk with her to her seamstress shed in the evening, introduces me to some of her sewing section. They make lots of jokes about being stitched together—tight as anything!—and I like their pleasantry. All of the sergers and machines are on small Lesson desks. The girls sit in chairs and work. It reminds me of Lessons so much, it aches. They even face a board with dates and lists scrawled down in chalk by their lead midwife.

Dinah says I can sit with her for a while before I go to the Ablutionary. I sit by her feet on the floor and watch her work the pedal, sew together a new dress, impressive and quick as any-thing. She turns the brown fabric inside out, grabs an iron to flatten everything smooth and precise. She makes a zigzag stitch to sew the front and back together, and a topstitch to attach her newly formed skirt to the body of the dress. "This can be for you if you like, Sable. It's your size."

"Thanks. But it looks small. Nothing is fitting right any-more." I bulge out my ever-growing belly, pinch the fleshy arm fat squishing out of my cap sleeves.

"We'll give you more breathing room, then." Dinah removes the stitches and starts over.

One of the girls is knitting a blue neck-scarf. She says it's for her midwife because she has bad circulation and is chilled even in summer. She says she chose blue because she's having a Boy and her midwife feels pregnant with happiness for her.

"That's so thoughtful," I say.

"Well, I get no letters from home. She's all I have now. I owe her."

Dinah shushes her. "You're too depressing, Melanie."

Melanie glares at Dinah. "Yeah, I tend to be. And no letters for me. Not one."

I wonder if Melanie did receive letters and they're just being held in the Domicile. Or I wonder if they're the ones Elspeth rifles through. "I'm sorry to hear it."

"It's all right. Have you gotten any? Bet you have. She's the strange girl, right, Dinah? The one who watched Harrio lose?"

"Right," Dinah says. Melanie smirks at me and my feelings aren't even hurt. I can tell Dinah thinks this girl is a complete doxy, a gossip with no brains.

"No. No letters for me," I say, only to avoid conflict with her.

Dinah doesn't correct me. She knows I got some from Lion, from Elspeth. "Well, I haven't either. My Match barely likes me," she says.

She means it as a joke, but I don't know if Colin really does like her and what He would do to her if He knew her child belonged to Garrison, not Him.

"They're not supposed to *like* you," Melanie says. She puts her needles down and stares long and deep at Dinah. "They *need* us. That's way more valuable, no?"

Dinah holds up the dress for me. "What do you think?"

"It's perfect. Thank you."

"I'd make one for Mamie, but I never see her. She only comes to talk to you, it seems."

"I think she's just tired. She works outdoors all day. And I think the chicken thing embarrassed her. She hates attention like that."

"It was good to treat the midwives," Melanie says. "They deserved that chicken. Someone had to kill it."

I leave Dinah with my new dress tucked under my arm, head to the Ablutionary. It's late and most of the girls have gone to bed. There are dresses and sweaters and underwear clipped to the clothesline around the perimeter of the room. In the almost dark, they look like people. A few girls sip from teacups in the loft. There's a clatter of cups and saucers when they hear me enter. I begin to take the dry clothes off the lines, fold them and place them in baskets. Not even five minutes pass before the girls descend the stairs and leave me completely alone.

CHAPTER 15

WHEN LION PRESENTS GREY WITH A LIVE PIG in the barnyard, none of us know what to do.

Mamie rushes into our cottage to tell us. Dinah is rinsing our dishes. I am scrubbing my teeth in the water closet. Elspeth has been ignoring me ever since Lion's visit. I think she scared herself with her own indiscretions. I could wring her like a sponge only to drip out a stiff *good morning*. Mamie's face is sallow; she looks as if she could faint. "Lion is making Grey do it. Everyone's going to watch."

I spit in the sink and rush to Mamie's side. Elspeth blushes and won't meet our eyes. "Elspeth? What do you know about this?"

"I didn't think they'd actually make her do it. I overheard Lion telling the other midwives after supper one night. I thought it was a joke." Elspeth looks perplexed. "What's the big deal with a pig anyway?"

"Slaughtering a pig is a punishment Lynx once used to give the women," Dinah says. "Pigs are a symbol of fertility. To force a woman to kill one is a great shame. I've never seen a pig slaughtering but my mother told me it's a horror show and makes the woman an outcast."

I feel a rising panic for Grey. "Why? Why her?"

"He suspects you of neglecting your DociGens, Sable. Enough girls have told Him. Flora told Him. You know she suspected it. He tried to get me to tell Him. He's punishing her for you." Mamie looks shamefaced as she realizes she's shared something she never wanted to.

Dinah grabs her by the shoulders. Their bellies touch. "Mamie, look at me. Did you rat out Sable? That time you were alone with Lion?"

"I don't know."

My heart is pounding. I don't want them to shame Grey like this. I think of Mamie and the chicken. He's punishing those around me, manipulating me, shaming those I love. Violent, malicious Sable—who doesn't want to be here, who doesn't believe in this anymore.

"When the pig arrived this afternoon, I knew something was wrong," says Dinah. "Lion saw me today in the sewing shed. He said He would have extra work for me tonight. You don't think . . ."

"You? Dinah, what would He have you do? We're all too pregnant to do that kind of labour." I feel my palms break out with sweat.

Dinah scrunches her hands into fists. "What if He wants me to help her?"

"You witches. You stupid witches. Lion hates you all," says Elspeth.

I lift my hand to get Elspeth to stop talking. "No, He hates me."

I need Grey. I need healthy-minded, busy, normal, dumb-smiling Grey to help me figure this out.

Dinah sinks against the doorway and leans on the wooden frame, damp from all the heat in the cottage. "I feel faint."

Mamie pours her a glass of water, hands her a peach from a basket on the table. "Do what you're told and you'll be safe," she says.

"I've barely spoken to Lion. I heard from my midwife that He wanted me moved into Domicile service, but I am too good a seamstress. Why is He asking this? What do they want?"

"They want a show. Pretend you're on the Trail. Like you just flirted with a Boy. Like you just got earrings. Act your way through. Be confident. Just do it quickly," Mamie says encouragingly.

I know it's because of me. The knife. The hidden pills. This is His way. He withholds letters to make us feel alone. I worry what Mamie might have told Him that evening in His office.

"Dinah," I whisper and touch her shoulder. "You know, you of all people, you can't say no. You can't afford to say no. If I angered Lion—if this is my fault you're being challenged, I'm sorry. I'm fiercely sorry."

"I'll do it," she says, looking at me with hollow eyes. "I'll help Grey. I know I have to do it."

Every muscle inside me aches with sorrow. It feels like the ceiling is sinking and I am suffocating. "I'll come with you," I say.

"I'll come, too," says Mamie. "The midwives better not eat it after."

"Oh, I bet they will. I hope they choke on it." Dinah squishes her peach and bright orange guts splay onto the floor.

I wipe up her mess with a cloth. "Dinah, this isn't about them. Target your anger at Lion, at Feles."

"Fern would smack you if she were here," Elspeth says, "for saying that." She pinches my arm. "You can't be angry with Feles. Even I know that."

Dinah skims her fingers along the hem of her dress. "Pig's blood will never come out."

"Sable, you're good with bloodstains, right?" Elspeth says, snorting.

"Says the real pig." Mamie sticks her tongue out at Elspeth.

Elspeth raises a fist toward her. I grip her fist and force it down by her side. "Everyone, just breathe. Forgive. And then shut up, please. We need to fix this. We need to be aligned together. To support Grey."

I hug Dinah. She feels foreign to me. She's such an angry version of herself. I feel a quick kick from her stomach. I smile at her. "Look," I say. "He's here for you. Your baby Boy. Nothing is ever so dark."

"He does that a lot," she says. She can't help but smile too. "He senses when I scream or cry."

"We're never really alone."

Mamie refills Dinah's water and she drinks two more glasses. I've never caused so many people at once such pain. Lion will get what He wants. The midwives will enjoy their fresh kill.

IT'S STILL QUITE LIGHT OUTSIDE, JUST BEFORE DINNER-time. Mamie and I go to the fence that surrounds the barn to be there for Grey and Dinah. The mud is thick and deep from the rain. A large bonfire casts some smoky warmth into the air.

The pig is in a wooden crate only a little larger than its own body. Lion watches from His balcony. I turn so He can see me. I cross my arms.

Other girls watch with their midwives by the large bonfire. Dinah's midwife, Fern, is there, too, seemingly unconcerned that

Dinah has been given such a dishonourable task. Grey walks across the field toward us. She looks ill already. I reach for her hand. I whisper, "You should knock the pig out. Knife it when it's unconscious. That's what I would do, I think."

Grey and Dinah pick up axes. Dinah is shaking nervously, her stomach round and cumbersome. She looks so tired. I know she is strong but she needs that strength for her Boy. Not for this. The midwives hoot and holler, excited to watch Grey dishonour herself.

Lion speaks to us all. "The Den is a place for lionesses, not pigs. Act selfish and rogue and there are consequences. For every girl. For her midwife."

The wind picks up and the folds of Grey's and Dinah's dresses flap, making bird's wings. Dinah's face is pale. She looks so tired and weighed down with stress. They shouldn't have to do this.

"Grey and Dinah will kill this pig because Sable has shown defiance. Grey, as her guardian, has failed to supervise her properly. Dinah, as her confidante, should have abandoned her. Sable has shown defiance to her body, to Harrio's body, to her Family Body. The best way to punish Sable is to shame her allies for what she has done."

I can't believe He's speaking of me this way to everyone. Mamie reaches for my hand. *Don't think of the blood*, I want to say aloud, but I am merely telling myself.

I want to enter the fenced grounds and help them. Mamie holds the strings at the back of my apron, as if she thinks I will leap out to help Dinah and Grey.

The pig is brown and large, a gash on its snout. Its eyes look like the eyes of a child, unstill and wandering. It squeals when Grey approaches it. She bashes it with the heel of her axe, unflinchingly, bravely. But this doesn't do much. The axe is too heavy for Grey's frail wrists. She catches the belly only. Dinah looks as if she is about to cry. The axe looks so heavy in her arms, with her pregnant belly and long dress. I can tell the extra weight is causing her back to wilt and ache. She has a firm stance, feet brave and wide apart.

"It's okay, Dinah. Just stand back. Be calm. I can do this," Grey says.

The girls around the fire and the midwives roar with laughter. They chant that Grey is unfruitful, barren. "Desert daughter! Desert daughter!"

I am afraid of them. How can they turn on their own?

Grey again tries to hit the pig's head with the blunt end of her axe. She cuts an ear and the pig cries out. The most horrible afterlife of cries. The animal thrashes in its crate.

Grey goes for another swing. The blade of her axe slits the throat, only a small portion. The blood fireworks. The pig reels and twitches at the wound. Grey puts her axe down, drawing in gulps of air.

"Stop. Please, Grey, we just need to give in. Tell Him we can't," Dinah says, lowering her hand toward the dirt, encouraging their surrender.

Grey swings again, plunges the axe deeper, this time right into its back. This isn't how it's supposed to be.

I turn to Mamie, who still holds the back of my apron. She's weeping. "This is disgusting," she says. "No one's shown them how. No one knows how to do this right."

I shush her and take her trembling hands off the back of my apron. "It'll be fine."

I feel an anger more potent than I ever knew possible, and a love for the two women who do this on my behalf. It comes to me that whatever I felt for Ambrose was based on convenience and permission, never this force of emotion.

I enter the pen. I ask Dinah for her axe and she, eyes wide, gives it over. She stands unmoving, watching me. The mud is thicker inside the fence. It smells like excrement but also of life. I face Grey. She wipes her hands on her dress. Her eyes are fierce and feral. I feel the same inside. I walk around the back of the crate, stare at the bleeding, twitching pig. It's bucking and shrieking but Grey is fast.

Grey raises her arms to the sky. She smiles at me both deliriously and with pride. We can defy Lion by succeeding in the killing. She raises and plunges the axe again. Grey does this over and over until it appears as if she can't feel her own arms, can't hear the shrieking of the animal or anyone else.

I take my axe and press firmly into the pig's neck, feel life and flesh tear, the muscles separate. My stomach aches, my back feeling warped and panging with tightness. I feel the skin and back of a creature split open. I watch it die.

There is blood all over us as we crouch down toward the pig. I feel horrible for this poor creature. I wish it could have lived. That we didn't have to kill it. Were we brave or were we cowards for doing this? I feel the stickiness of blood on the warm dirt. My world is blood and mud and Men. Blood soaks the wood of the crate, leaks in a pool out the gate where Mamie stands. She won't meet my eyes.

I turn up toward Lion. He smokes His cigarette, seemingly miserable at our efficiency, at Grey's strength. It was hardly sport. It was hardly entertainment. The blood on the edge of Grey's axe shines toward the midwives and other girls, whose cackling and jeering have ceased.

I am not just a woman with child. I am a woman. This is my child. These are my friends.

"Dinner," I shout at the midwives, leaving the pen, holding Grey's hand. I spit toward the bonfire. The midwives and girls are silent.

We lead Grey toward the lake. She sobs in my arms. We smell of blood. But we've won. Dinah sinks onto the sand. We all feel filthy and uncomfortable. "I'll dream of that fucking blood forever," Dinah says. "I'm never eating any meat again."

My new dress is soaked and ruined. Elspeth hurries toward us, tosses us each a towel from the Domicile. She looks nervous.

"Lion wants to see you three," she says. "After you bathe. I'm sorry." The empathy in her voice is unexpected and strange. "You were so brave."

I know I should be afraid but I am not. Grey looks scared and uncertain.

"He wants you to go to your quarters, Grey. To pack your things," Elspeth says.

Grey nods. "Where am I to go?"

"The Domicile for a short while, He says. He needs you there."

I am relieved Grey isn't being sent far away, to another Yard or exiled to Main Stream or something worse. She nods toward us and, still bloody, trudges off to her quarters. I want to tell her I love her but I don't.

"We don't have a lot of time. Let's go to the bathing shed," I say.

As the three of us walk, every girl we pass stares. Some smile tentatively at us. Most look disgusted, nauseous at the blood and disorder we caused. We pass the midwives cutting up the carcass on the grass with delight and precision. One thanks us for the protein and the others say nothing.

The bathing shed is near Mamie's medic tent. She wants to go to Ollie, her midwife, to ask for a DociGen.

"All right. Meet us back here," I say.

THERE ARE SOME SPARE BROWN DRESSES AND SHIRTS IN a cubby outside the wooden shower stalls. There is only one sack of water and it's probably very cool at this point.

Dinah and I strip and stand under the shower together. Our bodies are far less bloody than our clothes. We rinse and wash in silence, our teeth chattering as the icy liquid leaks down our backs, ignites our spines with cold and fear. The cloth of the shower curtains ripples in the lake breeze, water droplets weeping off our shoulders.

Dinah admits now that they asked her to mend Harrio's clothes. She didn't want to tell me before because it would upset me. "There were tears and blood smears all over them. I just didn't want to tell you, Sable. Fern delivered them especially to me. Her initials in the stitching of her robe, her brown dress. Her blue scarf had blood on the edges near the ears and neck. Some of the girls say they saw her leave in the morning. In a truck. But someone hurt her."

I hold my hands to my ears. They're ringing, screeching at me. "I can't hear this right now. I'm sorry. I can't think of Harrio right now."

Mamie is waiting for us outside the shed. She's sinking into a calmed drug trance. We hold hands and walk to the Domicile to see Lion. We pass the fence around the barn. The goats and chickens are loose from their pens. Flora is feeding them their supper on the mud where we killed.

Dinah looks back toward the forest at the far end of the Yard. The one that leads out. Her hands are shaking. "What if He knows?" She stops walking, squeezes our hands tight. "He knows about me. Doesn't He? Sable."

"I didn't. I wouldn't. Never."

Mamie drops Dinah's hand and looks at the ground. Her discomfort gives me a sudden chill. "He keeps our letters from us, the ones He wants to. Lion told me that He reads them to make sure they're appropriate for women to read. He had some from Isaac. I so badly wanted something from home. In one of the letters, Isaac asked me. He asked about Garrison and Dinah. Isaac makes me tell things—He terrifies me. You both know this."

Mamie speaks faster. "I just wrote to Him what you said—it's a secret. It was the DociGens. It was the DociGens that made me write it, I swear, Dinah, I swear."

Dinah can't speak. She has her hands on her stomach. She's heaving. "I have never hated anyone as much as I hate you right now. Or you, Sable. I bet you knew too. I bet you did." The thick sting of the word "hate" makes me feel sick.

I can't help but wonder who is guilty here and how Men have spun our worlds around.

"I'm sorry, Dinah," Mamie says. "You had to know. I'm sorry."

Dinah presses her hand to my belly. My girl is unmoving as if she can feel my stress. I picture her beautiful face and eyes and limbs. I need Grey. Dinah needs me. Mamie needs forgiveness.

◇◇◇

A MIDWIFE ANSWERS THE DOOR OF THE DOMICILE. SHE leads us up to Lion's floor. She says nothing. Lion is on His black couch, fireplace blazing. He's eating freshly cooked meat. Mamie gags audibly at the sight. Lion puts His plate down, gestures for us to sit.

"Brave girls, have you taken the lives of animals before? Stoned a robin to death? Lit insects on fire?"

"No," I say.

"Just that chicken," Mamie offers.

"You made it look so easy," He says, raising a glass to us. "Friendship is a weird inclination women have. It's all right. But I warned you before, Sable. Community matters more. Mamie practises this well."

Mamie has her hands in her lap. She is staring at the floor, at royal blue warhorses woven in the rug. Their harnesses, ash black. Their eyes, emerald green.

"I understand the need you have for friends," Lion says, "this push inside you to commiserate, complain, bond. But it creates disorder, hysteria. It isn't productive for The Den."

My throat feels chalky and dry. I think of the DociGens I buried in the mud. The ones that change us to be more like what Men want.

"Garrison," Lion says.

Dinah begins to sob. She can't even pretend. She's so tired of pretending.

"We have reason to believe Garrison is the Father of your child, Dinah. That you bred outside your Match, that somehow you slithered through the cracks unnoticed."

Dinah nods. "I'm so sorry," she whispers. She has her hands on her stomach. "I want my Son. I still want to have Him."

Lion forks an olive on the edge of His plate, sucks it a while before chewing. "But Colin knows. He'll know His whole life. A Man can't love a child that isn't His. And a woman cannot choose to be with someone unassigned to her."

Mamie hasn't spoken. Her face is firm stone.

"Harrio," Lion says, and I hate that He says it, "her mistake was her body's, not her mind's. Dinah, if you did what Mamie and Isaac and you yourself say you did, you will not be leaving this Domicile. You will be moved to the fourth floor here. You are not permitted to leave. There will be testing done in two days once we can get paternal evidence from both Men. To prove it. But by the looks of your guilt, you cannot go home to the Trail. Feles has banned you. You can't seduce what isn't yours, what isn't given to you."

Dinah's cries are intolerable as two midwives lead her down the hall. She doesn't struggle. "I love you, Sable," she calls back at me. "I'm sorry. I love you so much."

I stare down at the warhorses on the rug. They are leaping, their hooves up in the air, feral but trapped by thick, ugly reins. I've bitten my lip so hard that my teeth have sunk into a few layers of skin. Cool blood floods my mouth. I can feel the fire in my eyes and I think of their names, want to yell them out loud at Lion. *Harrio. Harrio. Harrio. Dinah.* My mind burns with their glorious names.

"Please, don't do this," I beg Lion instead. "She's a good woman."

Lion scoffs at this. "Like you? Like a girl who beat a Boy? A feral good *woman*? She's a girl. No women here."

Mamie stays silent.

I stand to face Lion. I tower above where He sits in His chair. He sets His dinner plate aside and sees me, really sees me. He reaches out and touches my belly, my girl, and I try not to flinch.

"Do you respect my Father?"

"I do," Lion says. "Do you respect mine?"

I swallow hard. "More than anyone."

Lion nods.

"But," I say, "can you answer one thing for me? Pretend I am George. My Father. What would you say to Him?" I stand tall and confident, pretend I am my Father. I am not afraid of Lion. "Why do you hide letters from us?"

Lion rises and moves past me, opens His door. "Why do you hide your DociGens?"

I turn and remain brave and sturdy, a Man's stance. "I don't."

"Good night, Sable. Good night, Mamie," Lion says.

MIDWIVES ESCORT MAMIE AND ME BACK TO OUR COT-tages. Grey is waiting for me and she says she's sorry over and over again for what's happened to Dinah.

"You don't even like Dinah," I say because I can't think of anything else. Grey looks hurt and leaves.

Elspeth is working on a quilt. She's lying on Harrio's bed.

"There were rumours for a while," she says. "Dinah told a few of the seamstresses that she had sex before she was supposed to. Also some of the girls on your Trail saw her go off with Garrison at night. Stupid girl."

I sit on the floor and unlace my shoes. It feels so good not to stand right now. My ankles are swollen and the heat has been miserable. I take my socks off. "She is a stupid girl. But she doesn't deserve this," I spit back at Elspeth.

"Doesn't she?" asks Elspeth. "Isn't this what Feles is preaching? Isn't this exactly what she deserves?"

"Why are you like this? Why are you so mean?" I ask, feeling fire grow along my neck and cheeks.

Elspeth sits up and tosses her quilt aside. "Do you know how hard it is, Sable? To suddenly have to be here?"

I nod. "But that doesn't mean you have to be so blunt, so prickly all the time. You're going to get your neck wrung when you get to The Den. You will."

Elspeth laughs. "Do you know how close my real home is? Do you know my mother is still there? Isn't that enough to make anyone bitter? It may as well be in another dimension. I'll never get to see her again."

I feel embarrassed for questioning her. She does have every right to be miserable. I watch the wind blow our curtains slightly. I watch two ants carry crumbs toward the gap under the door.

"What's it called? The place you're from."

"Bow Lake," Elspeth says. "Now leave it." She returns to her quilt, her eyes unmoving from each tight stitch, each ice-blue patch.

I AM TOLD BY ELSPETH THAT LION HAS ASSIGNED GREY to tend to Dinah in the Domicile, to leave me to fend for myself. As punishment for all my defiance. Elspeth says He thinks my behaviour has put everyone on edge. But it's Him who makes everyone on edge. He's diminished me through rumours. He's created fear from nothing.

Grey's final appointment with me in the medic tent is calm. Lion sends Fern to watch us. Midwives are not supposed to be as attached to their patients as Grey is to me. Lion thinks Grey is simple-minded, easily attached. But it's because Grey is kind. Because she's young. Because she cares about me and my girl, not just about her duty, her own safety.

I hate Fern now. She is brainwashed and lets fear guide her. She says good morning to me but she doesn't mean it.

"Good morning," I say back.

"Sable, it's our last appointment." Grey sounds shaky, unsure. "What would you like to learn here? What do you need?"

I can tell something is wrong and we need to speak alone. I can tell she is nervous. "I need to pee, actually," I say.

Fern mutters that I am rude.

"Sorry, but I do."

"Well," Fern says sternly, "you mustn't wake Elspeth while she's sleeping. You've all put her through enough trauma."

"Where am I to go, then? Not outside."

"Certainly not! You may go at the Ablutionary. You're a laundress, yes?"

I nod.

"And you have a key?"

"I do. But it's still dark outside. I'm scared."

"I'll take her," says Grey. "She doesn't need to go alone."

"Hurry back, then," Fern says. She sips her tea. "I have my own girls to tend to in an hour. Grateful, normal girls."

"Yes. Thank you."

We walk in silence along the lake until we're far enough from the other tents and cottages. I squeeze Grey's hand.

"Sable, I must tell you," she says. "Lion has received orders from Feles. If Dinah's baby is not from her Match, Lion is not just to abort the baby, He is to kill Dinah by a lethal injection.

Lion says I must do it to atone for my failure with you. Sable, I can't. I can't do it."

I stagger to a stop. I feel nauseous. Could this be true? Would Feles kill Dinah? Not just take away her baby, but take her life? Forcing Grey to do it is something I cannot bear to imagine. "Have you seen Dinah? Is she okay?"

"I haven't seen her. I heard from the other midwives at supper she's been compliant, quiet. Her room has a bed and a sink. They won't tell her family until after the injection. Lion Himself feels bad, I'm sure."

"That's madness for you to say."

"I know. But He's just a cog in a wheel in a lot of ways. I think He's hoping the baby isn't Garrison's."

"Well, it is."

"You're sure, Sable?"

"Very. I've known since November."

Grey nods. She grabs my hand tight and we make our way to the Ablutionary in the forest. I can't handle the idea of Dinah dying. I can't handle the idea of Grey killing her. I want to die too if this is what will happen.

I unlock the doors. I am thankful no one is here, it's so early. Water has dripped from dresses and coats hanging on their lines.

"Sable, what do we do? I can't kill her. I could never live with myself. How do we get her out? What do we do?"

"We stay quiet as long as we can."

"We stay quiet?" asks Grey.

"Yes," I say. "But first—right now—we must get loud."

Grey agrees to hate me.

◇◇◇

WHEN WE RETURN TO THE TENT, WE CREATE A BIG SCENE, a dramatic hatred, the appearance of a severed relationship, a hateful goodbye. We scream at each other. Even meek Grey is convincing. It's the right hour of the morning: all the girls are headed to their appointments and duties or free time post-breakfast. The field is peopled. It's an excellent time for a show.

Grey calls me selfish, says I've condemned my friend. "Dinah deserves better than you!" She chases me onto the sand near the lake. She slaps me on my face, which doesn't really hurt because I am in the moment and feeling quite proud of her. Maybe part of her means it. Part of her slap is for the way she has been treated since her miscarriage, the way she has been trapped at Ceres.

Fern follows us to the lake. She grabs Grey by the arm. "Grey, you can't touch her like that. Stop."

I spit at both of them, tell them I don't need a midwife, that my girl will be born in the sun and I will pull her out with my own two hands.

A group of laundresses passes. One reaches out her hand, says I will be okay without Grey. The others tell her to leave me. She listens. No one wants to be near me.

Grey stomps through the field and up to the Domicile. We don't finish the appointment.

IT'S JUST ME AND ELSPETH NOW IN THE COTTAGE. IT'S so depressing, I've lost my appetite. But I try to swallow food for my girl. None of this is her fault. I am so worried about Dinah, I feel sick. We need to save her before she is killed, sacrificed for the sake of example.

I have no access to letters anymore. I am not even sure the ones I send will be received. I write them anyway, leave them under the door of the Domicile. If Lion reads them He will see I am fine. They are full of propaganda, bliss. To every member of my family, to Ambrose. I am coping. I do not mention Dinah in them. He'll think I am choosing community, abandoning her, obeying.

On my way to the Ablutionary the next night, I pass the bonfire where Fern sits with other women. Fern, who thinks she saved me from Grey's abuse. She calls me pathetic to the others. I let her. I do not turn around. I pretend I cannot hear her. I pretend their voices are wind.

I miss Grey. She's been at Dinah's side. Elspeth says she sees Grey walking the hallways with trays of food, cups of tea. She says the room where Dinah sleeps is quiet and dark.

Grey will be in charge of administering Dinah's lethal injection when Lion says so. I hope it never gets that far. We hatched a plan in the Ablutionary. We're going to leave the Birth Yard. We're going to run away with Dinah. I am going to save us from the Men. But we're so swollen and so pregnant—I'm scared that it's a foolish idea. But I can't let Dinah die. I won't let her die.

MAMIE AND I SIT BY THE LAKE ONE NIGHT. WE'RE DRINK-ing the tea steeped from Feles's hair. Or rather, we pretend to sip it and spill bits of it onto the sand. She has stopped taking her DociGens, hands them to me to put in the hem of my apron. This has been hard on her. She resents the way they change her, but loves the way they make her feel. Some girls are peeling potatoes nearby. Others are snoozing on each other's laps. Some are singing to themselves, to each other and their stomachs. We have distance—we're on a log just outside their communal circle. We have quiet. I ask Mamie to come with us, to leave Ceres. I ask Mamie to atone for what she's done to Dinah and come, escape.

"She won't come if I'm there. I've betrayed her. You heard her. She hates me, Sable." Mamie takes a real sip of the tea, as if she deserves it.

"It isn't betrayal when you're afraid, Mamie. She would have done the same."

"Sable, I wish no one had ever told me about Dinah and Garrison."

"You needed to know. You're not the only one suffering from these secrets. You needed to know too."

Mamie's lips are chapped and she flakes off the dead skin with her teeth. Her eyes glow blue against the moonlit lake water. "I'm going to apologize to Lion, make things right. Have my baby here. Finish normal. Birth normal. Be normal, Sable."

"What's normal about Dinah dying?"

"Are you sure, Sable? Are you sure that's what they'll do?" Mamie says, chewing her lip.

The girls stop singing so we stop talking. All we hear are flames hissing at the sky, temporary and brilliant.

I DREAM OF IRIS FEEDING BIRDS. SHE'S WEARING A PINK dress, one I've seen in Gram's photographs. She's in Lynx's old backyard in Main Stream, sitting on a bench, breadcrumbs in her lap. She swells with my Gram Evelyn inside her. She isn't cold but there's snow falling to the ground. The birds gather around her and she clicks her mouth at them like Mamie does with the chickens. She tosses the crumbs into the air, lets the wind catch them and bring them to the frosted grass in front of her. There are pigeons that coo in flocks. There are hundreds joining her. She sings to them and eats a piece of bread herself. Then she's gone and I look down at a pink dress and my bulging stomach. The birds still approaching. I have become her. I am Iris but I am not free.

I wait for Fern to leave the cottage so I can sneak out tonight. Elspeth is exhausted. She is carrying a large child and is having circulatory trouble. She hasn't been feeling good. I feel fine, just sometimes cramped and awkward. I now have to lead my own stretches, coach myself for my birthing. Some days I skip my exercises. I take it as time to sleep, rest before we leave Ceres.

Grey is to meet me in the trees behind the Ablutionary. I need to get there without being seen. I count on the lulled sleep of DociGens. I count on the girls in the Domicile keeping Lion company. I think they're forced to lie with Him and please Him and I hate this but I can't fix it, can't save them, too. I count on midwives freed for the night and too tired to wait and watch. I count on Grey to make it out of the Domicile, quiet and unseen.

I don't wear my apron. I wear black pants from Dinah's drawer and a brown cotton shirt to better blend with the night. The grass is damp and muddy. My shoes make squelching sounds. I don't know if I should slow down to mute my feet or speed up to be unseen. I choose slow. The lights of all the cottages are off. The lights of the Domicile are off, even the lights from Lion's room on the fourth floor. It's dead with dark. I can barely see where I am going. The moonlight guides me, but barely.

I pass the dock where I buried Harrio's knife. I pass the bathing shed where I have not been since the pig slaughtering. Soapy water trickling from the cement floor onto the grass soaks my feet. I continue on toward the forest cottages, let my body be swallowed by the dense and unforgiving treeline. I have Ambrose's atlas under my arm.

I am more afraid of what could happen here than on my Trail. I am more afraid of Lion now than I am of my family's shame. I am more worried about my girl, forced to break the rules with me. She has no idea of the capabilities of The Den yet. She has no idea how frightened I am.

The forest is so blind to what happens within it, around it. It's so clean and fresh and powerful, innocent. I can never be as stable a home as the trees are to insects and birds, to their own budding arms. I pass Mamie's forest cottage and a communal dining tent. I wish Mamie could see me. I wish she were awake. I need to change her mind. There are dirty dishes in a basin outside the mouth of the tent. Flies buzz and land on pieces of unconsumed food. Someone has not performed their evening duty to rinse the plates and run them back to the Domicile. I am glad I am not the only woman overwhelmed by my daily work.

I make it to the Ablutionary, walk to the left of the building, behind to the circle of pine trees. I crouch under the shelter of the branches, in a quiet, better world. Grey is not here yet. I am tired from the walk, my ankles wet and puffy, my lower abdomen aching with the pressure of my girl inside me. I lean against a tree trunk. I watch ants collect dead nettles and bits of dirt, walk in a line back to wherever their home is. I open my atlas on the ground.

In time, a few red fire ants crawl across the pages, exploring. They walk over a page of mountains. Next, they walk on water. I hold out my finger to their small bodies. I know they bite but tonight they don't bite me. "Not even you want me," I say. I squish one with my finger. The others don't flinch. "Not any of you." Nothing on earth wants anything to do with me. Even my girl has been kicking less, making her presence quieter.

The pines rustle. "Grey?"

"Sable," she says. Grey's clothes are very dirty. She looks tired. She has a bruise on her cheek.

"What happened to your face?"

"Dinah," she says. "It wasn't her fault. I was trying to talk to her. I got too close. Her arms are tied to her cot but she was still able to kick me. She was asking me to save her and I didn't say anything."

"Is she all right?"

"Physically, yes. She's eating."

"Has Lion spoken to you?"

Grey drops her open hands as a way to tell me to speak more quietly. "He has," she whispers, lower now. "He's heard of our falling out. He heard of me hurting you."

"Good. Does He believe it?"

"Yes."

"Good."

Grey sits against the other side of the trunk. I reach for her hand. We face the world curtained by trees. I could live like this.

"How much time do you think we have?"

"Until the end of this month if I'm honest, Sable. Garrison and Colin have both received their paternity tests. They are under oath to be truthful and transparent."

"So if you inject, you kill both of them? Dinah and her Son?"

Grey starts to cry. Her hand tightens on mine until my knuckles feel sore.

With my free hand, I slide my atlas toward Grey. "Where can we go?"

"I don't know. I've never left The Den or the Yard." She flips through pages of the north. She points at lakes and wide swaths of land and pinpricks of cities and towns. "We can't go along the roads, first of all. Wherever we go, we'll have to take the woods."

"What if Lion or Feles sends Men to find us?"

"We try anyway. We're women. Aren't we good at staying hidden?"

She's right. I wonder if the Match whose child Grey miscarried still lives on our Trail. I wonder if He's had children since. The atlas has no real answers, no directions, just pinpoints of towns and cities we don't know. We rest and speak until early morning of how we can't wait to leave but how terrifying it will be. But more terrifying is Dinah dying under the laws of Feles. The sun begins to split through the clouds.

"I should go. I'll start the wash at the Ablutionary. I have no medic appointments anymore."

Grey hands me back the atlas. "I hope we can find a safe place."

"I'll take care of it," I say, though I feel hopeless. I thought my atlas would have an answer for me, that maybe Ambrose had known I would need it. Grey waits under the trees awhile for me to leave and unlock the Ablutionary. I picture her plucking apples or weeds off the ground, presenting them at the Domicile as an alibi. And it will be seen as gracious, a gift to the other midwives starting breakfast over the Domicile stoves. We're two people who haven't finished Lessons, who won't get to learn anything higher or deeper, going against what we've been brought up to believe is right and just. Then why do I feel so brave? Why do I feel so strong?

All the laundresses think Dinah is a whore, and I play along to keep from bursting with rage. I have to lie; it's easier and keeps me safe and quiet. When asked if I am ashamed of her, I scrub deeper into the coat or shirt I am washing, say yes, utterly, irredeemably, profoundly ashamed.

CHAPTER 16

ELSPETH TOSSES AND TURNS SO HECTICALLY tonight that I begin to feel sorry for her. I can hear her weeping, and I imagine she's frustrated and overtired. I've been avoiding her as much as possible, piling rations of food under my bed, stocking up on extra clothes from the Ablutionary. But her crying sounds so pathetic, so broken. It softens me.

"Can I get you anything, Elspeth? Tea maybe? Or milk?"

"I'm fine. I hate milk," she says. "I just can't fucking rest."

"Can I come up?" I ask. "To your bed?"

"Fine. But don't get queer on me."

"You're a shit person sometimes, you know," I say to her as I climb awkwardly up the ladder to her mattress, where she lies on her side with a thin sheet overtop. I sit at her feet. "What always helps me when I can't sleep is thinking of my mother, my sister. I try to pull apart all the ways we're the same and then I think of all the ways we're different, our own persons. It's soothing."

Elspeth nods and sits up. Her nightshirt looks tight and uncomfortable. "I think Dinah purposefully wrote out all my measurements wrong in the seamstress hut to torture me." She smiles. "She and I—we're very similar. Vindictive."

"I know," I say. "You both stress me out."

Quiet sinks in around us and I feel awkward being close to her. "Do you have a sister?"

Elspeth swallows hard. "No sisters. And thank goodness for that. They'd be as fucked over as I am here."

"I guess I was born fucked over," I offer.

"Sable, my Dad never used to believe this shit. That Men are better. He was always strict, but I don't know what happened to make Him snap. He just got really taken with The Den. Have you ever seen one of Feles's videos on male supremacy?"

I shake my head. I haven't ever heard the term "male supremacy." "Does that surprise you?"

Elspeth's eyes well up. "They're vicious. It's Him speaking directly into the camera, saying that we are nothing if we aren't controlled by Men. That Men can save us and return life to how it should be. That women are valuable but dumb, wicked if left to our own decisions. I can't believe people even buy The Den's water. That people can separate the product from His teachings. They just don't know. Like they aren't linked when it comes down to it. It's fucked. We're scapegoats."

"Well, it's all I've ever known."

"And then we moved to a small place where Men and their families follow Feles's teachings and wait there and learn about Him until the family is accepted." She smiles but I know it's a smile of pain. "Then you get knocked up with a stranger's semen stuck up your vagina and your Father watches and you lose everything, including your mother, and you're trapped here. You don't have a home."

"I'm sorry," I say.

She nods and wipes her dewy cheeks with her sheet. "I'll tell you more about Main Stream sometime. It isn't evil. It's definitely capable of evil, but it's capable of good too."

"Elspeth, why isn't your mum in The Den with you? Why is she at Bow Lake?"

Elspeth shrugs. "When Feles ordered me and the other new girls to breed, the Men didn't tell our mothers. Mine found out I was pregnant and she couldn't stand it. She couldn't stomach it all. She told our Father that we were done, that she wanted us home. He banished her. He forbade her from speaking to us again. She left the grounds Feles provided us. Now she's back in our old home, from before my Father became who He is. She's home. She's waiting for me. I couldn't leave because I'm too afraid of my Father. But one day, maybe I'll do it."

"Go to Bow Lake?"

"Yes. It's just a small town, but I miss it. I had friends. We used to ride our bikes and buy hamburgers at this little canteen, eat them along the river. And smoke my mum's cigarettes at night in the park. We did what we wanted. I was happy."

"And it's near here?"

"That's the stupid thing, Sable. It's so close, it's only hours from here by car. You could walk there in a day or two."

I don't know what makes me tell her but I do. Maybe I need to find out if there is someone else we can save. "Grey and I, we're leaving. You can come with us. We're planning to run away with Dinah."

"Are you that senseless, Sable? Look at your stomach. Look down at it. You can't go anywhere."

"I'm good for walking. We have to go. It's that or Dinah's dead."

"She's going to be killed? For having sex?"

"You said she deserved it. Remember?"

"I'm sorry. I'm sorry I said it. But they won't kill her." She looks at me, her eyes round. "Will they?"

We pause in the quiet of the night. My silence is an answer.

"You know, I lied when I said I was a virgin," Elspeth says finally. "I had sex before we left home. I had a Boyfriend, a Match, I guess you'd say. I chose Him."

"I chose Ambrose, but I wish I could've waited. I wish I could've chosen Him on my terms."

Elspeth reaches for my hand and this surprises me so much, I flinch for a moment. Then I reach back for it.

"Are you really leaving? Where will you go?"

"I don't know yet . . . Just away."

"Do you have any money? Anyone out there who can help you?"

I shake my head and try not to think about how hard this will be.

Elspeth tightens her grip on my hand. "Sable, my mother will take you. She'll help you. You just need to make it there. Give me your atlas. I'll show you."

I blush. "How do you know about my atlas?"

"I go through your things. It's fucking boring here. I thought you had an eating disorder with all the food under your bed."

"No, that's for—"

"Running away, I guess."

"Yeah." I climb down the bunk-bed ladder to retrieve my atlas. Elspeth gestures for me to come back and sit next to her. She shows me the walk along Peace River from here to her home.

"My mother's name is Abigail. Abigail Holbrook. She'll help you. She will."

"Will you come with us?"

"No, Sable, I can't do that. My Father—I just can't. He'll find me. He'd hurt us, my mother and me. And tomorrow I will take my DociGen and do my work and I don't want to talk about this again, okay? Don't ask me again. I just want to forget we've spoken."

"Okay." I take the atlas and go back to my bed. "I hope you sleep well. Think of your mum."

"I will," Elspeth says. "You tell her I think of her often."

"I will," I say. "I promise."

CRICKETS PURL NEAR OUR FEET AND WE ARE DUE SOON. I feel so heavy with my girl inside me. But it's funny how sometimes I forget she is there until I am lying down.

Sleeping has become impossibly hard, our mattresses not wide enough for us to turn and feel good. Elspeth has been crying in the middle of the night over how fat she is, how uncomfortable, that she'll never lose the weight and her Match won't want her anymore. I want to tell her she's beautiful. She is.

I need to keep setting aside food. I need to prepare my head. I need to do so many things and I find myself barely able to leave my bed. I am so scared, my body is paralyzed. Elspeth says I am acting weird and confronts me, saying the other girls call me the laziest laundress at Ceres. It's as if she's forgotten our conversation but I know she hasn't.

"I don't disagree, Elspeth. I am lazy."

"Maybe you're anemic," she says, popping a biscuit into her mouth. She ties her shoes.

"Maybe."

"In that case," she says, muffled by the food in her mouth, "you should've kept your midwife. You should've been calm."

She leaves for the afternoon. I am alone. She's right. I need to learn to stay calm.

Our time is over. The paternity test results arrive tomorrow. Tonight is the only chance we're given. Mamie is called to see Lion for her formal apology. She says I can follow her, go through with our plan while He is clearly distracted. This is her way of saying goodbye. She will play dumb and help, but she will not leave Ceres. She thinks I am stupid and she's angry but she knows I won't change my mind. I will not let Dinah die here. It's not their right. I won't let her die.

I eat supper with Mamie before we go to the Domicile. We eat in the communal dining tent and girls whisper and stare at me. Mamie leaves without finishing her fruit, walking quickly. I can tell she is nervous.

"I practised my apology to Lion at the lake today. I promised Him I'd be good and stay out of trouble from now on. It felt sincere enough. I'll speak slow, give you plenty of time to get to Dinah, to make your way."

She doesn't want to be hounded anymore by Lion or midwives, wants to deliver and live the rest of her time here in peace. Her craving for normalcy is understandable, because somewhere deep down I thirst for it too.

I forget sometimes that Ceres has been a place of refuge for Mamie. She has found refuge in regulated work hours, not caring for so many children, not dealing with Isaac's horrid abuse and hurt, not soothing her sick and aching mother's mind. I forget my own mother's face sometimes, but all the work she's done for me runs deep. All the kettles boiled, tea steeped, sheets folded, kindness, listening. But my Gram Evelyn was always a better listener. I hope she is well. She wanted me to excel, blend in, be fine here. If she could see me now with Mamie and Dinah, she'd lose her mind with worry and sadness. I would break her heart. I am going to break their hearts when I leave.

I kiss Mamie's cheek. "I love you," I tell her. She doesn't say it back. I know she feels abandoned by us, conflicted in her own decision to stay, maybe. She enters the Domicile and I picture her climbing the stairs to His room.

I head back to my cottage. From across the field, I see Lion's illuminated windows. I picture Him flattered to see Mamie grovel. I picture Him asking her favours she'll never be able to scrub from her brain. I am so worried, I hurt everywhere.

I have a canvas laundry bag stuffed with thick blankets, bread and fruit saved from the breakfasts I didn't eat, extra clothes from the Ablutionary. I stash it in the woods near the Domicile behind the thick trunk of a tree. But this doesn't feel planned enough. What if we run out of food? Grey is going to bring medicine, whatever supplies she can drum up. She has a filter for drinking the lake water. From Peace River as well. We can't stray far from water. I hope Abigail Holbrook will save us. I pray Abigail Holbrook will give us a home.

Now that the time has come, I am flooded with doubt. I ache to leave my mother, Kassia, Gram. I ache to never see Ambrose. But I would ache more if anything happened to Dinah and I did nothing to stop it. I promise myself I'll come back for Kassia and somehow save her from this experience and treatment. I promise myself I will make things right with Vale, my mother. I promise myself I will tell Gram Evelyn my story before she passes away. But most of all, I promise myself I will keep my girl safe from the Men who want to control and hurt her.

I WAIT ALONG THE TREELINE OF THE FOREST NEAR THE Domicile with our supplies so the other girls don't see me, don't see my bag or the way my body is littered with nerves. I feel unkempt. I feel as if they would know I'm leaving just by looking at me.

Mamie is still inside with Lion. I can hear them through the open window. She hasn't left. The plan is, Grey is supposed to take Dinah out for air while Lion's door is closed. The other midwives may see her, but Grey will say Lion requested that Dinah have a last stroll outside before her results, before the decision is made. Grey will lie, say that Lion is being generous, heroic. She will lie that He is humane.

Dinah doesn't know the plan but she will comply. I know she will. We will go through the forest. We will keep moving until we can't. They won't know we're gone until the morning. We have all night to walk. I rub my stomach and whisper to my girl to help me, whisper to her that I'm sorry if this is selfish, if this all doesn't work. I want to tell her I won't let her die but I can't say it. If we are caught, our fate could be the same as Dinah's, but we need to try. We need to try for her. Birth Yards are unjust. I will miss Mamie like crazy.

Grey and Dinah come out the kitchen door. They pause at the side of the building where the porch lights are burnt out, then make their way to the trees beside me. Dinah looks like a ghost. She wears a large corduroy jacket Grey found for her. Dinah clutches me tight. Her skin feels so dry, her lips look pasty and blue. She has turned to straw. She is a famine of a woman.

"Sable, He's yelling at Mamie," Dinah says. "I can hear Him through the walls. He's drunk. He's angry and drunk."

Grey nods. "Feles is forcing Him out of Ceres next Gathering Season. They blame Dinah, Harrio, everything, on Him, say that He has been an irresponsible leader, and that He let hysteria win. He got the news today. It was just before supper."

This was not supposed to happen. We're frozen in place. We need to go. We can't go. We'll go as soon as Mamie comes out. We'll go as soon as she goes back to her cottage and goes to sleep. We'll go after that.

"I've locked the door to Dinah's room," Grey says, rubbing Dinah's arms with her hands rapidly to warm her. "And the lights are out. He'll think she's sleeping until tomorrow. Until breakfast."

The air is foggy with summer's end. My body is so tired I want to sleep on the grass here in the dark. I want to float myself and my girl to my home—not my cottage here, but my home on our Trail, to my cot, watch the feet of my Gram twitch in sleep, wait for Kass to come in with tea and a story she's made up. I hope Kass has stood up for herself since I have been gone. I hope no one and nothing has bruised her mind or her heart. Kass is like me except that Kass is angelically good. I never want her to come to a place like this.

I have my atlas bookmarked, the three pages to where Abigail lives, to where we need to be. East.

Lion's balcony doors swing open. We hear the whining hinges. I can see Mamie and Lion at the edge of the balcony now. He's backing her up against the railings. Lion leans into Mamie. She's on her knees saying she's sorry. He says it's all our fault. He says we're greedy and we're whores.

Dinah starts to panic. "Sable, we need to get her."

Grey presses her hand to Dinah's mouth. "We can't move from here. If you move, you'll die. I know you know this, Dinah."

Dinah nods. Grey uncovers her mouth.

Lion yells at Mamie. "I've lost my reputation. All I've done is care. All I've ever done is care. About all your births. About every single woman here."

He has Mamie backed to the edge of the balcony. He has her by the arm. Her head is tilted back over the edge, her hair, her hair, hanging.

Mamie cries out, "You've buried us. You've buried us with all your care. What care?"

It happens so quickly. The sound is horrific. The single scream raises the hairs on my neck. Mamie's body makes a wet thud onto the grass. Her pregnant body is splayed and twisted, harsh and hurt. Her eyes open but sightless.

Without a word between us, we run. We run from her fall. We run from her lifeless body. We run into the forest and leave our dear friend. The trees close in behind us but I turn for one last look. Lion weeps from the balcony, looking down at Mamie, at what He did. At what we all did.

CHAPTER 17

WE HAVE NO CHOICE BUT TO KEEP MOVING. We travel through thick forest mud. We know we are going east. That's all we know. The moss so wet. The trees snagging our arms and cheeks. My breath is growing short. Dinah's is too. Grey leads the way. We keep moving. I feel so heavy and sore. It is so hard to move quickly and surely this pregnant. I don't know what's making me float with light but somehow I keep moving.

Mamie is dead. Her girl is dead. Lion did this. Drunk. What did she think, what did her body feel? We have no choice but to run. I want to. I can't process or think.

There are creeks rising above the mud. They speak in cool whispers but they do not calm me. We have time. We have nothing but time. Lion will be nowhere near thoughts of us, even by tomorrow. Through the trees, I see the track where the shuttle bus brought us here, when I sat on the bus with a feeling of certainty, pride even, carrying tradition with me, carrying my girl.

Dinah begins to slow down. She touches her hips, then clutches her arms to her belly. She says, "Too much. It's too much."

Grey and I sit with her on the ground and we let silence sweep over. Then everything that happened is back. We hold each other.

One thought creeps into my head—and I feel flooded with guilt over it—that it's nice to be in this forest. No Birth Yard. We will be boundless once we cross the chain-link fence Grey described. She said it's very tall and it might be difficult for us. Lion told her it was built to ward off animals but also to keep us in. The fence that frames the Yard.

An owl calls. I haven't heard one in some time. Wood bugs line a rotted log nearby, their small bodies close and fervent. A leaf breaks and falls near my feet. These small things that are always happening, constant. I am just a small thing. We're so, so big yet we're also unexceptional and small.

Grey chokes through the wind and her tears, "Mamie came to talk to me today. She almost changed her mind last night. She thought maybe she wasn't going to apologize. She was going to come with you, Sable. She told me. She thought she was going to change her mind and do it. She wanted out. She wanted to be with us."

Dinah swears at Grey. "You shouldn't say this now. Fucking don't."

I pull the blankets out from my laundry bag. "Let's rest. If we're caught, we deserve it." We all try to sleep beneath the firm, outstretched arm of an alder tree.

I see Mamie everywhere. I don't know when I finally close my eyes and sleep but I do.

WE REACH WHERE GREY ESTIMATES THE FENCE SHOULD be, where the land widens and the lake can be seen through the lush treeline. But there isn't anything; there is no fence within the forest. The Men only said it was there. We were never held in like we thought we were. Grey says we all believed it because we were told to believe it. I feel nauseous and sore but driven to keep going, to get out and farther away.

We cut east along the lake. We spend the morning walking, feeling watched and scared. We are hours away from Ceres now. We are in the foreign land of nature, nowhere I have ever been in my life. It's beautiful. We stop to drink water often. Grey stole a water straw from the midwifery quarters. It's for emergencies. You stick it in the lake and drink. It cleans the water. Simple.

As I drink, Grey tells me something she's been dying to tell me. "I think Lion won't tell Feles about us for now, or He'll have to tell Him about Mamie."

"It makes me angry that He might lie about her death," I say, wiping my mouth and handing the straw to Dinah. "It makes me sick."

"The girls and midwives heard it. We all heard it." Dinah's hands shake as she plants the straw in a shallow part of the lake. She sucks in water desperately.

"He could say she was foolish and fell," offers Grey. "An accident."

But I know what we heard. And we saw Him push.

Mourning has kept our appetites at bay. I imagine I see Mamie in the lake, kneeling and splashing water on her face. I see her spoon-feeding her mother on the stairs at home, putting her Brothers in their stroller, clicking her mouth at the Ceres chickens. I see her. I see her.

Grey hasn't left Ceres in over a year. There is a strange calmness about her. She holds our hands and guides us. She rubs our swollen ankles when we need rest. We're too pregnant for this but there's no going back. My arms and legs are dulled with the strain of having to keep moving. Grey assures us she will care for us. She tells me she loves me. I tell her I love her too.

I don't know if I should write Ambrose from Elspeth's home. Would He come to me if I did or would He reveal everything to Feles? I hope He will abandon everything for me and our girl. We can live in Main Stream. If He is still the same. What if He isn't to be trusted? What if Dinah and I die? Maybe to keep us safe I don't speak with Ambrose. Maybe I never see Him. The possibilities and unknowns bring numbness to my legs as we walk. I feel like we're dead too.

I crave salt. Grey has blood capsules and vitamins for us. We have plenty of apples and bread. There are blackberries growing wild for miles. I am grateful for them.

That night, Grey snares a rabbit for us. She says she did this often with her Father as a child. She made a snare with a coat hanger back at the Domicile. Wire and tape she cut with kitchen scissors. She jams the wire onto a weak poplar branch sagging low to the ground. She drives a thick stick into the ground across from it. She wraps her snare between. We wait far enough away to let a rabbit die peacefully and in private. It's caught by the morning. We're so lucky.

Grey has a quiet fire for us and we eat the dark, gamey meat for breakfast. It's not good at all. Grey says we should reach Bow Lake in a few days, that it won't be long and we need to hold on. She says we can arrive at night. She says we will be safe.

Dinah looks afraid. "How could Lion not be after us?" she asks.

"I'm sure He has His own tracks to cover." I say this but I am afraid He might find us, that our punishment will be death, that we won't ever find safety, that we won't ever get to be mothers. I wonder if there are Men hunting us or even Lion Himself, burning with rage and guilt. Every time I hear a rustle in the bushes or a bird call above us, I feel unnerved, an emptying, like this was all for nothing. That I'll have to face my family with such grave shame. Or worse, that I'll never see them again before we are killed by the Men.

If we do make it through, if we are never found here, I promise I will return to The Den. I will hold Mamie's mother and Dacey and all her siblings and tell them how she died. Resilient. Selfless. A good friend.

WE SMELL CAMP SMOKE THE NEXT AFTERNOON. WE'VE been walking since dawn. We stopped for berries and bread. From down the river, the smell of smoke is pungent. It smells like the burning of plastic and of animal flesh. Grey shifts off closer to the river, wades in to collect water.

"Don't!" Dinah hisses. "Someone's close. What if they see you?"

"We need to drink. You both need to drink."

I have been feeling very weary and terrible, my neck stiff and my ankles weak, but some sort of push thrusts me forward with every step. Maybe if we do get discovered, if we do see people, we will feel relief. Maybe we deserve to be seen, caught, returned to The Den.

But we drink up and listen to Grey. We hear rustling in the river and along the rocks. We hear the banging of a cookstove and thick, heady laughter. Dinah squeezes my hand and cuts off my circulation.

"This isn't the end for us," Grey says. "They mustn't see us."

We cover ourselves with dirt and hide behind a thick patch of reeds near the shore. It's murky and horrible. I urinate there because I am so afraid and cannot stop my body.

Not long after, the smoke scent thins slightly, blown away by the wind. But we hear the footsteps, heavy, thick. Men. I lift my eyes through the reeds and see them. Three Men. They are young— Boys. Maybe Ambrose and Isaac's age. They have a cooler. They carry fishing rods. They pass a cigarette back and forth between them. They have their trousers rolled up to their knees, carefree. Perhaps they could help us. Or perhaps they will bruise us.

I stand. The Boys see me appear to them out of the reeds. I am muddy and they stare, the reeds up to my waist, masking my belly. One cusses at the sight of me. One even laughs and rubs His eyes. Maybe they've been drinking. Maybe they'll help us. Maybe they think I'm not real.

Grey clutches the hem of my dress. She's afraid for me. Dinah hasn't budged. They lie face down and wait.

"Hey, what are you doing here? You lost?" one Boy with a stubbly chin and dark glasses asks.

"I live nearby."

He tramples His cigarette under His sandal.

"Whereabouts?"

My heartbeat quickens. I don't even know exactly where we are to tell them a name. The reeds are masking my belly. They cannot see Grey and Dinah. I do not want them to.

"That's okay. We get it. We're strangers. You don't need to tell us. We aren't from here. We're camping. Just finished university exams. Time to howl at the moon, drink till we're sick." Another Boy with curly blond hair lifts a glass bottle toward me.

"Congratulations," I say. I want to know if they can spare some fish. I want to know they won't hurt me.

"Are you all right? You're alone?"

"Yes, my friend died. I walked here for quiet. To remember her."

"Sorry," the second Boy says.

The third Boy hasn't spoken at all. They haven't moved closer and I pray they don't. "Her name was Mamie. She loved the water. And I found myself here."

They stand in silence, still staring at how filthy and strange I look. "I'm not crazy," I say, though I'm not sure who I am trying to convince.

"Grief takes you wherever it wants. I get it," says the third Boy. "We'll leave you, then. You sure you're all right?"

I nod and try not to cry. I am not all right. "Yes," I say.

The Boys wave at me and keeping walking toward a cluster of tents on a large hill. They didn't hurt me. They were never going to hurt me. They would've maybe even helped.

"What the hell was that for?" Dinah stands up and pushes me. "What if they raped you?"

"I thought you were going to get us more food." Grey stands too. Her face is black with mud. She wades out to the cleaner part of the river and dunks her face in.

"I wanted to. But then they'd know I ran away. They think I live close."

Though my belly is rumbling, I think of Ambrose. I think about how not all Men are made equal. Some can see me. Some will listen.

We rinse in the water and I feel satisfied getting the caked mud from my scalp. I open my eyes underwater and watch the dirt lift away, rejoin the earth. Dinah stays under the water for a very long time, until she needs so badly to breathe she heaves and sputters. When she rises, she says her Boy loves the water, kicks so hard, she doesn't want to re-enter the world when it's just the two of them and so nice and quiet.

We walk into the woods for Grey to set the rabbit trap again. It takes hours. One gets away, as the trap was set too low for the rabbit's girth and height. We have nuts and oats and jam from the Domicile for supper. I take two blood capsules. My girl kicks violently. I wonder why biology lies to her, tells her she wants to leave the warmth and solace inside me. Her first home.

Grey walks farther into the woods and sets another trap, waits nearby. We do not need a blanket tonight. It's a scorching evening. Dinah and I lie on soft leaves and try to get some sleep. Dinah's due date and mine are two weeks apart. Hers is first. But she thinks her baby will be late. She says she's surprised all of this hasn't made our babies climb farther up inside us somehow, in purely instinctual fear.

I roll to face her. "How are you feeling? I haven't asked you about your time. In the Domicile."

She reaches for my hand, places the other on my stomach. "Draining. But Grey fed me more often than she was supposed to. I refused to bathe, though. I thought it would kill me. That Lion would appear and drown me in the tub. I didn't even think about my mother or Colin or Garrison. I only thought of my Boy. How I ruined something that hadn't even started."

"I was never going to let you die. And you also know Grey wouldn't inject you."

"I wonder, Sable, if you didn't care so much about me and Grey wasn't so devoted to you, whether she would have."

Grey returns with a rabbit and skins it with her pocket knife. She sings a song her mother taught her. She wipes blood on a log and skewers the rabbit. "I'll wake you when it's ready. Rest."

"She wouldn't have," I whisper to Dinah. "She wouldn't have been able to."

I SIP WATER FROM THE RIVER WITH GREY'S FILTER. THE water is tinged green the farther we walk, but I know it's safe to drink. I feel fine. The straw is working. The sun is burning wonderfully. I am dizzy with it all. I squat in the water and my crotch and waist are wet. I see how long I can stay like that until my legs give out. My cervix has thinned, dilated in the past few days. I feel it. My cramps and back pain are fiery and strong, especially at night. The grass is more comfortable than the mattress in my cottage ever was and it's both funny and infuriating. I still fear we may be caught. That we are being followed. I still fear we won't make it. Dinah has had trouble sleeping because she dreams of being injected still. She dreams of never being a mother. I don't dream here. I just want us to be safe. I'm always watching for lights in the evening coming through the trees. Feles's Men coming to bring us what we deserve in their eyes. Hysterical women don't deserve to choose. They don't deserve to leave. Sometimes I think about this as we walk and walk. What do we deserve? Is it better than this?

I WAKE TO MUCUS LEAKING OUT THE SIDE OF MY UNDER-wear, clear with a few soft streaks of blood. I know what this means. I keep quiet and moving.

Dinah sneaks off farther into the woods most mornings because she doesn't feel well and needs to vomit. We worry she's not hydrated enough. Grey doubles her water intake and watches her drink it. Dinah also complains of her clumsiness as we walk.

"Your joints are loosening," Grey says. "That's what happens when you're almost due."

Since her miscarriage Grey has been obsessed with learning about childbirth, something she will never be able to do herself.

We walk and sleep, walk and sleep. Time is no object. We walk at strange hours. We sleep during the day. It feels like forever and I kind of like it. If we were the only people on Earth, we could survive and we'd be happy. We could start over with our babies and so on and so forth. We could repopulate the Earth differently and boldly. Maybe this is what I want.

I CAN'T WALK ON OUR LAST DAY, WHEN WE ARE SO CLOSE, and I tell Grey. Every muscle in me is tight. My uterus pinches, then releases and the pain is wild. I wade in the lake awhile though it's daytime and we should keep closer to the woods to avoid being seen.

There are clusters of impressive fish, their shadows, the glint of their gills. One flips into the air and back in the small, soundless space. I have another contraction. I call for Grey and she wades into the water. She holds my hand, rubs my back. She's also cussing.

"You're my first patient, Sable," she whispers.

"I trust you."

Dinah doesn't know what to do. She watches from the shore. For once in her life, she has nothing to say. She begins to cry. I know we're both thinking of Mamie. I know we're both afraid of not knowing where we belong anymore, not knowing what kind of people our babies will become. I am afraid of not surviving this birth.

The pain is electric and it inches down my legs and abdomen. I yelp each time the waves course through, but being in the water is numbing and healing. I sit in the lake and the water is so green. I am earlier than I was supposed to be. Will my girl be born here? No Yard, no midwives carrying her away for testing. No one comparing her to someone else. She will be mine here. I can praise my own body, thank my own body. Grey slips me more blood capsules, a couple of pain-numbers.

"Remember how many women have done this. Remember how many will. Remember how strong a body can be. Remember how strong you are. You need to leave the water with me now. I will try to carry you the rest of the way."

I nod. "Okay."

"Dinah, please help me," Grey instructs. "The best you can. Carry our things. I'll try to lead Sable safely."

"How far?" I ask as Grey guides me back to shore. I holler once again. The pain is deafening, like the worst monthly cramps combined with stark bursts of fire, a flaming.

Grey points past a cove. "I think it's there. If you look really closely, Sable, you can see smoke, chimney smoke, around the bend there. That's where it should be if we timed this all right. If I read the atlas right." I don't even care if it is Bow Lake. I know Grey will find us some kind of safety. She won't let us suffer anymore.

Dinah holds up the atlas before packing it into our travel bags. "It must be here. We're so close. To Abigail."

Through wincing pain, I bite down and lean on Grey. She

can't fully carry me, she is too small. But she guides me for the walk around the bend as I am all sweat and tears and aching.

I focus my eyes on a thick line of chimney smoke in the distance, the black rising of it against the white, cloudy sky. It feels so welcoming and perfect. Bow Lake. Abigail Holbrook.

When we reach the bend, we enter the town through a metal gate where the shore meets the grass. The sign on the fence says Bow Lake Park. Children wearing bright colours scream and run. People play games. People yell. People splash along the water. Others lie in netting tied to trees. There is loud music crackling and blaring. I smell burning, smoking meat. Car exhaust and screeching of tires. More children running in a single chain, their eyes bright, hands held. Brilliant kites with patterns alight in the sky. Grey closes the gate behind us.

I can't keep the pain in. I cry out again. I feel I am about to faint. I collapse my entire body against Grey.

A young Man in a shirt ashes a cigarette and abandons His chair beside a woman, His Match maybe. He runs toward us. "Is she okay? Is she in labour?"

"Yes," I stutter. "I'm having my girl."

"Here, I can hold her," the Man says, relieving Grey of my weight against her body. Boldly, kindly, He picks me up, cradles me like I am a child. He smells different than any Man I've ever been close to. He smells like melon and beer. Grey and Dinah say nothing. They don't know what to say or do.

The Man looks me up and down, studying my dress, my apron, my face. "Sorry, but where did you come from?"

I shake my head. "Nowhere."

His Match runs over. She's holding a portable phone to her ear. "Bow Lake. The park. I think she's going to faint." She hands me a bottle of bright blue liquid. A crowd starts to lace around us. "Drink this, sweetie."

I shake my head and wince at the electric-looking liquid.

"It's just a sports drink, hon. No alcohol. Ambulance on its way, okay, hon?"

I take a sip from the bottle. It's sickly sweet. It's good.

Grey reaches for my hand. "We're getting help, okay. This is okay," she whispers to me.

Another contraction lurches inside me and I holler again.

"Can I lie down?" I ask the Man. "Until they come?"

"Babe, can I have your towel?" He asks His Match. She obliges and lays a flowery-patterned towel on the grass by the fence. He lays me down gently.

Dinah holds one hand and Grey holds the other.

A crowd encircles us—*How old is she? Where's the father? What is she wearing? You think they're sisters? One of those Mormon communities, maybe. Did anyone see where they walked from?*

Dinah clears her throat and finally speaks. She asks the entire crowd, still watching us. "We need someone. We're looking for an Abigail Holbrook. Does anyone know? An Abigail? Holbrook."

My pain is so loud and waves in and out. Moments pass and no one offers much help. But then a Man. An older Man. A Man pushes through the crowd—a Man with white hair and a toddler on His hip. He speaks up. "Abigail Holbrook." He raises His hand. "Abby, she's my daughter."

Dinah squeezes my hand tighter. "Elspeth. We come from where Elspeth is," she says to Him.

The Man approaches us and begins to tear up. "Elspeth. Is she all right?"

Dinah nods. "She is. Right now. But we had to leave. She told us Abigail could help."

The Man lowers the child down and leans in to us. He places a hand on my forehead and the feeling is kind and cooling. "You're very brave, girl."

I can hear the siren screams of a truck reaching us. I can see flickers of blue and red in the corners of my eyes.

Grey rubs my arms and stomach. "I'm still your midwife. I'm with you, Sable," she says.

I breathe even and deep and feel the voice of my Gram telling me I will be a beautiful mother, the kindness of my mother telling me I am smart. The cruelty of some Men. The kindness of some Men. I stretch my legs out straight. I lie with my stomach to the light. I lie with my head to the sun.

ACKNOWLEDGEMENTS

F OR MY WEST COAST LITERARY COMMUNITY WHO are more like family, particularly Jocelyn Tennant, who saw this novel in its infancy and gave me her time and talent to better it. Thank you to Selina Boan, Mica Lemiski, Jessica Johns, Rachel Jansen, Shaun Robinson, Megan Fennya Jones, Kyle Schoenfeld, Carter Selinger, Kayla Czaga and Adèle Barclay for their fierce and loving friendship, for showing me how to be kind, available and an active listener.

To Christopher Evans and Sasha Singer-Wilson—the best coffee-shop writer companions and dear friends. Thank you for chatting this project through and for your thoughtful silence as we worked side by side.

Thank you to my generous editor, Jennifer Lambert, for taking on this journey to the Birth Yard with me and for loving and taking care of Sable through the whole process. Thank you to Iris Tupholme and Melissa Nowakowski and everyone at HarperCollins Canada for their enthusiasm and support for my first novel.

Thank you to my agent, Denise Bukowski, for challenging the manuscript in its early stages to help it grow in a way I never thought possible as an emerging novelist. You are incredible. Thank you as well to Stacy Small for your correspondence and care throughout the publishing process.

For Margot Wallace, Joanna Lepiesza, Rachelle Bourget and our beautiful Lauren Richards—I love you all and your families infinitely.

Thank you Marcel, Ann, Marc and Gabrielle LeBlanc for loving me and welcoming me into your family and for sharing joy in my writing process with me.

For my mum and dad, Susan and Jeffrey Tater, for never questioning my passion and always showing me you really are my "number one fans" since I was nine and entering short story contests in Ottawa. Your care, attentiveness and patience are voracious—I am very lucky.

Monica, Meredith and Madeline Tater—thank you for absolutely everything. The strength of the women in this book stems from you.

For my husband, Curtis LeBlanc, who makes me a better writer—more, a better person—for cultivating support and warmth in our home. Thank for your participation in this book in the way of conversation, for thoughtful meals and for prose-dreaming with me in our little rowboat, *Rosamund*. I love you so much.